PRAISE FOR BLUE DESERT

An exquisite story about a woman finding her place, in the outer land-scape of her surroundings as well as the inner landscape of her heart.
— Jennifer Rosner, author of *The Yellow Bird Sings*

Blue Desert sweeps us into Alice's astounding modern odyssey, transporting us between Northern Africa and England, between childhood and old age, between the riveting external world and its secret internal workings. With sensual detail, Jeffries blurs the boundaries between countries, between violence and desire, suffering and compassion, art and reality, until we're aching with the narrator to reach home. But Alice's Ithaca is no geographic place. It's the landscape of love: complex, deeply tuned and spanning worlds, a passage home you will never forget. — Chris Jacox, author of *Bears Dancing in the Northern Air*, Yale Younger Poets' Series

Crossing continents, cultures, and history, this story of one woman's ordeal and renewal is filled with hope and generosity. Alice is a remarkable character whose bravery and determination are as much a part of her survival as her expansive heart, curiosity, and capacity for forgiveness. "The desert is a palace of winds. A palace of space," Alice recalls about her years away from home. The same can be said of *Blue Desert* , an exquisite, expansive, and transporting novel.
— Hester Kaplan, author of *The Tell*

Though I have never been to Africa, thanks to Celia Jeffries, I have now crossed the Sahara on a "dun-colored camel" and slept beneath the desert's "sequined sky." This novel is, in a word, gorgeous. Just like Alice, who loses herself in the beauty of the desert, I lost myself in the beauty of this story of love, loss, loyalty, betrayal, redemption, and forgiveness. This book will astound you. — Lesléa Newman, activist and author of *I Wish My Father*

Blue Desert is unflinchingly adventurous, unashamedly feminist, deeply human and thoughtful. Jeffries seamlessly weaves two narratives: eighteen-year-old Alice with the Tuareg tribe in wartime Sahara and seventy-eight-year-old Alice in London—to a compelling conclusion without sacrificing the lyricism of her prose, lush grounding in the natural world, or the heartbreaking complexity of her characters.
— Ellen Meeropol, Author of *Her Sister's Tattoo*

Blue Desert , a page-turner of exquisite beauty, ricochets from the heyday of England's colonial power to the majestic Tuareg of the Sahara Desert. This book tunnels through time and our hearts when a young English woman finds a love that transcends the codes of two societies. Prepare to be transported. — Jacqueline Sheehan, *New York Times* bestselling author

Page after surprising page, Celia Jeffries carefully metes out clues to the puzzle of Alice's extraordinary life, from London to the Sahara Desert and back again. *Blue Desert* is a mesmerizing and unforgettable story. Once you start reading, you won't be able to stop.
— Ellen Wittlinger, author of *Someone Else's Shoes*

In sumptuously detailed prose, Celia Jeffries weaves a fascinating, troubling tale of cultures colliding. She lures us deep into the desert, deep into the past, and deep into her imagination. A wild, gripping story, well told! — Debra Immergut, author of *Captives* and *You, Again*

Blue Desert is a sweeping epic of family, adventure, love and the people and places that leave indelible marks on our hearts. Told in vivid, lyrical prose, and spanning decades, cultures, and continents, *Blue Desert* is a fierce, unflinching tale that is both deeply historical and uncannily relevant to our era. Beautifully written and deeply felt, Alice's story of life in the Sahara desert among the Tuareg—and all that comes after—opens a window between two vastly different cultures that will enchant and transport readers. — Joy Baglio, Founder of Pioneer Valley Writing Workshop

BLUE
DESERT

BLUE
DESERT

A Novel

Celia Jeffries

Rootstock Publishing

2021

BLUE DESERT © 2020 Celia Jeffries

Rootstock Publishing 2021

Published by Rootstock Publishing
an imprint of Multicultural Media, Inc.
27 Main Street, Suite 6
Montpelier, VT 05602
www.rootstockpublishing.com
info@rootstockpublishing.com

Design: Lisa Carta

Cover image: John Singer Sargent, Bedouins, 1906
WikimediaCommons, Photo by the-athenaeum.org

Title page painting detail:
Carl Hasch, The Libyan Desert, 1897.
WikimediaCommons. Photo by Dorotheum.

Map: Great Trading Routes of the Sahara, 1889
World Digital Library, Library of Congress

ISBN 978-1-57869-044-2

Library of Congress Control Number 2020917150.

FOR JASON

Author's Note

This is a work of fiction: names, characters, places and incidents are the product of my imagination, or are used fictitiously. Any resemblance to actual events, locales, or persons, living or dead, is coincidental and unintentional.

Tuareg Language

The Tuareg speak Tamasheq and write in the Tifinagh script (vestiges of which have been found on rock art and on the walls of the tomb of the Tuareg matriarch Tin Hinan). However, it is far more likely they would speak Arabic to foreigners; thus for clarity and consistency Arabic is used throughout this novel.

GLOSSARY

Amenokal	The supreme Chief of a Tuareg territory.
Bismallah	Arab phrase meaning "in the name of Allah." English equivalent "in the Name of God."
Caliph	Title used for a temporal or spiritual head of a Muslim state.
Cheche	See Tagelmust (below).
Djinn	In Arab and Muslim mythology, an intelligent spirit of lower rank than the angels, able to appear in human and animal forms and to possess humans.
Guerba	A water bag made of a goat's hide.
Jellaba	A full loose garment (of wool or cotton) with a hood, sleeves and skirt of varying length.
La	Arab word meaning "no."
Marabout	A Muslim holy man or hermit, especially in North Africa.
Palanquin	A covered litter used to transport people. It can be carried by people or by animals.
Salam 'alek	Arab greeting: "Peace be upon you." English equivalent: "Good Day."
Shukran	Arab word meaning "thank you."
Souk	An Arab market or marketplace; a bazaar.
Tagelmust	(also known as a *cheche*) An indigo-dyed cotton, sometimes ten meters in length, used as a veil and turban by Tuareg tribes in the Sahara. The material protects them from wind-born sand, and the indigo that rubs off from the material is believed to protect the skin. Because the dye can permeate the skin of the wearer, the Tuareg are often referred to as the "blue men of the desert."
Tende	A drum—and the music associated with it—among the Tuareg people.

THE SAHARA, 1910

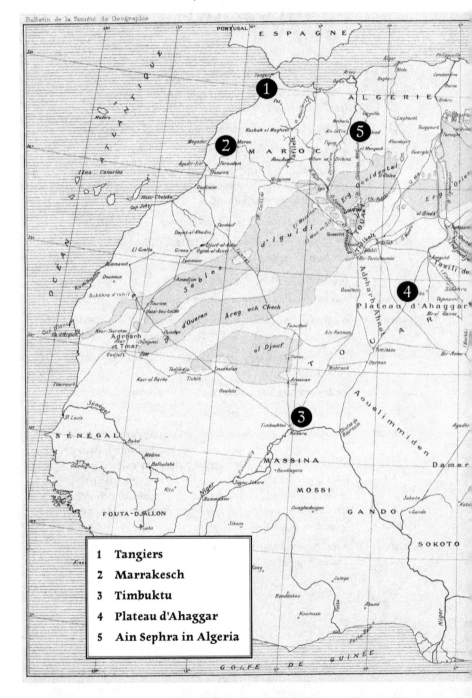

1 Tangiers
2 Marrakesch
3 Timbuktu
4 Plateau d'Ahaggar
5 Ain Sephra in Algeria

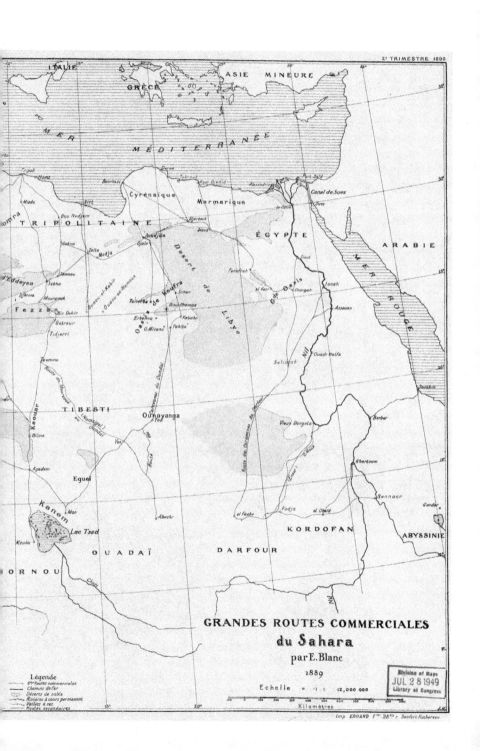

GRANDES ROUTES COMMERCIALES
du Sahara
par E. Blanc
1889

Echelle = 1 : 12,000,000

Kilomètres

Légende
6ᵗᵉ Routes commerciales
Chemins de fer
Déserts de sable
Rivières à cours permanent
Vallées à sec
Routes secondaires

Imp. ERHARD Fᵣᵉˢ 35ᵗᵉ r. Denfert-Rochereau

LONDON

June 6, 1970

"I WISH FOR ONCE THE POST WOULD LAND UPRIGHT in the box." Martin bends over to retrieve the day's missives. He's an exact man, neat to a fault. His pens and pencils line up on his desk and papers are always sorted and piled like an oversized *mille-feuille*.

"Anything for me?" Alice calls.

"Everything for you, my love," Martin says.

"I don't want everything," she laughs. "You may keep the bills."

He smiles and walks over to hand her a heavy cream envelope.

"Oh Lord, spare us," she whispers. "An invitation to the Hobsons."

Martin shakes his head. "June is fast upon us," he says. "Garden party, no doubt. Everyone is competing with Buckingham Palace."

Alice begins to rip the edge of the envelope. She sees Martin purse his lips and tosses him a wide smile, then moves nimbly over to his desk and picks up his letter knife. She slips the ivory-handled spear under the flap of the envelope. She doesn't have to look up to know that his shoulders, which had seized a bit when she began to tear at the envelope, have now relaxed as she

1

makes a clean slice through the vellum and pulls out the printed invitation.

"Indeed," she says in her most impressive House of Commons voice. "The Harris-Hobsons request the honor of our presence in the patch of lawn they have stuffed with roses and vicious dahlias."

Martin laughs. "No doubt we are busy on that date."

"No doubt," Alice says.

Alice turns as Martin holds out a yellow envelope.

"What is that?"

"A telegram. For you."

Martin hands it to her, still smiling as she slips her finger under the envelope's flap, pulls out the yellow page, and unfolds it. He watches as she goes completely still.

He stood in the entrance to the tent, his back to the dry wind. He squeezed his eyes as he peered into the dark interior. I was crouching in the far corner of the octagonal space, my white skirts fluttering against the red and green of the unfolded carpets like the flag of a surrendering army. Although the tent had been standing for twenty-four hours, the air was still thick with the fragrance of juniper branches laid down beneath the carpets.

From the entrance to my corner was only a few strides. I knew once his eyes adjusted to the light, he would see that the blankets and pouches had been strewn about and a line of defense had been set up with the large seating pillows. Behind him the tent flaps inhaled and exhaled slowly like a tense beast.

The man sat down in the shadows of the tent and stared at me. He was nothing but a pair of eyes. Fabric, yards and yards of fabric, and a pair of eyes. His eyes were blue, stone blue. The longer he stared at me, the darker they became. He did not seem to blink, nor did he seem to breathe. He was a heap of cloth with a pair of eyes above. The fabric didn't move. Not a rustle. It was so still in the tent. And warm. I dared not blink, he was too quiet. He was waiting for something. He was waiting for me. It was so warm in there. My feet ached. My body was heavy. We had been walking for so long before the driver met this man. I dared not blink. He was still staring. Now his eyes were black. Black sparkles beneath the turban. Black sparkles above the blue cloth. I dared not blink, I dared not move. I must be as still as he was.

Hours seemed to pass. He got up and left the tent. I collapsed into sleep.

"Alice, are you all right?" Martin is standing at the door staring at me.

I lift my head and listen to the words leaving my mouth. "Yes, I am all right," I say as he crosses the carpet towards me.

"What is this?" he says, pointing to the telegram.

"It is not for you," I say and see the alarm in his eyes.

"It is not for you," I repeat and sit down, then fold the paper into my lap.

"You have no color and your hands are trembling." He pulls out the chair beside me and lowers himself into it, then puts his warm hand over mine and softens his voice. "What is the news?"

"Abu has died in the desert."

"Who is Abu?"

"My lover," I say, surprising myself as much as him.

DEVON, ENGLAND

1910

I WAS SIXTEEN YEARS OLD, told I was possessed of a "danger-ous will," when life unhinged its jaws for me. We are moving to Morocco, Father announced. All five of us: Mother, Father, Edith, James and me. Just in time, I thought. I knew Mother was already casting her eyes about for a suitable mate. Dances and dinners were definitely on the horizon.

The apple trees were just about to blossom when boxes and barrels appeared on each landing and the cupboards were emptied of linens, glasses, china, and cutlery. Aunts, uncles and cousins dropped in at odd hours, tea was always available, and Mother was much too cheery. Edith and I followed the servants about, watching them collect the household goods.

We sat on Mother's bed as her maid Judith did an inventory of the family jewelry.

"Three pearl necklaces, one with diamond clasp, one with gold clasp, one without clasp."

"What is Morocco like?" I asked.

"Hot, I should say."

"Hot like summer?"

"No, hotter. The place is really just sand."

I had read about the Sahara in *Goulding's Geographical Atlas.*

It covered most of Northern Africa in yellow. Morocco was pale yellow along the coastline, divided from the deep yellow by jagged marks representing mountains.

"One brooch in the shape of a butterfly. One set of opal earrings."

"Why are we going to Morocco?" Edith asked. Although she was two years younger than I was, Edith was always assumed to be the oldest of us three. Her gaze was pensive and her questions precise. We were an unlikely team.

"Mine is not to know. Business, I would think. For your father's business," Judith said.

Father called himself a cloth merchant, but most days he sat at the breakfast table, ate an egg, read the newspaper, then bowed to Mother, pulled his chair away, and said, "Off to the office, my dears." I watched him straighten his back and walk to the study in the front of the house, where he stayed behind closed doors until tea time. Other days he took the train to the city and returned late in the evening or a day or two later.

"Three rings, one ruby, one sapphire, one opal in the shape of a half moon."

"Oh, let me see that," I said, reaching for the opal.

"Goodness, girl, give that to me. We're making an accounting here, not playing dress up. Give that back," Judith said.

Mother entered the room holding a piece of paper in front of her.

"More news from the ministry," she said. "Any trousers that provide a wide range of movement are acceptable. Gauzy material is best, something the air can pass through, but nothing the eye can see through." She read the description without comment. Trousers were for men only. The idea that women would wear them was quite startling. Mother continued to read to herself, then explained that the trousers were actually undergarments, that a long robe-like dress called a *jellaba* was worn over the trousers, and a large piece of material was wrapped around the head and face.

"Where is the woman?" Edith asked. We were staring at a picture of the outfit being described.

"Inside the material," I said. "Inside all that material. See, the eyes are showing."

"Must be hot."

"Well, I don't know about that," I said. "It doesn't say anything about corsets. And the material is light. It looks like they are floating inside it."

"It looks hard to walk in," Edith said.

Mother laughed. "You don't have to worry about that. We won't dress that way. Only the natives dress that way." She leaned over and patted our heads. "We'll dress the way we've always dressed." Something in my chest sank at her words. The way we always dressed was cumbersome and hot and as far from floating as one could imagine.

MOROCCO

1910

T HE SEA WAS ROUGH as we approached Gibraltar. Most
people had gone below to sip ginger tea and bemoan their
fate. I held tight to the rails on deck, determined to do as I had
read Hercules had done: to stand in one spot and with a turn of
the head look one way to Europe and another to Africa.

"Alice!" Mother called to me. "Step away from the rail! It's
too dangerous." I pretended not to hear her. A moment later
Father stood beside me and put his arm around my shoulders.

"Look," I said and pointed to the right.

"Africa!" we both shouted.

Three hours of turbulent sea lay between Gibraltar and our
arrival in Tangiers.

Just before departure Judith had said she "lacked the courage"
for such a voyage and declined to join us, handing Mother the
valise containing her jewels. Kate, our indomitable cook, came
on board clutching her potato masher. As we approached Africa,
Kate and Mother stood side by side, each holding her most
prized possession.

In 1910 there was no real harbor anywhere along the coast
of Morocco; thus ships anchored offshore. We stood along the

9

rail watching a flock of small boats approach, filled with waving cloths that at first I thought were sails. Before we knew it, the boats had surrounded our ship, berobed men were climbing the ropes, luggage and goods were tossed overboard onto flat rafts, and general pandemonium broke out. We waited at the rail, assuming some gangway would be lowered. When none appeared, we managed to descend on rope ladders, our skirts waving wildly about our legs. We landed amidst the din in one of the small craft. Two very dark men yelled and pulled on oars, and we were taken close into shore. As Mother sat mouth agape, and Kate grasped her potato masher to her chest, a fresh horde of berobed men crashed through the waves to our little boat and took us in their arms. Kate screamed and began calling on the saints and all above. Mother remained mute. I laughed as black arms reached out of vibrant cloth and lifted these frantic women to carry them through the waves to shore. Father stood tall, remonstrating with the men, then stepped over the bow into hip-deep water and walked straight as a wet ramrod onto the beach. A pair of arms reached out for me, and I put my own arms around the muscular neck of the man who carried me from one world to the next. He walked beyond those who had been deposited at the water's edge and leaned down as he placed me gently upright. "Thank you," I said. The man bowed deeply and turned away.

I looked back for Edith and James and Mother and Father. There they stood among a bedraggled line of proper British subjects, staring back to the sea from whence they had come, the women still smarting from the touch of "heathens," the men unable to take charge as their belongings were hauled across the sand like carcasses pulled in from the depths. I could not tell the difference between the shrieks of the gulls, the only familiar sight to me, and the general shrieking of the men and the black-robed women who lined the walls into town. It was as if, my father later said, we had boarded the ship in 1910 London and debarked in Tangiers in the Middle Ages.

Kate kept hold of her potato masher in such a grip that all who encountered her bowed to the wooden shaft with zigzag prongs as if it were a holy talisman. In some odd way, these people understood her stance and respected the power of a sacred cooking implement.

Three days later we stepped into the compound in Marrakesh. The first time I saw a movie in which the scenery went from black and white to technicolor, I understood that was what had happened to us in Marrakesh. "It's the Garden of Eden," I whispered to Edith. She grabbed my hand, and we both closed our eyes and took a deep breath.

"Identify," she commanded.

"Roses, viburnum."

"What else?"

"Jasmine, lemon."

For days we plucked flowers and put them in our hair, made necklaces and diadems and bracelets as we roamed about the grounds intoxicated with the color and fragrance.

Mother was too exhausted from the trip to leave her room for the first few weeks. Kate decided her idea of potatoes was not to be had in Morocco and booked the first passage home, leaving her precious masher behind. James and I hung it above the courtyard door and watched as Alif, the cook who supplanted her, bowed to it each time he entered or exited.

While Mother recovered from the journey, the three of us spent days getting lost in the maze of rooms connecting one to the other, running our hands over the extraordinary woodwork, the blue-green walls. We walked soundless and barefoot across rugs laid one atop another, strained our necks to see the carved ceilings, and tripped back into childhood games of hopscotch in the stenciled shadows the latticework threw across the many courtyards. Everywhere we went, fragrance followed us: roses, oranges, lemons, jasmine, and mint.

When we found the stairs to the roof, we rushed out into the open space and stood gasping. A fiery sun was setting in the west. To the east, upside-down feather dusters stood in golden boxes lined in front of sparkling mounds of sugar.

"Palm trees," Edith said.

"The Atlas Mountains," James said.

"Beauty," I whispered.

Our first weeks in Morocco I could barely breathe. The air was hot and dry, cold and wet. All at the same time. I knew the moist salt air of the seaside, the acid coal-stink air of the city, and the gentle, clear air of the country. But this was something my lungs couldn't fathom. Each breath brought in a different atmosphere. It was as if there were no barriers—east or west—to the wind. It came across the Sahara, dragging the fertile earth of the East up and over the mountains of stone ground down for longer than man had lived, and swept down the coast to curve inland and startle us with the salt of an ocean open all the way to the other side of the earth.

Edith and I spent as much of our days in the garden as we could. The two of us left off our corsets and walked barefoot most days. The warmth, the fragrance, the light—it entranced us.

"We're becoming natives," Edith laughed.

"We live in an inside-out world," I said.

There were walls and windows and doors, but the house was open to light and air in ways no building in England ever was. The smell of roses and lemons and oleander followed us inside when we were called to continue our studies. When the library shipped from home arrived, we dutifully opened our Latin to spend desultory afternoons translating Ovid, always aware of the tantalizing garden outside the window.

The kitchen is the place to learn the ways of the world. In Devon Kate kept life humming between the long wooden table and the pantry. There was always something simmering on the stove, a cup of tea at the ready, stories to tell, a smile at the sight of me. Here the kitchen was an open courtyard, the work table a spot on the ground. The courtyard was always full of women and men coming and going, delivering vegetables, chasing chickens, slicing, dicing, poking the fire and chattering away.

The first time I stepped into the kitchen courtyard, everything went silent. Alif stood, bowed deeply, and stared at me. "As-salamu-alaikum," he said. I bowed and smiled back at him, as the women twittered, trying to hide their laughter, turning their faces away.

The color and fragrance stunned me. It was everywhere: oranges, lemons, greens, mingled with the burnt umber of small piles of spices. I stood mute, looking around at the hands chopping and mixing until I realized all activity had ceased. Alif was standing silently. I involuntarily shook myself as I realized he must be waiting for orders. Or perhaps for me to leave. "Oh," I said, and pointed at a pomegranate. He handed it to me; I bowed and turned to leave. As I passed through the doorway a buzz arose, and the chopping, mixing, sweeping and chatter once again filled the courtyard.

I continued to visit the kitchen now and then, despite Mother's disapproval. "Alice, please try to conduct yourself properly. These people are not our kind. Do not interfere."

13

Edith just shook her head each time I headed to the courtyard. Finally my presence no longer discomfited people, and Mother decided my visits were useful—I could teach Alif how to make "proper" tea. I knew that was never going to happen, but why tell her? Thick, syrupy mint tea continued to appear at the table until she gave up and sent me in to commandeer a pot of water to make her Fortnum and Mason Earl Grey myself. A day later Alif presented me with a battered old teapot and a space by the fire. Making tea with Alif became my passport to a new world of herbs and spices, sounds and smells, to a more sensory world than I could ever have dreamed of.

James dropped the tattered tennis ball a few inches from my feet. Edith swung her racket back and forth in a lazy arc, then swiped my backside as I bent over to pick up the ball.

"Ow," I cried and twisted around to toss the ball in her face.

She swung wildly and I jumped away. "Can't catch me," I called as I ran across the dirt we'd been using for a court.

"Don't want to," she called back and threw her racket in the air with one hand and caught it with the other.

"Stop!" James yelled, and we both stood still as statues. "Can't you play the game?" he cried.

We both laughed at his mild tantrum. Twelve-year-old James was the sweetheart of the family, always smiling, ever eager to follow us about. We ran up and threw our arms around him.

"What game?" I said.

"Tennis," he sputtered. "I want to play."

Poor fellow. We tousled his cornsilk hair and giggled. I could see Ahmed behind the oleander bush and motioned to him to join us.

"You need a partner," I told James. "Give Ahmed a racket."

"What?! We can't play tennis with the staff."

"Why not?" I said.

Edith turned to look where I was pointing. "Alice, you can't mean him? From the kitchen?"

I walked over and handed a racket to Ahmed. When he put his hand on it, I pulled him from the bush and led him onto our court.

"Alice," Edith hissed. "What are you doing?"

"Playing tennis," I said and bounced the ball off my racket.

James stood beside Ahmed and showed him how to hold the racket. I watched as Ahmed moved around the court in his long robes, reaching up and then bouncing back in shock when the racket strings connected with the ball.

"Yes!" James cried and ran up to the line we had cut in the dirt, dust puffing up around him.

"Edith," I yelled.

She ran sideways and we were volleying and laughing and the blue sky and crunching footfall broke through the boredom of the afternoon. Ahmed grunted and coughed and began sending powerful returns. Edith and I were sweating, but it felt good.

James was everywhere, calling to Ahmed, swinging his racket wildly. "Stop!" he cried as Ahmed ran across the line. "No, LA!" he called and pointed to the line. "Don't cross the net."

Edith and I stood, catching our breath and shaking our heads as James explained the game. Did he think Ahmed spoke English? Or was sport a universal language? I watched the two boys—one fair and short, but fully confident in his instructions. The other tall, slim, and dark, seemingly amused. Ahmed nodded and smiled and held the racket in both hands.

By the end of the week it was clear Ahmed had added one

hour of tennis to his daily duties, and James began to complain that Ahmed was letting him win.

The paints came at just the right time. Edith and I had explored the entire compound, we had identified every plant in the garden, and I had run my fingers over the spine of every book in the library. As much as I loved the light and air in our new home, I was beginning to feel the confinement. I missed my tramps through the fields at home. I needed space.

"For you," Alif said, handing me a package. It was postmarked London and had a return address I didn't recognize. He stood silent and still, waiting for me to open it. I shook it, then held it up to my nose. Alif pulled a knife from his robe and handed it to me. I put the box on the ground and slit the strings, then pulled the paper away to reveal a wooden box marked "L. Cornelissen & Son, 106 Great Russell Street." When I lifted the lid, Alif gasped.

"Paints," I squealed.

Alif knelt down as I lifted the cool tube of cerulean and rolled it in the palm of my hand.

"Thank you," I whispered, then put the box aside to look for a card. And there it was:

Paint me a kitchen
~ from Kate

I burst out laughing, and when Alif looked puzzled I pointed to the potato masher above the door and said, "Kate! It's from Kate!"

A week later Sir Henry agreed to post the painting I had made of Alif standing below the potato masher holding a bowl of reds, yellows, oranges, magentas, greens—the "kitchen."

Protection was everything in Morocco. If one worked for a foreigner, one was automatically under his protection and not subject to the taxes of Morocco itself. Gathering provisions meant hiring someone's friend, brother, or ally, all of whom were eager to be taken under your protection. Mother was undone by it all. A simple request for afternoon tea meant a stream of people crossing the compound, like a line of ants arriving at a picnic. We adjusted, eventually, but the compound itself seemed to be full of people day and night—always deferential, always polite, but never quite known.

The truth about Morocco in 1910 was that only misfits and demigods would go there. It was not a colony or a country, only a place no one could contain. The French colonized Algiers and the Sudan and were sparring with Germany over Morocco, but it was still a no-man's-land. There were a few odd Europeans, drawn to the crudeness of the place, to its potential. I never quite knew what drew my parents there. Business, I thought, but what business could a cloth merchant have in a land of dust? I overheard vague references to duty and country, but no one ever came out and said we were there for political purposes.

I had always been an eavesdropper, getting my information from what was said and not said, mostly at the dinner table. "The Moor is afraid of our empire," Sir Humphries announced over boar stew with pomegranate sauce. He was one of those leftover explorers, a man who had headed out to the farthest reaches of the Empire and couldn't quite find his way back into the drawing rooms of London. Father knew him at Harrow and was thrilled to find him here in Marrakesh.

"They are a tribal society. Right and wrong is a loose net for them; they only know brute force."

"Oh, come now," Father said. "All men want freedom."

"Not our kind of freedom," Humphries said. "They are like children, playing with the rules. No pork, no alcohol, but they will take it any chance they get, then fall to the ground five times a day and praise Allah."

"Surely they don't want to pay tribute to those sultans? Such a traveling circus they are, with all their wives and horses and rifles and such." Father wiped the grease from his upper lip.

Humphries laughed, a wide-open mouth of a laugh that shot spittle onto the table. He lifted the linen napkin from his lap to his lips, pressed and held it there before looking directly at me.

"When I first came to Morocco, I dressed as a Moor, thinking it would be easier," he said. "I wanted to go to Agadir—Santa Cruz when the Spaniards had them in their grasp—it's a port the Moors had closed to foreigners to keep trade to themselves. I had a letter from the sultan saying I was to be accorded respect and given safe passage. I never got beyond Mogador. *We cannot guarantee safe passage*, I was told. *We cannot honor Sultan's wishes.* I knew it was a ruse to keep me away."

"Did you ever get to Agadir?" I asked.

"Of course I did. You've got to play their game. I found El Hussein, the best muleteer around. He had me dress as a Turkish doctor, swathed me head to toe and rode me around the outskirts of the trail for hours to get me and my clothes dusty enough for deception."

"What did you find in Agadir?"

"The most beautiful Jewesses ever to be born to the tribe of Israel."

A short "hmmph" came from Mother's lips.

"No wonder they closed the port," my father laughed.

"Girls, you may be excused from the table," Mother said.

I pretended not to hear her. "You said the Moor is afraid of our empire. Why is that?"

"Alice, do not pester Sir Humphries."

Humphries ignored her and turned his body as well as his eyes toward me. "They have put up with emissaries and consuls from all corners of the earth—Guatemala, Buenos Aires, America, Italy, always some scrapper who shows up with credentials, raises a flag, and settles in to enjoy the good life provided by protection. It's quite a symbiotic relationship, always works well until the local chieftain finds something to take offense at and rides in with his rifles and swords to reinstate himself as grand pooh-bah. We, however, represent real trade. We bring our own goods, our Manchester cloth, our rifles, our navy. They can see we are not here to play."

MARRAKESH

1912

"GIRLS," MY FATHER CALLED, "I am waiting." Edith put her hat on as she stepped through the door. Mother reached out and touched her shoulder, an unfamiliar gesture, then turned to me. "Alice, don't keep your father waiting," she said.

I dropped my umbrella into the porcelain holder, smiled at her, and waved my goggles as I headed for the car.

"Don't run," she called after me. "A lady doesn't run."

"This lady does," I laughed, opening the car door.

Edith and I sat in the back seat, dusters over our dresses, hats on our heads and goggles over our eyes. Edith hated wearing them, but Mother insisted the Moroccan sun would ruin our eyesight. I loved them. I felt exotic in my eighteen-year-old body and ready for anything with my goggles on. Father sat in front, speaking loudly and slowly to the fellow who had come to replace our regular driver that day.

We waved to Mother standing on the front steps and I fell back against the seat when the driver started up abruptly, obviously unfamiliar with the machine. We were heading out to visit a client of Father's. It was blazing hot and as we passed the medina, I envied the people in their light layers of gauzy fabric. My linen dress and heavy duster may have kept the soil from the road off me, but I was too warm and I unbuttoned my collar to get some breeze on my neck.

When we left the city and moved up into the surrounding hills, the air cooled a bit and Father told me to sit still, but I kept turning around in my seat to see the city. After two years, I still relished the long vistas, the open expanses of light and color. The road became a dirt track once we crossed the ridge, but the driver did not slow down. The dust became so thick we kept our heads down and wrapped our scarves over our mouths to keep the grit out of our teeth. I could see panic in Edith's eyes.

She leaned forward to tap Father on the shoulder and motion that we should slow down. He turned to the driver and made an effort to yell something, but the fellow never even turned his head. My father reached out and put his hand on the driver's arm. I saw the reflex action, saw the driver jerk his arm away, turning the steering wheel sharply to the left and I saw— before it even happened—I saw the car flip over and my sister fly out the side and my father fall like a log into the driver's lap, and I saw the windshield shatter and my goggles fly up in my face and the sky and sand change places before me. But I didn't feel a thing. Not a thing. My first sensation was of silence. No voices, no motor, no wind. Just immense silence. I was on my side, my arm thrown across my face. I moved my fingers, then my toes, then my legs. I pushed my arms into the sand to raise my body and turned my head.

The car was upside down. My sister's bonnet was sitting on the upturned wheel of the car as if she had casually placed it there while she stepped away to take care of some chore. When I stood and moved forward, I heard a groan, and, thinking it was my father, I ran to the other side of car where I found the driver lifting himself up from the ground. I shrieked when I saw my father's arm sticking out from under the car. I dug my hands under the side of the car trying to lift it. I shouted and clawed at the sand until I felt a hand on my shoulder. I looked up at the driver, who pulled his hand away but kept it held out to me. The sun directly behind him outlined his hair and lean body.

I do not remember what happened next. I have had plenty of time, plenty of days and hours, even years, to bring back that scene, but all I can recover is the driver holding my hand as we walked, bent forward in the wind. I don't know how long we walked. I didn't know what happened to my father and sister. I told myself that they were dead. It was the only way to step forward in life. It was the only way I could have walked off into the desert hand-in-hand with a man I had never met and whose language I could not speak.

I had left home that morning in Marrakesh a proper eighteen-year-old British girl, dressed in white, covered in a pale blue duster. Within twenty-four hours I was orphaned, bereft of hat and gloves, and standing in front of what I could only assume was an oversized bird. Before me rose a full-throated vision of dusty expanse, a head of the deepest blue imaginable and eyes that sparkled in their sockets. The driver pulled at me roughly, put his hands on my shoulders, and began jabbering to this mythological being before us. Only then did I connect the dusty robes to the swirling blue above and realize the eyes were human, the figure swathed in material that rose and fell as a hand reached out and took hold of the driver's arm. Once again the driver began jabbering, cackling, the only recognizable sounds the *inshallah* that broke out every few seconds. The person before us raised his head the slightest degree and tightened his hold on the driver's arm. It was like watching someone turn a radio dial.

The driver's voice diminished with each press of the hand until he stood mute beside me. Only then did the blue man turn his eyes to mine.

The driver fell to his knees, babbling and bowing, clearly begging for mercy. I stood alone in the sand and looked directly at the man before me. I know now that he was startled by that, that he thought I was mad, driven to the edge by my journey into the desert. I think now I was never as sane as I was in that moment. This was not the face of a stranger. My body, my mind—dare I say my soul—recognized him.

LONDON

June 6, 1970

IN THE LATE AFTERNOON MARTIN STANDS at the window. Alice is in the garden again. On the ground. In the dirt, her fingers kneading the earth. She looks up and sees Martin.

"Come join me," she calls.

Thirty years ago he called Vincent Grove at the sight of Alice on the ground. Today he takes off his jacket and waves to her. "I will be right there," he says.

Martin kneels down beside Alice and smiles. She can feel the heat he generates and finds it still pleases her. He is the perfect man to advise the government. He enters a room quietly, deferentially leaning over as if his height has bent him forward. Eye contact is easy, people are put at ease. Then he speaks. How can a thin instrument deliver such a deep, imposing symphony? He is never interrupted, rarely debated.

Alice stands, and he rises and puts his arms around her. She allows him to wrap her in his warmth, waiting for his pronouncement, but he remains silent. They hold onto each other, Martin conscious of how odd they must look, Alice completely at ease.

"Alice, I am worried about you." He takes her hands. "This telegram. Your hands shake, you are cold. You've been murmuring. What does blue signify?"

How can she tell him? The Tuareg. The blue men of the desert. How can she open up that world?

"Ask Edith," she says, then immediately regrets it. *Oh My God, why did I say that? Ask Edith? That is not a good idea. Not a good idea at all.*

Martin pulls away to look at her. "Alice, how can I help? You are distressed. Perhaps I should not go to the Paris talks."

She looks at this kind man. Tall, thin, watery blue eyes, white wispy hair. Distinguished is what such men are called. And his voice, always comforting no matter what he is saying. Did he develop that for negotiating skills? Did he learn that in the war? Twice in his lifetime people tore up European soil and buried multitudes. To save the world and to destroy it at the same time. He has spent a generation walking between those who want to save the world and those who want to destroy it, both of whom think it's the same thing. *Have I been an asset to his career or have I been a liability?* He squeezes her hand.

"Martin, I will be fine," she says. She notices he asks nothing more about the telegram. *Where is it now? Where did she put it?* She startles a bit when she feels it in her pocket.

"I will be fine," Alice says. "It is written."

"What is written?"

She laughs. "That's what Dr. Omer taught me. Play with words, play with color. Sometimes I play on the easel, sometimes on the lined page. Please don't worry." She withdraws her hand and laughs again. *Color. The color blue. The blue of the sky, of the morning light, of the bottle of gin.* "Is it time for our blue bottle of gin?" she says.

Martin looks directly at her, and for the first time in their marriage she finds herself avoiding his gaze. He squeezes her hand again. *"L'heure bleue,"* he says and winks. He puts his arm around her waist and leads her inside to the drinks cart, and they settle into the evening ritual.

LONDON

June 7, 1970

THE SUN HAS RISEN. I feel the pale warmth on my hand and look up to the open window. On the table before me the telegram rustles in the breeze.

"Progeny to arrive, Friday, June 12."

Did I not read that? Have my eyes failed me again? *Progeny.* Is that a poor translation? Abu is dead. Does our child live? Is he well? Who is he now that Abu is dead? Where is he? Who sent this? The tribe? What else could they want? What else could they take from me? I fold the telegram in half, then in half again, and yet again, as if pressing the paper together will force the words to face each other and not me.

"Does Edith know this?" Martin is standing in the doorway again, this time dressed for a meeting. I glance at the clock and gasp. It is half ten. I will miss church service. Where has the day gone? The sun is high in the sky.

"Does my sister know what?"

"About the telegram. About the life you had in the desert."

"Well, yes, she was there, in Morocco."

"Yes, I know that," he says.

"The desert, I don't know—no—I don't think she knows

29

about *my* desert," I say. I look up at him, expecting to see arms crossed, eyes searching. What I see is concern. No, what I see is fear. How much did I say last night?

All these years I have kept my silence, never going beyond "Yes, I once lived in Northern Africa." I know the family was glad of that. They never wanted the truth. I came back across the Mediterranean, through the plains of Spain, crawled up the face of France, and when I arrived at the place we call home, the family went mute, allowed the world of breakfast, lunch and dinner and tea with the Vicar, allowed that world to wrap itself around us like a cocoon—or was it a shroud? It was difficult at first. I felt like the Ancient Mariner, ready to accost strangers in the street, wanting to shout my story in their faces. "Look. See these scars? Let me tell you what happened to me."

I didn't, of course. I learned to live inside my head, to be my own audience, even with Martin. By then I had lost the words for what I held within and began to believe that the truth that comes too late can only do harm.

I get up and walk to Martin, give him a kiss, and wish him a good meeting. He embraces me a bit more tightly, a bit longer than usual, then turns to the door. "See you at *l'heure bleue*," he calls over his shoulder.

Blue is what I will live for now. The blue of the sky, of the morning light, of the evening shadow. Of the cloth that covered Abu's head. A long indigo swath that covered Tuareg men of distinction, a color so deep and penetrating it seeped into their skin, became the identifying pigment, the element that announced their mastery of the desert: the blue men. I was mesmerized at the sight of such blue. The mind can only take in so much in one day.

I will sit in silence again, awaiting the sun. I will turn to the East and bow to that first light. God willing, we will have sun, we will have that sacred light in our pewter sky. Nothing is present to me now. Only the desert. Only Abu, and our son, and the life I abandoned fifty years ago.

I learned to be silent in the desert. It's a skill I have used well. Here. In this noisy island. People are reeling from the youth set loose in the streets, the masses demanding attention—women are demanding rights, the docks are closing, the Irish are bombing (good on them). People say London is dying. I say it's just coming alive. This nation of shopkeepers is throwing open the doors and paying attention to the life on the street.

I am silent. I am listening. I can hear a heartbeat out there. The Queen's horses still clip-clop along the road like some nursery rhyme come alive. The rain still splashes on all and sundry, a sound I will never take for granted. And the newsboys still call out useless warnings of men trying to change the way the world revolves on its axis. Under it all I hear a drumbeat, a murmur, a pressured percussion. Something is afoot in the world. I half expect to see Mohammed stop and feel the sand, put it to his lips to taste the measure of its movement. Man may drive upon it, slap it with his feet, stomp it with his four-footed beasts, but the only way to know what is coming is to touch the earth. Skin to dust. Touch the earth and it will tell you its truth.

THE SAHARA

1912

TWO FEET WERE ALL I SAW that first morning in the desert. Two mahogany feet, the toenails like cracked shells, when I opened my eyes and looked across the pattern of reds and golds in the rug I lay on. Then one of the shells separated from the others and the fabric shifted sideways and my fevered mind—which had been comfortably constructing the floor of a familiar home with a beautiful rug and statuary and drapes— shook itself slowly into another realm, into another picture. The man who had taken my hand from the driver waited for me to open my eyes and look up. But I didn't. I could not look up into the face of my captor.

I lay quietly, watching the toes grow larger in my field of vision, beginning to believe I was Alice in Wonderland and everything that was now so much larger than life would soon— if I just waited quietly, if I just remained immobile—become so much smaller.

That whole first day in the desert I could not swallow or blink. I didn't know what color the sky was, what color the land was. That whole first day in the desert I did not know where the sky and earth divided. My eyes failed me. My ears failed me. Everything throbbed. My legs were dull stumps, my arms were cold and useless. Only the goats and camels were real to me. The warmth of their flanks. The smell of their breath. The sound of their packs shifting from side to side. I did not register the number of men surrounding me until we stopped for the night and I was taken from protective cover and left to sit amidst the baggage while they pitched the tents.

Finally I understood. I was alone. Separated from home, now separated from family. I was out in the world alone. I had heard the stories at the dinner table of white women abducted into the desert, of people who "went missing." My parents and their friends lowered their voices when they spoke these names, as if speaking them aloud would pull the threat closer to us, seated amidst plenty while outside the forces of need pressed closer, threatening to pull us apart one by one. I was alone now, with no survival skills. Polite manners, proper conversation, and the right fork and spoon had no power here. Was my name being intoned *sotto voce* at the dinner table miles to the west?

A few days must have passed, though I could barely mark the time. My world now was what I could feel at the end of my fingers, what I could taste on my tongue, what I could see beyond the blackness of the rug.

Fire and water were the central elements of those first desert days. The fire was what saved me. The fire roared as the men talked and sometimes drank, some getting up to dance and sing, others sitting quietly to watch. I remained in the tent, listening to the fire crackle and warp, the constant wave of sound almost as mesmerizing as the waves at the seaside when, as children, we were wrapped in blankets and allowed to sleep on the beach up against the gorse while our parents sat in folding chairs facing the black expanse of the sea. I began to look forward to the fire

all day, to the time when the men gathered together and I passed
out of their view and was allowed to assume the same unspoken
presence as the animals tied to the posts beyond my tent. I could
hear the camels breathing on the other side of the fabric, steady,
deep and constant.

Water appeared. Wrapped in a rug, attached to the camel, I was
surprised that the thirst wasn't overwhelming and my thoughts
of it were few. I didn't hunger for the taste, only the sight. The
few times I could open my eyes and look towards the horizon,
I was always surprised it wasn't there, the ocean that surely
should have been at the edge of this sand. We stopped a number
of times throughout the day. I was passing in and out of consciousness, rocked by the camel's movements, then slid off its
side to awaken within a scratchy placenta of wool. Each time, I
opened my eyes, and without a word, the *guerba* was offered and
care was taken to lift it to my lips and tip it gently so each precious drop hit my tongue like the beginning drops of rain. I was
never allowed to touch the water bag. He would lift my head if I
was lying strapped to the camel, or bend my head back if I was
seated on the ground, his touch gentle but firm, moving my face
towards the neck of the *guerba* and each time, without thinking, without will, it seemed, I would close my eyes and allow
the hand of my captor to provide me with the one thing that
allowed me to live another day in his captivity.

Night again. Days and nights ran into each other. The only
marker I could see was the change of terrain when I opened one
eye like a telescope to look through the threads of my wrapping.
One day the camels walked sideways up a dune, slipping here
and there, ever so slightly. The next day they plodded sure-
footed over hard dirt, until one day they picked their feet over

flat brown rocks that lay before us like spilled chocolate bars.

No one had spoken to me since the driver went prostrate and Abu had taken my hand. Every morning before I came fully awake, the rug was wrapped around me from behind, a strange comfort. Alone in my cocoon I listened at the shores of a great silence, breathing in the heat. My body shut down for hours at a time. No hunger, no need for elimination. Then came the moment when I was lifted off the camel, carried into a tent, and the moment when I was unwrapped and the air hit me like a rogue wave, washed me over and left me gasping, unable to move, unable to stay calm. I listened to movements in the blackness until my eyes regained sight. I kept silent and still when Abu appeared. I became the animal that I am, every particle of my being suddenly alert, the body abruptly alive with hunger and thirst.

I listened with every inch of my skin, aware of what went on behind me, beside me, in front of me. At first I grasped at every syllable, every strange utterance, trying to connect it to something, trying to make meaning. I began to listen more clearly and to understand what I did not know.

It was at night that my life returned to me, when my body was returned to me. My mother's voice came to me then, reading whole chapters of Dickens or Eliot to us as we lay in our beds, eyes closed, covers pulled up to our noses, drifting through imagery and sound. Alone in the darkness of a strange language I went back to those stories, willing myself to remember them again, night after night. In that sea of sand I listened to the water as Pip stood in the marshlands of Kent, and Maggie and Tom Tulliver succumbed to the River Floss.

During what seemed to me now a normal day's journey, perhaps a week into my captivity, something changed. My camel's pace quickened. The air darkened. Suddenly sound came from everywhere at once. Up, down, ringing around my head. The animals hooted, and my camel shrieked. I could not see through the rug that enwrapped me, could not see why the beast I was attached to was trying to shake me off. I had nothing to hang onto, nothing to grab. I could feel things loosening as I was bounced back and forth against the side of the camel. I opened my mouth to scream but nothing came out.

Then all was dark and I was weightless, released into space for a split second or a lifetime—how to define the movement through that wall of noise? The rug unraveled, and I tumbled out into light and heat and an unbearable stench. Sand flew around me, spitting into my eyes, my nose, my ears. Tornadoes of dust enveloped moving trees. No, not trees—legs, camel legs, here, there, twisting in front of me, beside me. I curled myself up awaiting the inevitable strike of a hoof as the camels thundered off, men and beasts galloping and running until all was still and silence surrounded me. I stayed curled, covering my eyes from the intense light, gasping for breath. I felt the earth thump as someone or something approached me. From the corner of my eye I watched a camel approach softly.

Then all was still. The camel's leg went straight, and robes dropped down from above and a hand took hold of my arm and pulled me upright. The dark eyes of the man in front of me went wide; his dirty turban fell askew from a mouth that sputtered and shouted. I pulled my arm away, but he clenched tighter on my wrist and dragged me away from the swirling dust. I stumbled and the man threw his arm around my shoulder, lifting me off the ground, my legs flailing beside me. He dragged me up a hill, the noise diminishing slightly as he lifted, pulled, dragged, and finally threw me to the ground.

He put one hand on my collarbone, lifted my skirt with the other, and began tearing at my undergarments. I twisted and grabbed at his face, clawing at his eyes, but the slap across my face made everything go hazy. I blinked hard and gasped for breath again. I bared my teeth, trying to find a way to bite the hand holding me down. Suddenly a rush of air passed my face, the assailant cried out, and I was lifted up to look down upon him, now bleeding on the ground from a wound to the head.

Abu kicked the assailant aside and looked down at his hands holding mine. He lowered his eyes, let go of me, gently pulled my skirt down, and turned away.

The next morning Abu came to me in the tent and motioned for me to rise. He pulled the rug away from me and opened the flap of the tent. I kept my eyes on his and followed his gaze, then looked into the world beyond and lowered my head at the rush of open air and light. Men were milling about, loading the camels. I looked for the driver among them—the one person I could connect to Marrakesh—but these men all looked the same to me. Dark arms jutting out of their robes, eyes sliding sideways at the sight of me. I turned to Abu, who held his arm out directing me to step outside before him.

He nodded when I put my foot out, then held my elbow as I stumbled. Every eye was upon me; I felt the glances like pin pricks and watched the men's stance stiffen. Abu pulled my hat from a pack on the ground and held it out to me. I put it on my head and walked forward, holding the rim down to avoid the men's eyes. Abu moved ahead and mounted one of the camels seated in a row before us. As soon as the animal rose, a man hit the other camels' legs and each of them lifted in a jumbled line and moved off. I followed, each step a struggle to stay upright and keep a forward movement. I looked up and counted four camels in front of me. A while later I looked up and counted six. Then ten. Until I could not count the number ahead of me, a line of tall slim dancers sashaying through the heat.

I must have fallen. Abu took my arm, and I shouted and pulled away. My arm was on fire. I could see men closing in. I continued to shout, or was I mumbling? The men circled me and stared. I pulled my duster tighter about my body and reached for my hat pin, then realized my hat was no longer on my head. "*La*," I yelled. "Keep away! Do not touch me! I will kill!" I grabbed at my coat and the buttons fell off. Abu stepped in front of me and reached out again. I slapped his hand away and saw the men step forward. Abu pushed his hand back behind him, and in one movement the men backed up. I saw a smile in Abu's eyes and heard him speak. *You are alive,* he said, *your animal is awake.* I did not know those were the words. What I knew was that the men had turned away and Abu filled the horizon.

From behind Abu stepped a young boy, rags on his body, face bared to the world. Abu spoke to him, harsh sounds that kept the boy's head bowed. Another man appeared, an aged man leading a large, slow camel. Within minutes the camel was folded on the ground, a large wooden hoop was attached to the blankets on its seat, the hoops were covered in cloth, and I was settled inside to ride the rest of the day in relative ease. From that moment on, the boy remained by my side.

The first time I saw a camel whole, I was repelled. It looked like a mistake. Someone wanted a horse, but somehow the legs got too long, the back curved the wrong way, the belly distended, and the neck just went haywire. But the eyes were mesmerizing. Deep, dark and intelligent. I knew this animal saw me clearly and understood me better than most humans. In the distance, on the skyline, a line of camels is like the white curl at the top of a wave, moving forward in an undulating line, folding over the edge of the horizon. And once I was part of that movement, I still could not believe how graceful it was.

Each animal had a value. Each one was the most prized possession a man could have in the desert. My camel was beautiful. She spat at me and bit me and swung her smelly tail at me and taught me that in the great chain of being, she was worth more than I was. When the driver had stood that day before Abu and tried to trade me for a camel, Abu had laughed. A white woman for a camel? Surely a fool stood before him. I could see Abu was annoyed when the driver pushed me out in front of him. Abu stepped closer to me and met my eyes. The driver became excited, gesticulating and talking loudly. The man in front of me, the man who became Abu, laughed, then drew himself up and put his hand on the sword by his side, his anger obvious beneath the language in the air. The driver pulled back a bit at the force of his words.

I stood still, aware of my own anger rising from my tired body, and listened to the rough vowels flying in the air about me. The driver lifted his shoulders, opened the palms of his hands, and leaned his body forward as he sputtered and spat out foul-sounding syllables. Abu remained still, then looked directly at me again while speaking more softly to the driver, who then raised his hands and shook them in front of himself, babbling violently—pointing at me.

When the driver reached out and pulled my skirt above my knee I saw my father's hand reaching out in the front seat, saw the world turn upside down again. Fury rushed through me and I shouted, thrusting a fist at the driver's chest. But I wasn't strong enough. My whole body ricocheted from the impact and I tumbled to the ground.

There was no bargaining that night. I was bound in the rug in the tent, the driver was never seen again, and the camel he had pointed to became my life boat, rocking my sore body through the heat of the day and sheltering it at night. I began my days in the desert as a parasite, strapped to the side of a beast, painfully aware that the universe as I had known it was now operating inside out.

I learned to read the tilt of Abu's head, the expression in his eyes. I came to know each man in the caravan by his gait, by the way he carried his body through space. Mohammed, the oldest, was the most graceful. Even though his legs were not visible under his robe, the length of his stride and the turn of his shoulders belied his years. He moved across the sand like a walker on water, hardly a ripple in his skirts.

The boy was all disjointed energy. I could feel him before I saw him, jutting through the space between us, his knobby knees pumping forward of his body. But Abu was the one I was most attuned to. First in fear, later in anticipation. He moved with purpose, no wasted energy in the movement of his arms and legs. And a strange dignity in the way he carried his head above his body as if it were a crown, or a nest of eagles.

And me? How did I move? As in a dream, I suspect, at first hopeful that one morning I would awake and the dream would be over. Until I became a believer, one who lives within the dream of the desert.

Once I was released from the rug, I tried to stay close to the animals, some of whom I knew were female. I did not want to be alone among the men, not for fear of what they might do to my sex, but for lack of something more elemental, some way of breathing and being that I now know is unique to the feminine. At the same time, I watched them, the men in their *mufti*, wrapped in such layers they were only identifiable by their eyes. We had been warned about such eyes. Eyes that seemed to look straight through you, eyes that took your measure in one swift glance. I must have been like a startled animal at first arrival in Morocco, my own eyes wide and stunned, until the warnings took hold and I learned to keep the blue of my own hidden from all but those I knew well.

I did not use the *palanquin* for long, perhaps two or three days. The boy arrived one morning dressed in the manner of the others—a long robe, a scarf wrapped around his head, although it hung down below his chin, revealing a grand smile. He handed me a pile of cloth and motioned for me to put it over myself, then turned and stood outside the tent with his back to the opening. I hardly needed to do more than pull at my dress before it fell off in shreds. I lifted the cloak over my body and laughed when it fell to the ground like a clown's costume. The boy turned then, and put his hand over his mouth to keep from laughing himself. I motioned him inside and said "Please fix this." Here I was, speaking in my own language, assuming there was something in the vowels, the sounds, that accompanied by hand gestures and raised eyebrows could convey my needs. The boy stared hard at me, then bowed. He didn't laugh, but stepped behind me and reached around to tie the voluminous material back with rope. Then he touched my shoulders gently and I understood to lower myself to my knees while he wrapped the *tagelmust* about my head. He moved in front of me and put out a hand that held a stick with black resin on the tip. He pantomimed painting his eyes, and I gingerly rubbed the stick around my eye sockets.

When we left the tent, no *palanquin* was mounted on my camel. Mohammed assisted me in mounting, and I rode in my *mufti* with the rest of the caravan.

Now that I was part of it, I watched the caravan more closely. What had been simply men and animals was now a well-ordered parade. What had at first appeared to be clumps of travelers wandering through a bare landscape now came into sharp focus.

What might have been a month into the journey, I watched as Abu moved through the line. He did not speak, but his presence was obvious. Mohammed, the aged camel tender, turned, then a young man whose *tagelmust* was always slack, then the yellow-eyed goat herder—each one stood taller, walked straighter, as Abu approached. The next week I watched as Abu sat beside the fire. He was relaxed and laughed and sang with the men. They seemed comfortable with him, but not a one of them moved from the fire or changed position until Abu stepped away.

I knew Abu was more than a leader. Every species has a pecking order. Every group has those with power and those without. Then there are those who are trusted, whether they lead or not, whether they hold power or not. Abu was the trusted one. Every eye turned to him. He was the one who could hold the space of safety; every man and beast within his sight knew that. Although he watched the moving line, although he looked straight at each one of the men, he did not look for direction. He took us in as he took in the length of the clouds, the reach of the hill, the color of the ground. We were information. We were to be assessed, to be taken into account, to be accounted for. Could I be fooling myself if I thought there was more to it than that?

The sky opened farther and farther, and a million suns came forward. I heard the sounds of morning, felt the folds of the tent pick up the breeze from the east. Sand surrounded us but still I could believe we were near the ocean. Sometimes the air carried a density I knew only exists at the place where sand meets sea. As I did each morning, I stretched one toe at a time, pointing towards the tent opening, then stretched out a finger on each hand, extending myself back out into the world one extremity at a time.

The day was still relatively quiet. I got up, wrapping my garment tightly round me, and for the first time since I joined their journey, I opened the tent flaps and stepped outside by myself. The camp was calm, but a hum of energy flowed through the area. The animals were stirring, I could hear them in the distance. The ashes of the fire glowed white and red, sometimes sparking when a stray bit of wind passed. The men were still spilled about the fire, curled on their rugs, their bodies completely covered.

I stood like a statue, afraid any movement might awaken the bags of bodies around the campfire. To the right was a larger tent I assumed was Abu's. Turning to the left, I stepped clear of the sand that had been diligently swept away from my tent entrance by the boy and headed toward the rustle of the animals. They were hobbled some distance from us. I could barely see them in the shadow of the dune. I wondered if I had become smaller. If the stricture of my days, the heat of the desert, had diminished my size. I had no gauge. These people were not of my kind. I could not say I was taller than one or shorter than another. I could not compare myself to people so unlike my own. How did they see me? As a part of the load, an object of trade, ballast for the day?

I sat down on the sand facing the camels and began talking

to them, cooing almost. "You are the pretty one," I said to a pure white camel who swung her head around and batted her long eyelashes at me. She tried to stand, pushing her tied-up front legs before her. "I'm sorry I cannot help. It must be so frustrating to be tied, I know, but Mohammed will be here soon. He will untie you." I slid myself down the dune until I was next to the white camel and reached out to pat her neck. "You are strong and graceful and move like a queen." I kept talking, telling this folded up beast about the green fields in Devon and the fat of the cows and the strutting chickens. "You would not believe it," I said. "They are so spoiled compared to you." The camel turned her head sharply and opened her mouth to make the sound that drove most people away, a sound that starts out as a rumble, then moves into a strong growl, and finally bursts out into a multi-layered belch. I heard a laugh behind me and turned quickly, then gasped and slipped in the sand trying to stand up and move backwards at the sight of Abu.

He reached his hand out to me, and without thinking I took it. Once again he pulled me upright, this time with delight in his eyes. He laughed again and turned to the camels, saying something as he pointed at the white one. I did not move and did not take my eyes off him. He turned back and smiled down at me, and I followed him over the dune to where Mohammed was and watched as they talked and laughed and Mohammed headed up to take care of his charges.

In the desert the sky was tissue, a thin, vulnerable casing for a pulsing hot earth. It covered the heat with a cool blue membrane that kept us from losing ourselves. When the heat and dust threatened to overtake me, I focused on the sky, staring through the blue veil of my Tuareg headdress. More than once that line at the horizon where sky and sand met had kept me sane. When Abu turned to look at me I sensed it, but I did not look at him. I kept my eyes on that line, and something in the clean geometry of the desert straightened my spine, filled my lungs and allowed me to inhabit this place on earth more fully than I ever did in the security of my family and friends

Each of the days that followed my visit with the camel, I waited for Abu to turn to me and to speak, knowing I would be able to grasp little of what he said. I waited for the men to look over at me. They were aware of me, a curiosity, something strange added to their care. At the end of each day I waited for the camels to stop, as if on instinct. If I had a watch I am sure it would show they stopped at exactly the same time each day. Certainly the quality of the light seemed the same each evening when they lifted their long forward legs and brought their furred feet to a final rest for the night.

And so I made my way into the Sahara. In the desert I was small and large at the same time. I was an ant, an insect, crawling across the floor of the world, and I was an Amazon, the only woman among men, the only white among dark. I would never be so distinct again.

LONDON

June 7, 1970

"ALICE, MY DEAR, WE'RE BOTH impersonating normal people."

Martin pours the gin and tonic, folds himself into the chair across from his wife and raises his glass to her. Alice raises her glass, then smiles into the elixir. Martin sighs deeply. Life is full of surprises. Alice had always been and always will be the biggest surprise. Just when life had become a slow slog, she appeared in the garden at Bournemouth. Even now, decades later, she can take his breath away. Across from him sits a woman in her eighth decade with the bright eyes of an eight-year-old. She dresses appropriately and knows how to dine properly, but there is always—like now with her first loud slurp of the gin and tonic—the recognition that this person could eat you alive.

But what is happening now? She's awake all night, scribbling and sketching, referring to Dr. Omer. This does not bode well. Martin can still feel guilty about the hospitalization thirty years before. But what else could he do? Thank God they didn't use the electric shock, he made sure of that. When she turned a corner without it and came home with paint and paper, he saw her work was good and told her so. Others did too. But she would not put any of it in a gallery. "This is my world," she said. "It's not real, but it's better than nothing."

He understood that. We're both refugees, he thought. It helped him in negotiations, this ability to see the world as unreal. The ones who had trouble at the table were the ones who took it seriously, who thought the world should have strict borders and tight rules. Sands shift, life wobbles. Sometimes if you fear the worst, the worst is summoned. He won't fear the worst now. Alice seems refreshed by the drink, as always. Still, this may not be the best time to leave her alone. And that telegram. She may deny its importance, but he will have Richard look into things.

Martin smiles at his beautiful wife. She smiles back.

THE SAHARA

1912

DUSK ARRIVED QUICKLY ONE DAY. The wind grew stronger, whipping sand into the sky like sheets of taupe stretched across the horizon, erasing the line that defined our journey. The caravan stopped, encircled by dust and heat. Abu took hold of my camel's harness and pulled her, along with the others, into a circle. We dismounted and sat facing inward; the animals folded themselves down on their haunches, providing shelter for us with their dun-colored backs. I looked around at my camel and saw her top and bottom eyelashes, long, thick and straight, fold and interlock, shutting out the sand that was now swirling about us. The beast remained calm. I bent over and wrapped my head completely, pulling the cloth over my ears and leaning into the side of my camel to break the high whistle of the wind. Time disappeared. Consciousness disappeared. A wall of wind had passed over our circle as if we were a bump in the road. Finally the storm took its dust and sand with it, leaving us in silence.

I opened my eyes and found Abu sitting close beside me, his robes intertwined with mine. He smiled. "God is great," he said.

"Yes," I said. "God is great."

Prayer surprised me in the desert. It came unbidden, prayers to the strange gods of Allah and Canterbury's Archbishop. *The Lord be with you now and forever more. Al-ham-du-li-lah. The lord is my shepherd I shall not want.* As a child I thought it was some apologetic bowing and scraping one had to do before begging. The Lord, my shepherd, I-don't-want-to-bother-you kind of thing. Only now was I beginning to understand it meant I shall not have any needs. That was all that came as I put one foot in front of the other, as I watched my toes harden and the nails scrape off. I needed a shepherd, I needed a rod and a staff. Maybe not to comfort me, but to hold me up. It didn't take long for me to fall to my knees and bow prostrate before the East every time the boy did, to fall forward, allow my head to drop, my body to release its struggle to hold me upright. To fall forward toward the light, to fall forward in the heat, to fall forward and feel the light on my back. Even the animals rested, prostrate, calm, quiet, ready for the bipeds to become quadruped, watching as we fell forward on all four appendages, as we drew our bodies back, spread our arms forward, and became one of them.

This is what the desert can do to you. It can spread you across the earth, flat to the land, can make you understand the earth is the only lasting thing in your world, and even the earth is subject to change.

Aleece. Abu looked directly at me and spoke again. *Aleece.* My name. How did he know my name? I talked to myself, or rather I talked to the animals, and I talked to the boy, but I had never dared to address Abu. This time I did. *Abu,* I said, and smiled to see his scarf loose around his chin, his teeth white against his dark skin, his lips dancing as he spoke my name a third time, more softly, *Aleece.*

Was it then that language began for us? Before this our communication was through our eyes—questions, concerns, whole
conversations took place between a lifted eyelid or a dark squint.
Aleece. It was like a benediction, spoken slowly and with
care. To this day I can feel the complete calm that descended on
me. From that moment on I felt myself move with a determination, an acceptance of myself I had never had. Or perhaps had
had one time, and had lost within the walls of school and church
and parlor.

When Abu spoke my name, I heard the sound of it as I
heard the wind through the leaves at home, as I heard the rustle
of grass beneath my feet, as I heard the air above me and the
crunch of stone beneath me. Once again I was solid on the earth.

LONDON

June 7, 1970

EDITH IS ON THE PHONE. "Hello Alice, how are you today?" I know that forced cheeriness. My sister calls out of duty, not interest.

"I am fine," I say and wait for her to reveal the purpose of her call. It will be a bit of a wait. Edith is direct in her purpose but indirect in her method. That is one thing that has not changed. As a child she sat politely at table making all the proper conversational comments. While I most often blurted out my questions and ended up reprimanded or ignored, Edith calmly chatted away until she got the response she had been angling for. Kate the cook used to say, "Edith got the British genes."

I am laughing to myself as I listen to Edith talk of the garden, the weather, the grandchild, as she circles around and around. Finally I say I must get on with my day. "I have an appointment," I say (with my paints and my canvas, I don't say).

"Oh, the reason I rang you is to ask if you'd like to go to Devon this week. Jane and Benjamin are coming and with Martin away I thought—"

Martin must have called her. I told him to call her, didn't I? I've made this complication, haven't I? So he is rallying the troops. And they have made decisions. We are going to Devon.

I understand now. We are all going to the house by the sea for a few days while Martin is at the Peace Conference. "You are tired," he had said. "You need rest, sea air." And he was right; I am tired. All these memories, all this scratching with paper and ink. Although I'd rather be alone, I cannot resist the idea of a seat in the sand and an open horizon before me. We will all go to the house in Devon. Has he told Edith of the telegram? Or has he left that piece of work to me?

What does he know of our truth? We are sisters who used to speak the same language, used to see the world the same. Now I rarely know what she's talking about. I gave up trying to understand long ago. When did that slight hint of anger begin hissing out the side of some words? When did she begin to sigh at the end of each sentence?

It takes patience to listen to her. I gulp air and cannot wait for her to finish talking, I jump to make sense of things before she finishes speaking. I just don't have the time to listen to her. I am too impatient. That has not changed.

You do not need to force life, Aleece, it is always coming to you. Relax, Alice, there is time.

I want to keep my sister by my side. *Keep your enemies close.* Are we enemies? We bicker. We disagree. But we are of the same blood and bones, we traveled the same passageway to enter this earth. And that counts for more than anyone ever wants to admit. I don't want to keep these secrets anymore. They're heavy and bite my neck and constrict my throat and maybe I was wrong in thinking I would lose Edith if I told her the truth. You can't really lose a sister, can you? Misplace her? Displace her? Keep her outside of your secrets, maybe.

"A visit to the sea sounds perfect," I say. "Thank you."

Edith puts down the phone and calls to Jane, "She is coming, prepare yourself."

Jane comes to the doorway and laughs. "A week with Aunt Alice by the sea. Delightful. I'll go get Benjamin sorted." She winks then turns away.

Edith begins calculating. Three adults, one child, how many sheets, which bed to make. Is there enough toilet paper, what staples are in the larder? Summer used to be such bliss. When the family packed up and headed to the house on the coast, she and Alice spent hours at the edge of the water collecting stones, identifying marine life in the tide pools, teasing James. Although the journey from their home to the house by the sea was not far on the map, the geographical change was surprisingly vast. The whole family relaxed once there. But life was different with staff. Picnics, a proper tea. Time to enjoy the air, the sunlight, time to read.

Edith can hear the thud of her own pulse as she lifts herself out of the chair and walks to the closet to find the large over-night bag. Martin was cryptic. "I don't think Alice should be alone while I'm at the Paris talks." He didn't really ask, nor did he explain. Something about a telegram. "Alice will talk with you," he said. But he is coming with her, taking the train down, then returning immediately, which is odd. His taking the time to accompany her.

Edith pushes her eyeglasses up her nose and sniffs. How old is this luggage? There is a crack down the side of the bag. Edith runs her finger along it and sighs. Since Frederick died and Jane divorced, a visit to Devon means a house full of women. And Jane's little Benjamin. Alice will entertain him, or be entertained by him. "I need a good night's sleep," Edith says aloud.

LONDON

June 8, 1970

M Y NOTEBOOK IS TUCKED into my large tote bag. I pull
it out as the train rocks forward and Martin lowers *The
Times* from in front of his face. "You're sketching?" he asks.

"Yes, sketching."

He lowers the paper to his lap and smiles at me.

Martin thinks her remarkable. He loves her face when reading,
when drawing, when in repose. He is not a surreptitious husband; he has always been open with Alice, or so he believes. But
he cannot ignore his training. While she slept he had opened
the folded yellow page and read the future. He understands the
silence that had surrounded their marriage has been broken.
He knows Alice has a hard journey in front of her, one she has
alluded to over the years but never fully revealed. He must be
patient, he must not force her, but again, he cannot ignore his
training.

"I'll miss you this week," he says.

She flashes her bright eyes at him and raises her hand in a
salute. "The world needs you," she says.

"Do you?" he asks.

She startles at the tone of his voice, the unexpected words.

"Yes," she says quietly. "I will always need you."

Martin nods his head, then raises *The Times* to review the state of the world.

I pull out my pen and set to work.

Deepest darkest Africa, it was once called. My Africa was warm and brilliant. Blues that defied the British imagination, gold and ocher. The colors were astonishing. Once, in the rail station at Putnam Crossing, I saw a tribesman standing tall and thin in his robe. It was as if a flower had bloomed in a back abandoned garden, seeing this tall stalk of color in the middle of black coats and hats and brollies. Now I've lost the word, the word for illusion in the desert, when the constant blinding scene before one leaves the mind craving something unique, something different, and the hallucinations begin and it's so common there is a word for it, but it escapes me.

The map of Africa is a giant jigsaw puzzle, the pieces changing every year, different colors, different sizes, different shapes. *The Times* had an article just a couple of days ago, an article on death, plague, whatever, and the requisite outline of Africa was there, looking like a black smudge, something spilled just below Europe with a long stain spreading down the page.

I root about in my bag and—here it is—my map of Africa. I stopped at the bookstore this morning on the way to the train and asked for one. They actually had a roadmap! A Michelin Guide to the desert. Extraordinary. I burst out laughing and the salesgirl, no more than nineteen I imagine, with hair the color of a rusted-out coffee can. The girl didn't see anything funny about that.

"I could have used this fifty years ago," I said, laughing away.

"That's two pounds," she said without looking at me. They don't make eye contact anymore, the people who take your money.

I gave her the two pounds and she shoved the map into a bag and handed it over in my general direction, already turning away to chat with the boy behind the counter.

Imagine that. A road map of the desert. Of course it is useless. But there are names on it. *Tamanrasset. Timbuktu. Aïn Séfra.* Actual places rooted in the shifting tides of sand. Places with water and trees and buildings and people. Places like dots on a line, the geometry of travel from one oasis to another. Now I remember the word. *Mirage.* Hallucination in the desert.

DEVON

June 8, 1970

JANE MUST HAVE BEEN FUSSING with the family cottage again. Blue striped wallpaper in this room. Matching blue striped spread, ticking on the pillows. I feel like a nasty old woman complaining of the comfort. It was much more rustic when we were children. Or was that just in contrast to the linens and drapery at home? They are all being so kind. Martin sitting quietly with me all the way down on the train. Edith and Jane at the station, smiling and cooing "Oh it's so good to see you, it's been too long." Sweet of them. Benjamin put his arms around my legs and held me tight—the best greeting of them all. Then Martin's goodbye and the admonition to rest, have a lie-down before tea. It's just so damn soft in here. I can hear the waves outside, spitting the rocks up the beach. I can hear the gulls screeching. I can feel the light crossing the window. And here I lie like an Easter chick in an overstuffed nest.

It's warm and sunny and I am glad to be by the sea, despite the décor. Then I remember the news, and my heart begins to race. Throughout my life when I was anxious about an imminent event—an exam at school, a surgery scheduled—I would be reassured by the passage of time. In two weeks this will be past. In three days this will be past. It settled me. Time was something

61

I had no control over. There was nothing to do but let the sun cross the sky, let the moon follow its course, and then I would be through it, on the other side. But time cannot settle me now. In six days, "progeny" will arrive. Maybe this is a mistake, or a joke, a bad practical joke. But now I hear Edith coming down the hall and my mind flips through the lifetime I have lived since Saturday, and I think in a few days Martin will be on his way back from Paris and I know this is not something time will take care of. My heart begins to race again and I wonder if this tired body will live six more days. What should I tell Edith? My breath begins to deepen and my heart feels full and soft, and I can believe it is a separate part of my body and will keep beating six days and more no matter what my being wants to do. By the time I rise from the bed, my heartbeat is so loud the gulls, the surf and the wind sound a thousand miles away.

LONDON

June 8, 1970

MARTIN IS NOT A FEARFUL MAN. He has seen man at his worst on the battlefield and in the boardroom. He has learned to take the long view and to value what is his. But today, on the afternoon train from Devon to London, Martin sits in fear.

"Abu." "The desert." And the lightwave emerging from Alice's blue eyes. I've seen this before, he thinks. The doctors said it was hysteria, delayed from her time in Morocco. I should not have listened to them, he thinks. Alice never lies. She may not always make sense, but she never lies.

When he leaves the train, Martin does not go to his office. He walks past it, assessing the situation. The invitation to attend the Paris Peace Talks was just that, an invitation, not a command. Vietnam was the booby trap the French and Americans had stepped into. For once Britain had kept her sticky fingers out of the problem. Martin is not interested in power except as an abstract equation. Others lob bombs across a no-man's-land, dig tunnels and strafe vast reaches of land. When it is over and the weapons laid down and men—always and only men—sit around the table with merely words to lob at each other, Martin is invited to sit with them.

He watches and listens while people fight over their placement at the table. He considers the character of each person present, his eyes often unfocused so he can listen and watch without assigning the body to its country. In this way he analyzes the table like a particularly intense chess match. He watches the body language, he listens to the timbre of the voice, he keeps the focus on solving the puzzle and, like a sapper listening to the ticking of a bomb, he waits for the solution to reveal itself. Who will acquiesce? What words will appease? What pattern of conversation will click everything into place?

Today he listens to his own footsteps tapping on the sidewalk, moves cleanly through the throngs, and focuses on Alice's words. *Abu, desert, my lover.* And the one word that rattles him: *Progeny.*

THE SAHARA

1912

THE WIND IN THE DESERT WAS INDIFFERENT. Gentle
and caressing one minute, lethal the next. It seemed like
a lifetime, not months, since I had sat under the acacia tree in a
white linen dress with a white sun bonnet and sipped tea. I stud-
ied that image in my head and it was as if I were looking at another
person. I looked down at my hands, stained by the red dirt that lay
just below the surface, the dirt that had become a part of my skin.
Not the sand of the seashore, but the deep, dense earth the sand
released as it swirled around us. My skin was dry, sere really, and
I was thinner. Sometimes when I stood and moved about I was
unsteady, unused to such a light body. I knew I was to keep well
covered. To protect me or to incarcerate me?

The night was over. Dawn was not yet on the horizon, but
the cold that blankets the desert at night was beginning to lift.
The animals were always the first to arise, raising their heads
towards the east. I sat quietly in the tent waiting for the boy
to bring me the morning tea. All my meals at that point were
silent and solitary. I surprised myself with my enjoyment of
that. After the tea, so strong that I choked the first time I took
a sip, I washed in the corner of the tent and wrapped myself up
for the day, covering my unruly hair with the lightweight blue

cloth, winding it around and around as the boy had taught me. It's stunning how quickly one can adapt.

The sun came up. Mohammed spread hay across a blanket in front of the camel's hobbled knees. A few men bowed to the East. The air thrummed with the vibrations of man and beast coming awake. I was loaded onto my camel, felt the heat penetrate my wrap, and lost myself in the rocking cradle until at some point the caravan came to a halt and all was lowered to the ground, fires lit, tents raised, animals hobbled, and the sun's light and warmth passed from the earth. Even in what I assumed was sleep, I could feel myself rocking, constantly rocking through the desert. The truth is, the Sahara hypnotized me.

In Marrakesh the tea was often bitter, so hot we couldn't lift the glasses. My brother James thought it was funny to have tea in glasses, with leaves, huge green leaves, stuffed inside. Mother insisted on regular English tea, but James and I took to visiting the kitchen courtyard and having tea with Alif and Ahmed. We learned how to hold the teapot three feet above the glass and pour a steady stream, then tip the spout back at exactly the right moment, never allowing a drop to fall outside the glass. James shaved sugar. "I'm skiing off the mountain," he would say, slicing the knife down the side of the cone onto the blank paper it sat on. Mother warned us our teeth would rot, but we grew to crave the dense, thick syrup of mint tea in Marrakesh.

I lifted my glass and looked at the boy, just about James's size, if not his age. I tried to remember my brother—his face, his long arms and legs—but his image was fading. Edith remained clear to me, and when I saw her again, she was Edith. But James faded. The photo on the mantel when I returned might as well have been a generic soldier-in-uniform photo from the Sunday photogravure. I could never recover the James who laughed and shaved sugar and drank what he called "swamp tea."

I didn't know I was hungry until they put the goat on the fire. The last full meal I had had with others was Sunday breakfast, before we set out in the car with Father. Mother had worked for weeks after cook left, trying to explain scrambled eggs and toast to Alif. Bacon was out of the question. By that day, the day we drove off with Father, breakfast had become a common board of scrambled eggs, flat bread, and an array of condiments: chopped tomatoes with onions and cumin, walnuts in honey, carrots and preserved lemons. Mother had managed to acquire some Fortnum and Mason plum preserves that gave her such pleasure none of us ever touched it.

Hunger is for the living, for those who can recognize another day on the horizon. But then they put the goat on the fire, and the smell of meat wet my mouth. The boy came to me with a shallow bowl filled with grain, vegetables, and pieces of meat on top. He set it down on the rug before us and dug his hand in, lifting the food quickly to his mouth. Then he nodded to me. I had seen the kitchen crew eating this way outside the cooking room. I almost laughed the first time I came upon them. How many times had our nanny slapped our hands in the nursery when we reached out for the platter? How many times had I been reprimanded to hold my fork the correct way, to keep my hand in my lap? And here were these people squatting around a huge platter, reaching in and taking food. I watched in horror, then in awe as I saw that not a single grain, not a single morsel of food was dropped. The entire process seemed delicate. Like a circle of cranes leaning in, the group ate silently, bowing as they reached forward, leaning back to swallow, not spilling, not jostling each other, but humming and smiling as they nodded at the goodness of the meal.

"Praise *Allah*," the boy said. "The first goat of the journey."

I reached out.

"*LA*," the boy said and gently put my left hand down, then lifted my right hand. I reached out again, holding my fingers in the slight scoop I saw him make, then lifted the mix of grains, vegetables, and meat to my mouth, spilling most of it in my lap. The boy laughed. I wanted to slap him, but the nursery discipline was strong in me. I put my left hand in my lap, reached out again, and took two tiny grains between my thumb and forefinger, brought them to my mouth, and swallowed. Hunger is a good sauce. I leaned over again and reached for a piece of vegetable. Then a piece of meat. Then another and another. My hand was scooping now, my mouth open before the hand had returned to the platter. The boy watched me, then shook his head. "Slow," he said. "Slow. Or you will sicken."

Goat. Strong meat, smoky from the fire. Our diet had been mostly vegetables and grain, some flat bread, and at the outset of the journey, cheese, eggs, goat milk. It was a pleasure to work one's teeth, to chew on bone, to—what is the word?—to masticate. Eventually I came to know how long into a journey we were by what Mohammed served. Every few weeks, I would see him walking among the herd, poking the sides of the goats, and I knew soon we would have a roast. One goat, one good-sized goat, fed the entire caravan. We slept well after a roast, our dreams calmer, quieter. The next day the men would joke and tug at each other. They seemed stronger, quick-paced, as if each bite of the goat had transferred that sure-footed, bleating beast into their own bodies, and for a few hours, perhaps a day or two, the caravan moved forward with a palpable energy.

Sometimes the longing hit me. I wanted to step lightly down the stairs and turn the corner into the sun porch where the table had been laid with fresh scones and jam and a pot of fragrant Earl Grey. I longed to see my sister sitting calmly by my side, eager to reach for the Devon cream, holding her cup with one little finger pointed out to the right. I longed to put on my squishy boots and my black slicker and tramp on the soft earth of the garden in March and marvel at the first buds beneath the beech tree.

The boy put the tray with mint tea on the rug in front of me and smiled. I nodded and watched him turn and step out of the tent. Then I laughed aloud. What would Mother think? A man—well, a boy—waiting on me? I raised the glass to my lips and then choked on the sip I took. Mother had not appeared to me for weeks. Not in dreams, not in memory. And here she was now, standing in the doorway of the back hall. I was sitting on the bench pulling my boots off.

"Alice, a lady doesn't tramp about alone." Her voice was sharp.

"What do you mean? I always walk alone. Well, I don't really walk alone—there's always a dog or a cat or a cow or a chicken, and sometimes there's the barn owl and James's donkey, and once there was a ferret who walked beside me down by the brook—"

"Alice." Mother's voice was rising. "It's not proper. You are a young lady now, it isn't proper. Look at you. You are muddy and flushed, and no man wants that."

I stood up and laughed. "Why do I care what a man wants?"

Mother wrung her hands in front of me and I stepped back, thinking for a moment she was about to slap me. "Alice," she said, "you don't understand the world. You must settle down. You must make yourself attractive."

"Do you think I'm unattractive?"

"Of course not. You are a beaut—a very good-looking girl. Young woman. And that can be a dangerous thing if you don't manage it well."

I heard her swallow the word "beautiful," and I could hear the agitation in her voice. Something inside me wanted to tease, but something else told me to be wary.

"I don't understand," I said. "Manage the fact that I'm good looking?"

"It is a great asset for a woman. You will be sought after. You have been well brought up, you can make a good impression and that can lead to a good—alliance," Mother said. "A good alliance in life."

"MARRIAGE?" I said. "Is that what this is about? Marriage?"

Mother dropped her arms to her side and sighed deeply. "Perhaps we should discuss this with your father," she said.

I stiffened. Mother and I did not "discuss" things well. How many times had I been sent back to the nursery as a child, reprimanded for my "sassy" mouth, my "rude" words, my "willful" behavior?

'Yes," I said between clenched teeth. "Let's discuss this with Father."

But we never did.

Then came the day I stepped forward in the heat of midday and stood in confusion at the sight of people approaching from the west, people in trousers and hats, carrying guns. Abu was by my side instantly. He motioned to me to cover my eyes with the *tagelmust* and then stepped in front of me. I did not recognize the syllables of my native language until the voices were only a few paces away.

"Where are you going?" the men asked.

I heard my native tongue and did not think it odd until later that these sunburned men came upon us in the emptiness and assumed Abu and the others spoke their language. I did not offer to translate; I did not offer to use the words I had gathered, each a precious commodity in this barren world. I stood silently behind Abu and heard the frustration in the voices of the men as their anxious demands were met with calm silence.

"Where are we?" demanded a red-faced, portly man sitting astride an aged camel. "Can you tell us how far it is to Timbuktu?" Abu bowed his head to the men and made gestures to the boy to bring water. The men slid off their mounts and grasped the water bags greedily. Only one of the three bothered to look up and nod "much obliged" before draining the bag. No one in the desert gulps water. The body evaporates more water in the act of gulping than it takes in. Besides, it is unutterably impolite. I found myself cringing as the men, at Abu's invitation, unloaded their beasts and prepared to spend the night with us.

I should tell them who I am, I thought. I should tell them where I came from, who my family is, that I have no idea how long I have been wandering in the desert and I do not know if anyone remembers me. I wonder, did the family think of me on my birthday which surely must have passed by now? Are they looking for me? But I remained silent, confused by my own inaction. Although Abu did not seem concerned, I chose not to sit by the fire that night. I sat in the tent listening to the white men talk among themselves and waited for grief and homesickness to overtake me. It did not happen. I did not yet know how much Abu understood of my language. He afforded the men all the hospitality a man of the desert always offers a fellow traveler.

The men were made comfortable, offered food and water and places by the fire, but although there was much talking and laughing during the evening, there was no point at which you could say there was conversation. Abu remained quiet, and the three Englishmen continued to talk, mostly to each other, sometimes in raised voices to the others. It seemed they were from London. Their talk was of the wealth they thought was hidden in Timbuktu. The reward at the end of their journey.

Later that evening a note appeared on my tray, put there by the boy no doubt. It was in English. It said, "Do you need help?" I stared at the letters on the paper and ran my fingers across the ink stains. *How did they know I was here? When did they see me? Which one of them wrote this?* The boy had retreated from my tent before I opened the note, and to step out after him seemed unwise. I sat with the slip of paper in my hand and tasted a new fear, a fear that immobilized me.

Why did I not act on this offer of help? Fear gripped me, but fear of what? Fear of being offered a new life? The ability to become a completely new person? The chance to shed the layer of skin grown in response to those who fed me, clothed me, told me what they expected of me? But I was a captive. Yes, I was, but I also felt freer than I had ever been in my life.

The note in my pocket was a hot coal burning into my flesh. Through the night I prayed. I prayed for guidance, for direction. Strange prayers, strange words, a new language unfolding, folding, pulling and pushing words "Our Lord who art . . . Allah . . . Allah . . . Alleluia." My head throbbed from the weight of a mixed vocabulary of French, English, Arabic, Tamasheq, vowels and consonants and grunts and twitches and a mouth that moved separately from my tongue. The more I understood, the less I could speak. Was this a dream? Were these incantations? In the morning when the boy brought the tea I asked where the note came from, and he smiled and showed the sack of money he must have gotten for delivering it. Pennies, ha'pennies, useless in the desert, but to him a fortune. "Where are the white men?" I asked. He shook his head. They were gone. They had left at daybreak, supplied with dates and camel's milk and thick rugs, gifts from Abu.

Why did I open myself to the desert so easily? It all seemed to happen as if ordained: the car overturning, the wind rising, the driver leading me away. I see it all now quite clearly. Still, I can't make sense of it. I once walked into a full-length mirror and after the shock of bumping into myself, so to speak, I laughed to think I—Alice—had almost walked through the looking glass. I stood there holding my fingers up to the fingers in the glass, and I swear I almost believed I could step through. Perhaps that's what actually happened on that rough road beyond Marrakesh. I stepped through a looking glass in Morocco in 1912 and placed my foot in Abu's world. There are days that makes as much, if not more, sense than any other explanation for what my life became.

The camels were calling. They could smell water in the air, although there was no green on the horizon. We turned down into a rock canyon and their low calls reverberated as we passed into the chill of a wet chasm and came upon the wonder of a gorge of fresh water. The caravan was moving at a hurried pace, to where I did not know and could not ask. Abu stayed close to me through the days. I was still learning to believe I was safe in this new world. Old voices told me the world was ruthless, it could break, cut, maim me, in unexpected ways, mostly physical. With Abu I was learning to believe in the world as a place to spend all of me, all the time. Not just an afternoon in a garden, or an hour in a walk, but every minute, every footfall, every breath was here for me to explore the world. I was still learning to believe that what I felt—safe—could be what is true.

We seemed to stay en route longer than usual, stopping for very short periods and not setting up camp until just before the sun set. Day after day we kept up the same pace until this day, when the camels breathed in the moist air of the gorge and began their incessant rumbling. The caravan stopped, and beast and man stepped into the water with relief and delight. I watered my feet, then stepped away to relieve myself behind a rock and came upon the three British men again. This time I recognized my own language. My back muscles spasmed at the first open vowel.

"Hallo Miss!" the portly man called, as sweetly as if we were passing on High Street. "Did you get the note? That little bugger took our money but never gave you the note, did he?" The man's voice became coarser; he spoke crossly. "Everyone on this continent is slicing off his piece of the pie."

Fire ran up my spine, furious fire that opened my mouth before I could think.

"Please," I said. "Leave me alone. Leave me be."

"What's your name?"

"Where are you from?"

The three of them prodded me with questions, moving in closer and closer. "You don't belong here."

Good God, I thought. These are my people? These ridiculous men. They were fools. Foolish white men. Their thoughts walked across their faces like cartoon characters. I knew immediately they did not have the best intentions.

"I don't need you," I said, almost under my breath.

"What's that, Miss? What are you doing here?"

I looked into the burnt face before me and saw the face of a man who assumed he knew the world, who didn't even try to show respect to beast, to woman, to sand and sky, to the world above and below him. *Now or never* went through my head, *now or never*. Visions of tea and crumpets and tight corsets and endless chatter inside damask-covered walls. My chest tightened.

"Perhaps you like these dark men?" The fat man leered at me.

Red flashed across my eyeballs.

"You don't belong here, Miss."

"What are you YOU doing here?" I shouted. "YOU don't belong here." I saw them exchange looks.

"GO," I yelled. "Go away." I put my palm straight out in front of me.

The squat one reached out. I kicked out hard, hitting him on the shin and sending myself off balance. I fell to the ground. The men's hands were reaching down. I rolled away, kicking up sand like a swimmer, screaming at them.

"She's crazy," the fat one yelled, throwing his hands up. "She's just plain crazy. I'm not dragging her out of the desert, she's not worth the money."

"Go away," I screamed, rolling and crawling to my feet. "Leave me be. Go back to your bloody King."

At that the red-faced fellow laughed. The squat one kicked sand back at me and pulled the others away. "Let her go. Let her rot out here."

"Your name," the red-faced fellow said, almost kindly. "Tell us your name."

"I have no name," I said, backing away from them. I picked up my *tagelmust*. "There is no name for me," I called over my shoulder. I swung the *tagelmust* over my head and twirled it a couple of times. "I'm nameless." I laughed and waved. The men shook their heads. "Crazy," the squat one said. "I told you, the desert makes people crazy. Leave her here."

I walked back behind the rocks, then stood on tiptoe to watch as they moved away. When I turned around Abu was standing there.

"*Inshallah,*" he bowed his head. "You have chosen."

We traveled for days after the encounter with the British men. When I questioned the boy, he shook his head and turned his eyes away. Although I had come to understand some of their language, I could not understand their silence. The fire burned at night and the men sat around it, but there was no singing or dancing, no storytelling. Even the animals seemed to know more than I did. Their ears pointed forward and they moved with a tension I had not felt before.

A few times I thought I saw lorries on the horizon, but each time we turned ourselves sideways to the sight and it faded before I could be sure. The desert was becoming stone. The high dunes gave way to flat coarse ground, covered with a thin layer of sand. The camels and goats left quick imprints that were blown away before we had stepped a few feet forward from them. I was beginning to think of our water supplies. The last watering ground we visited was long ago. And the nights were getting colder. I wondered about the men lying beside the dead embers of the fire. Were they cold? Were they lonely? Where were the women of their world?

DEVON

June 8, 1970

"YOU WERE SUCH A BEAUTIFUL LITTLE GIRL," I say at tea.

"Alice, you're not making sense. You're too tired," Edith says.

"No, thank you for your concerns. But I'm not tired, I just had a lovely rest on the train. I am remembering. You had such golden blond hair. The servants gasped when they first saw you in Morocco."

Edith looks at me, then turns away quickly to hide her blush.

"They did, they truly did," I say. "I don't think they had ever seen people such as us. Ahmed always called you 'sun child.'"

"How could you know that? They didn't speak English."

"Oh," I laugh. "You're right, they didn't. But I remembered what Ahmed said, and later I asked Abu what it meant and he said 'sun child.' I told him how people would stare at you, and Mother made sure you were completely covered whenever we left the compound. He loved hearing that story. Of the sun child. Do you remember? How the servants would give you the sweetest meat, the ripest fruits, how Ahmed would fold your clothes with gloves on his hands?"

Edith stares at me. "No," she says. "No, I don't remember anything like that."

77

She gets up to clear the table, then turns and asks, her voice an octave higher, "And Abu, who is Abu?"

I grabbed the hem of my robe to wipe my mouth. Mother. And Edith. And Father and James. Where were they now? I lifted the robe to my eyes and pressed against the lids to tamp down the threat of tears.

When Abu entered the tent I turned my face away to hide my distress, but he saw it immediately. He saw everything.

"You are not calm," he said. "You are beginning the day with distress."

Always a declarative sentence. A statement of what is before him. Not an interrogation. Not a judgment. Like the animals, Abu remained in the present. He leaned down, placed his hands on mine, and lifted me to standing, gently brushing my robe off my face. He stood there looking into my eyes.

"Aleece, you must trust yourself. We live in our own worlds. You cannot live in other people's worlds. You must live in your own world."

Is he telling me I cannot live among his tribe?

In time I understood. His words came back to me as I lay in the midst of the Sisters of Blessed Mercy. They came back to me again in Vincent Grove. And here they are once again, as I try to talk with Edith. *Trust yourself. You must live in your own world.*

I go cold. I stutter, mumble, then turn to Benjamin. Edith stands for a minute, then follows Jane into the kitchen.

Benjamin is holding up an apple slice and looking through the empty core ring.

"What do you see?" I ask.

"The stars," he says, "over my head."

Benjamin loves to talk in rhyme.

"The stars over your head? Is that what you said?"

"Yes, the stars over my head when I'm out of my bed."

"And where are you led by the stars over your head when you're out of your bed?"

We play this game as long as we can. Volley poetry, I call it.

"When I'm out of my bed with the stars overhead I'm led to the edge."

"To the edge?"

"Yes, the edge of the world."

I look at the apple slice beginning to brown at its edges and stare at the perfect star in its center.

"Auntie Alice?"

"Yes, Benjamin?"

"Did I lose the poetry volley?"

"No, I lost this time," I say. "You took me to the edge and I couldn't return."

Benjamin gives me one of his five-year-old gazes and I watch as he bites into the apple and giggles.

"I win, I win," he crows.

I put my hand softly on his cheek and say, "Yes, you win."

I stare at the star inside the apple on the plate.

The stars were almost upside down in the desert. We must have been quite far south. I couldn't find a constellation I could identify. Couldn't find a familiar star. There were so many in the sky, it was like losing your friend in Piccadilly Circus on a rainy Saturday afternoon—so many people under black umbrellas, the familiar ones are lost to you.

"This isn't the same world," I said to Abu.

He laughed, a quiet, amused rumble deep in his throat.

"No, Aleece, this is not the same world."

"No," I said. "I mean this is not the same planet, the same universe. You live under a different sky here."

"We live under the same sky, Aleece, we just live closer to it than you are used to."

"How can you live closer to the sky?"

"There is not so much between us and the sky as there is in your world. We have not cluttered the in-between air."

Sometimes what Abu said made no sense until I had listened long after he spoke. Listening in the desert was standing as still as an animal and waiting until the person speaking came to a complete stop. At home so much of what I thought was listening was really just waiting for someone to take a breath, waiting for someone to leave an opening rather than waiting for them to reach their meaning.

I pick up the last apple slice on the plate. "Look, Benjamin, the star is not so far."

He laughs, a half-swallowed chuckle. "The star is not so far from the apple's car."

I snicker at him. "The star is not so far from the apple's car but very far from Benjamin's jar."

"Your rhyme is sloppy, Auntie," he says.

"Yes, Benjamin, my rhyme is often sloppy."

Jane collects Benjamin and I step into the sunroom with my notebook.

This house feels alien, the surroundings so clean and beautiful and coordinated. Not like the tent, where things were definitely rectilinear, the poles rigid, the skins taut against the structure but then the surprise of pillows and rugs and the jumble of low tables and lanterns that somehow erupted from the baggage and got set around the inside. It never ceased to startle me, like those play sponges Benjamin has for the bath. A flat dry cake one minute, then drop it into the bath and up pops a bright pink and orange island complete with palm tree, floating in the water, bumping against Benjamin's knee. That's what it was like at the end of a long trek, the men descending from the camels, unloading the beasts, untying the shafts, unrolling the tents, and within no time, there it was, a complete room, bright and inviting, floating on the sand. If I had not seen them do it, I would have thought it was a mirage.

THE SAHARA

1912

MID-MORNING, SOMETIME DURING my second month with the caravan? I had bled once, maybe twice, since entering the desert, and had ripped excess cloth from my robes. This time the boy saw my soiled cloths. He looked scared and raised his eyebrows, then lowered his eyes. "Not long," he said. "One more day."

The next day the caravan came to a complete halt at the sight of a flower. I was touched that these tough men would bring their relentless pace to an end for a moment of unexpected beauty. I watched Abu approach the blossom. He looked up at me and smiled. "Āman," he said. And then I understood. A bloom in the desert indicated the presence of water. The camels were always the first to sense it. Something in their gait changed, imperceptibly at first, then their flanks filled out and their fuzzy ears pointed straight forward.

We came upon it early in the day. A green sinew curving through the light brown valley before us. The animals quickened their pace, and even I breathed more rapidly in anticipation. The change from arid to humid was seamless, as if the high desert dune before us had rolled over in its sleep, shifting its coverlet of sand to reveal the soft green wave of the grass.

The iridescent blue of sky reflected in the imperceptible glide of water on the move.

At its edge, the water was murky brown, silt floating up to the top, churning about as the animals and men together waded straight in. "What?" I gestured to the boy. "What is this? I cannot go in here." The boy wasn't listening. He was dragging the leather water bag through the disgusting river of dirt—the water bag that would sustain us on our journey. My stomach began to heave and I turned away, fearful of adding my vomit to the ugly sludge before us. *This cannot be, I thought. This simply cannot be.*

I have no trouble imagining the oceans boiling away and sand overtaking the world. When we arrived at that oasis, I watched as the men untied the animals and allowed them to walk straight into the brown water. Abu saw my distress and reached out his hand to guide me away from the commotion. He pointed upstream and walked me along a rutted path under the palm trees.

We stood side by side in the edge of the water, and I laughed at the sight of our feet. His were barnacled boats, wide and calloused. They looked as though they were floating in the current. Mine were so small in comparison, but they too were calloused, and the color of weak tea. I could almost believe they were growing out of someone else's body.

Abu bent down and thrust his hands in the water, splashing his feet and the hem of my robe at the same time. Without thinking, I kicked my foot forward as we had done at the seaside in the shallow waves, splattering each other and shrieking like loons. He grabbed my ankle with his hand and I tumbled, knocking him into the stream and falling face forward after him. I gasped at the shock of feeling my whole body wet and cool. Abu's laugh bellowed from below. He took hold of my arms and lifted me above the water, raising me above his head. His wet robes flowed out from his shoulders. "You are a bird," I cried. "You are a raptor!" He pinned my arms against my body, pulling his fingers in as if they were claws. Gentle, soft claws. What could have been painful was playful. I laughed but I could not dispel the image that arose of Abu's hand slowly turning the driver's wrist until he fell to the ground.

When the boy came upon us Abu was standing in front of me, slapping the water with his feet. I tried to pluck the wet robes from my body and walk as demurely as I could away from the shock and fear in the boy's eyes. Abu had been laughing and splashing in the water with me. Our bodies had touched. And the boy had been a witness. I turned away, not wanting to see the wrath I was sure would erupt. There was silence all around. Then I heard a great roar and I turned to see Abu lunge at the boy. "Don't," I cried, then went soundless as I watched Abu lift the boy by his knees, catapult him into the water, and burst out laughing. I left them there, kicking and splashing, and made my way back to the encampment.

This was all some sort of miracle—fresh, astonishing. No longer did the men watch me, wary of my every move. I became a willing member of the caravan, and, most amazing to me, I began to understand more and more of the language. When the men spoke to the animals or to each other, it was as if my ears realigned themselves and the sounds filtered in with a significance I grasped.

At night I sat by the fire, beside Abu, and warmed myself while the men sang and joked and contented themselves. I longed to sip the drink of the men; my thirst to be a part of it all was immense, but Abu did not drink the spirits, and I was of Abu, so I did not. At times I forgot the differences between myself and the others. No longer male, or female, or British, or Tuareg, no boundaries of class, culture, geography, intruded in the space that surrounded us.

I scooped up sand and spread my fingers wide, bathing my feet in the abrasive powder. My toenails snagged on the hem of my robe as I began to dance. I slipped in and out of placement in those first months, listening to the wind, the clear bell of air that puffed my earlobes or clapped the side of my face.

A cough behind me sent my shoulders up, but the strangled sigh of the camels calmed me. Abu was everywhere then. At the head of the caravan, back behind Mohammed, speaking sharply to the boy. I always met his eyes, although fear kept me from looking at the others.

"You are too direct," he told me later. "Your eyes are too clear. You must learn to tame them."

"Tame my eyes?"

"Yes, a woman should not see too much in this world. A woman carries life. She should not see the things that threaten life."

I laughed. A full-throated laugh. Abu pulled back and for an instant I thought he might slap me, but his hand fell softly sideways and he stopped short of a caress.

"Aleeeece," he said. "You have already seen too much."

I opened my arm to gesture towards the camp.

"No," he said. "I do not talk of the desert. You have already seen too much before the desert. Here you can rest your eyes. Here perhaps you can use new eyes."

I laughed again and circled my thumbs and forefingers over my eyes like goggles.

"Is there a word in your language for a woman like you?" he said. I shook my head.

"No," he said. "There is no language for a woman like you."

I watched Abu for weeks before I understood he was training the boy. Like a shepherd with his dog, he put the boy through the paces of finding his way through the caravan: a nod of the head, the turn of a shoulder, and the boy could separate one camel from another or place himself beside a man who for some reason needed to be watched. I didn't really know what I was seeing until one day I watched the dance between them and remembered Angus on the downs and recognized the intense silent exchange of man and beast.

The boy was eager and agile, and although he was always called "the boy," I could see Abu cared for him and in many ways had a respect I didn't see in his interactions with the men. It should not have surprised me to learn Abu was teaching him to read. First the stars, then the sands, and eventually, words. I must confess to some jealousy at that point. And fear. In the pecking order of the caravan, the boy was clearly below me, at my service even. What would happen to me if that pecking order changed?

I was following the baby camel. He was all legs and eyes, like an overgrown praying mantis. I saw him tottering away from the camp, his legs taking him in one direction, then suddenly in another. I sang to him, nursery rhymes, which made his ears twitch and his hips go out of alignment. I was lucky to have such a sweet white thing to follow about the dunes. I kept imagining he was a cross between a lamb and a horse, tight white fuzzy fur and elongated neck. As I sang, I managed to decrease the distance between us until I began singing *Frere Jacques* and he stopped and let me approach.

I stroked him and sang another verse, then took off my *tagel-must* and tied it around his slender neck. *No nose ring for you fella, not yet,* I whispered.

We stood together swaying for a moment or two; then I raised my head and looked back from where we had come. A shrub, a rock, a mound of sand. I looked to the west. A shrub, a rock, a mound of sand. To the south. A shrub, a rock, a mound of sand. Everywhere I looked, the same vista, the caravan nowhere in sight. I had been stupid. Utterly stupid, to set off without paying attention to the light, to any feature I could return to.

The camel nuzzled me. He was hungry. I could feel the panic rising up my throat, could feel the pressure pushing down against my backbone. *It is written. In S'hallah,* I murmured to the camel. *The lord is my shepherd,* I began intoning, *I shall not want. He maketh me to lie down in green pastures.* I opened my eyes. No green pastures in front of me. I closed my eyes and leaned against the little camel. *He restoreth my soul.* I opened my eyes and took a deep breath, then turned to the baby camel. *Yea, though I walk through the valley of the shadow of death, I will fear no evil, for thou art beside me.*

The camel snorted and pulled his neck away. *I will fear no evil,* I said, and let the scarf loosen between us. The camel began walking and I followed, my skin on fire. I watched the sun move down toward the horizon, felt the wind coming up and knew it was erasing our footprints. The 23rd Psalm was gone from my head now. The camel turned to me and I realized I was moaning, a low heavy sigh. I sounded like the cows in Devon, groaning under the weight of their own milk.

The sun was behind us now. We were walking into our shadows. When was the last time I had water? My lips were scratching against my teeth. The baby camel was teetering now, his legs stumbling into each other. I took hold of the scarf closer to his neck and whispered into his ear. *We are far from home, my friend. And alone. In the desert.*

Did I think stating the obvious would change things? The camel was tired. The light was dimming. My legs were moving out of habit. I was not thinking, I was just moving. Then I was on the ground, underneath the baby camel. He was shrieking and flailing, his legs kicking. I covered my face and curled as tightly as I could but could not avoid the white legs—one hit me in the thigh, the other hit my upper arm, the force of it rolling me over the side of the dune we were on.

When I came to a stop I stayed frozen, listening for the baby camel. *Please God,* I prayed, *please, he did not break a leg. He did not hurt himself.* Finally I pulled my hands away from my face and sat up. At the top of the dune the baby camel stood tall, snorting and stomping his front leg. I tried to stand but my legs would not hold my weight. I lay down and covered my head with the first layer of my robe. There was no sun on this side of the dune. The temperature was dropping quickly. I rolled back and forth, digging a burrow for my bruised body. At some point consciousness left me.

I awoke to the chill before dawn, that time of cold when the sun is still to come. My feet were swollen and my head ached from dehydration. I lay in the discomfort, staring at the dune before me, watching it move. Move? I blinked, then rubbed my eyes. The dune twitched. I sat up and stopped myself from yelping. The baby camel was lying on his side, the swell of his midsection rising and falling before me.

God is Good, I whispered, sliding my leg under me to rise up quietly. I put my weight on my left leg and a pain cracked up my spine, sending me back to my knees. The baby camel twitched again, then started to struggle to his feet. I grabbed the scarf that was still around his neck and held on tight, as his struggle pulled my own body upright.

"So, sweetheart, we are together, we will not part again," I cooed. He flicked his ears front and back, and I kept cooing into them as much to keep myself from my pain as to keep him calm. "Yes, my little one, we are traveling together again."

I could not walk. He could not hold my weight. The sun was above the horizon now. We had only two or three hours before the heat would take both of us. I ripped the hem of my robe, pulled a thread to open the cloth and fashioned a long train. "Here my sweet, you are going to wear this, and I am going to ride your tail."

When they found us, the baby camel was walking east, straight into the sun. They thought at first that he was eviscerated, that his entrails were dragging behind him. That made more sense than what they were actually seeing—a young camel dragging a young woman through the desert.

I named him Hercules. Abu kept him for years, until the legend drew too many people to view the "camel who fell in love with a woman." Abu traded him, but the legend continued and was ascribed to any number of young camels offered for trade.

The men treated me with respect now, and I had work. Not what I would expect women's work to be. No cooking or cleaning or laundry. Laundry was not such a concern in the arid world of the desert. Nothing got all that dirty, or maybe my tolerance for grime had grown. Omar did the cooking and Mohammed took care of the camels, along with me and the boy. He gathered them and hobbled them for the night, but I settled them.

"You do well," the boy said. "They listen to you." The men laughed.

"A camel listens to no one," Mohammed said.

The boy started to protest. "They do," then he stopped and winked at me. I had taught him to wink. It was our secret connection.

At night I sat next to Matilda, my camel, and talked to her. Indeed, her ears perked up and although it was too dark to see her expression, I could see the reflection of the fire in her eyes, and I believed she was listening to me. I told Matilda she was grand. The grandest animal I had ever met. Much larger and smarter and meaner than any animal in England. She liked that.

Matilda my camel. She was a puny shield against the world of the Sahara, but she spoke the truth, thrusting her knobby knees forward and spitting her rage. I tried it myself a few times, collecting the saliva in my mouth, then letting go of it in one scattered glob. Very satisfying. Abu came upon us one day, having a spitting contest. Matilda was folded down for the night, her ironing board legs pinned underneath her. I was standing beside her, both of us expectorating to the West. Matilda pressed her tri-cornered lips together and let go with a huge blob, sending her load at least six feet. I pulled myself upright, took a deep breath, and forced out a meager stream covering a distance of two feet at the most.

"Unpack the cord," Abu said from behind me.

'What?" I turned, my lips still wet with spittle.

"You must unpack the cord," he repeated, then put his hand in the center of my shoulder blades.

"Watch."

I watched as Abu lowered his *shesh*, wet his lips, and to my amazement, forced them into a triangle similar to Matilda's. He then lifted his arms above his head and pressed them out to his sides, lowering them like a bellows, at the same time releasing a full stream from his lips that arced across the sand in front of us.

I burst out laughing. Although I wanted to, I could not tell him it was a perfect match for the other stream I had seen released from a lower orifice.

No one in my world had talked to me of the dangers hidden in my own body. Of the treasure I must guard, must keep tightly locked until my wedding night, when, my mother assured me, my husband would unlock it. I didn't know anything about sex when I went into the desert. I knew about babies and I knew a man and a woman would be intimate, but I did not know how. I knew that my body woke me up at night with strange cravings for touch, and pulsing, throbbing sensations. I did not tell anyone about this or ask anyone why my body was behaving so differently. Nurse had given me clean strips of cloth when I told her about the blood. And Mother took me to the dressmakers when she saw how tight my bodice had become, but I knew enough not to ask after the first time I began with "What—" Mother said, "Don't fret. Your husband will show you."

I had seen the cows in the field and the mare tied to the stall, neighing and banging against the slats when they pulled the stallion into the barn. I had a sense that the act involved a lot of thrashing about and screaming and bulging eyes. It didn't look like anything that could be done in the white starched sheets of my parents' bedroom.

Abu watched me now. I could feel his eyes on me. When I turned to catch him, a small smile crept over his countenance. The longer we traveled, the more defined the men's features became. At first they all looked alike, figures in fabric moving, shoving, sometimes shouting. But now they each stood out for me and I could recognize the cook, the camel caretaker, those who commanded others, those who followed. And Abu, of course. Always Abu. He came to me now whenever we stopped for the night and watched as the boy helped me descend from my camel. He waited while my tent was set up. He became an easy presence beside me, one I came to expect. Sore from the ride, tired from the heat, I stood in silence and listened to the sounds of camp and kept my eyes down until the boy nodded for me to enter my tent. It wasn't long before I started looking for Abu when the caravan halted and kept my eyes on him as he approached. He always looked directly at me, then turned to scan the horizon.

This went on for a couple of weeks. My body was catching up with me. I could feel my muscles tighten and my heart beat more quickly now. It was as if I had been holding my breath and now exhaled deeply for the first time. I found myself breathing hard and blushing in the presence of Abu. If he noticed the first time, he didn't show it. And then the throbbing began and my body became so hot I had to loosen my robes, and he noticed. He stood closer to me now and began to speak softly, words I didn't quite understand, but a tone that was unmistakable.

Finally there came a night when Abu entered my tent and stood beside me. There was no light. "*Inshallah,*" he said, "we make our destination in two days." *Inshallah*. God willing. I did not ask where our destination was. I was completely undone with the yearning in my body, the yearning for him. I reached out for him and in one motion we were encircled in a twirling dervish of cloth and arms and legs, laughing and cooing as we released ourselves from the stricture of loose fabrics, then fell on top of them.

"You are sweet," he said. "Like a fig." I did not listen to his words so much as his touch. He relished me. He began with my eyes, closing them gently, a kiss on each to seal them shut; then his fingertips played across my cheeks and down my neck, his tongue cooling the heat he had unleashed. Down my breast, and around each nipple, his body held high above me to allow the breeze to play with us both, then the soft tangle below until I could no longer contain the moan and rose up to meet him, biting his lips.

Sex came naturally when it finally arrived in my life. No thrashing, no wild-eyed beast, unless you count me. Maybe it was all my time with the animals, maybe the close heat of the desert, but once I tasted that primal moment, I couldn't get enough of it. Abu was my true lover. Other men enjoyed my body, some abused my body, some, including my husband, succeeded in pleasing me. No one has actually touched me, no one except Abu.

DEVON

June 8, 1970

I AM SITTING IN THE SAND, TIPPED BACK in the folding chair with my legs stretched out and my toes buried in the gritty beach of my childhood, when I hear their voices coming from above me. Edith is sitting on the bench at the top of the stairs to the beach, talking with Jane.

"Alice slept on the floor the first few months after she returned," she says.

"She did?"

"Yes, Mother's maid was furious that she had to make up her bed every day even though Alice was never in it. The maid complained to Mother, who told her to change the sheets every day anyway."

Once again I'm stunned by the level of Mother's denial.

"Why didn't you tell Alice to sleep in the bed?" Jane asks.

"Oh for heaven's sake, what could we say? Half the time we didn't know what language would come out of her mouth. She was like some untamed creature. We didn't know what to do with her."

Edith thinks I can't hear her. People do that all the time, sit up there above the beach, high above the sea, and discuss all sorts of intimate things. The surf can drown out many things,

95

but Edith's voice is not one of them. I'd rather listen to the wind and the waves, but wind and waves have nothing on Edith when a willing ear is nearby, and she has one now with Jane.

"Martin found her with the telegram. She wouldn't let him have it. He tried to talk with her, tried to get her to come back to bed. She stayed up all night sketching and writing and told him strange stories. He called me the next morning."

There's a pause. I try not to turn and look up.

Edith continues. "I've been waiting for her to tell me what happened. One has to wait for Alice. She does things in her own time. Always has, even when we were children; the family was always waiting for Alice. 'Where's Alice?' Mother said every tea time. Tea never began without those words, 'Where's Alice?'"

"Mother?" Jane says. Firm. Determined. "The telegram. What did the telegram say?"

"Oh yes, the telegram. Can you imagine? Fifty years ago we knew what that meant. But today, who sends a telegram?"

"Mother? The telegram. What did it say?"

"I have no idea, Jane, you will have to ask Alice."

LONDON

June 8, 1970

MARTIN WALKS ON, ACROSS PARK LANE and into the park. At the Serpentine he sits on a bench and stares at the water. There is a time for everything, he thinks. Now is the time to call Witherspoon. When he stands up there is a determination in his stride; his head is high; he passes through the tourists as through a throng of birds and heads for his office.

"Miss Patchett," he says as he walks briskly past her desk. "Witherspoon—on the phone—get him please."

Miss Patchett looks up startled at the tone of voice. "Witherspoon? Yes Sir, I am getting Witherspoon on the phone. Now."

Martin stands in front of his office window taking in the slant of light cutting through the brick walls and concrete bands across the road. Although he was waiting for it, he startles a bit when the phone on his desk buzzes. He picks up the receiver and begins talking before the cup settles against his ear.

"Richard," he says. "I need a favor. Personal. I need to know who sent a telegram to Alice last Saturday."

Martin is not surprised to have the answer within hours.

The Night Ferry from Dover to Dunkirk is no longer the luxury mode of transportation between London and Paris, but it's still Martin's preferred passage. He settles himself into his compartment and takes out his notebook and Mt. Blanc pen. Sisters of Blessed Mercy. Mother House. Rue du Bac 49, he reads. He could count on Witherspoon to respond without inquiry. If he knew the contents of the telegram, he wasn't going to discuss it unless asked. Martin didn't ask. It will be revealed. In time. In place. Martin is sure of that. He has learned patience. He puts down his notebook without making any notes, hangs up his suit coat, and folds his shirt. After splashing his face in the miniscule sink and brushing his teeth with care not to bang his elbows against the walls, he tucks himself into the no-longer-comfortable bed provided by the Night Ferry.

Everything changes. Change is what we need, he thinks. He gets up out of the bed and retrieves his notebook. From the back pocket of the binding he pulls a photo. Alice at Bournemouth. Her hair blowing in the sea breeze, her hands wide open, her smile directed at the camera, at him standing behind the camera. He takes a deep breath as he gazes at her, then slips the photo back into the pocket of the notebook, turns out the light, and closes his eyes. Sleep comes easily, a blessing he never takes for granted.

DEVON

June 8, 1970

J ANE AND BENJAMIN HAVE GONE TO DINNER with the Trowbridges, leaving Edith and me to dine alone. I look at the well-set table and the remains of our meal.

"We had no dish detergent in the desert," I murmur. "We swirled our rough plates in the sand, abrasive cleansing. The only utensils were our right hands, fingers folded over the bread to clasp the stew like soft paws." I laugh quietly, remembering. "Meat, we shredded from the bone. Milk was squeezed from the pouch. Water from the goatskin."

Edith recoils across the table. We are having wine with dinner. To calm our nerves, Edith said. The sea calms my nerves, I said. Wine loosens my tongue, but I do not tell her that as I raise the glass to my lips.

"No wonder you were so odd," she says.

"What do you mean?"

"Your first night at home. It was so embarrassing. You reached out for the platter, your long, thin arm straight across my face. Everyone stared. I had to put your hand back in your lap."

"Yes, I remember those looks. All those eyes on me. It took quite a while to remember the uses for all that cutlery. The

Sisters of Blessed Mercy understood. They didn't give me any utensils most of the time I was there. But it was the food at home that confused me. Slabs of brown meat, fruity sauces, white mounds—what were they, potatoes? And the bread. Fluffy, salty stuff that stuck in my throat. And then they brought that pink and white thing."

"Stop being so contrary. You know perfectly well what that was, you know it was trifle."

I look up at Edith and shrug my shoulders. "I felt like I was eating a Sunday bonnet," I say, and am relieved to see Edith laugh.

"Well, you certainly were strange," she says. "I was scared. When I first saw you at the dock, I wanted to turn and leave. You looked like a wild animal, a feral cat, wrapped in white linen, your hair all loose, your eyes so wide I could hardly look at you."

"Hmmm," I murmur and lower my head, my eyes resting on the scar in the inlet between my thumb and forefinger, where the dagger passed through my hand on the way to Haddad's neck. I can hear Edith sniffling but don't want to raise my head, don't want to look at the hurt in her eyes.

"You never told me anything," she whispers. "I never knew what happened to you."

I look up to see Edith's face tight, drawn in on itself, and am not surprised when she begins tapping her fingers on the table.

"Even now, the telegram. You haven't said anything. Who was Abu?"

"My—" I cannot say it. "The man who—"

I must say it.

"My lover."

Edith stares at me. "Your what?" I do not respond. She takes a deep breath, her cheeks turn pink. She stands up from the table and turns as if to go to the sink, then swivels back around. "Your lover? In the desert? Of course you had a lover. You had everything. Why not a lover in the desert? Alice this, Alice that. We were always being told 'Alice is going, Alice is doing. Where is Alice? What is Alice doing?' Then it ended. When you left…" Her voice is rising now, spiraling up her fingers twitching. "You left me!"

I reach up from the table to take her hand. "*Audhu-billah,*" I murmur. "*Audhu-billah.*"

"*Ooo hoo bee la,*" she hisses. "What on God's earth does that mean? There you go—off into your own crazy universe. '*Ooo hoo bee la.*' How am I supposed to know what that means?"

I slump back in my chair. "It means 'May God protect us,'" I say.

"God protect us?! What are you, ordained now? Are you in the desert again? Back in that crazy world you carry in your head?"

"NO," I say. "I am in the kitchen. I am in the kitchen with my sister. Where this family has *told* me to be!"

We are standing now, squealing at each other, two old women, anger stiffening our already stiff arms, weakness keeping us from hitting each other.

"You always had everything, got everything," Edith sputters. "Even when you were gone, everything was about you." She looks directly at me, her eyes triumphant. "There was one thing you didn't get. I know he never told you he courted me first. Did you ever know that? I could have given Martin children! That's one thing you never did."

We both go silent. Edith puts her hands in front of her mouth and stares at me, her fear palpable.

I turn away and pull out the chair at the table.

Edith lowers her body onto the rocker beside the window. We sit in silence for minutes, the only sound in the room my shallow breathing and the creak of her chair as it rakes across the warp in the floor.

"I had a child," I say quietly. "In the desert."

DEVON

June 9, 1970

I'VE LIVED MY LIFE AS A CHILDLESS WOMAN. I've watched people's eyes go soft and watched pity appear. I've learned to await the inevitable question, "Do you have children?" And I've learned to dissemble. "I was not blessed," I used to say. Then, "Unfortunately no." Then, "I have nieces and nephews." And finally, "No," with a direct gaze that sent the interrogator scuffling off to find another subject.

It used to hurt, that simple lie. My stomach cramped, my legs ached, I felt a drop in my nether regions as if my body were shrieking at me. "Liar," it cried out. "You remember this, you remember the cramp, the spot on the cloth, the rush of water, you remember the cry that escaped your lips. How could you forget? How could you lie? You remember when all the women gathered round and put their hands on you and smiled and clucked. They did. They clucked like hens. Such tenderness. How could you lie about that? And then the pain, the gasping for air, and the women who massaged your belly and sang to you as you lay, propped up on the rugs in the tent. And the fear. Not of the pain, or the coming child, but of the dirt. The women were clean, but there was the desert. There was dirt.

I listen to my body and wonder at the memory that exists

in every single cell, I wonder about a body that knows I'm lying. The sore breasts, I swear I had to look down at my blouse to be sure it wasn't damp with milk. I used to blush when I made this lie. People were kind, assumed something was wrong with me. I managed to live a childless life in England. A barren woman. One the gods overlooked.

Until this telegram arrives and my body remembers the lie and these tired breasts ache, and the private world between my legs grows damp and I have to go check that I am not bleeding. My ears begin to reach out for the sound of a cry, for the squeal of delight of the women in the tent, and my heart begins to pound at the memory of that perfect face gazing up at me, and I want to die, not for the pain of that childbirth, but from the pain of that fifty-year lie.

THE SAHARA

1914

WALKING THROUGH THE MARKET was always painful. I could live for days and weeks without any particular necessities, but when we came to the market I could see through the gauze of my wrap coffee urns, rugs, leather bags. I could taste the confines of home, could feel the weight of the coffee pot, could hear the clink of the china in the dining room, could feel the Persian carpet under my bare feet as I dressed for breakfast.

I walked close to the boy out of necessity—it was so crowded, and after the space of the desert, this proximity to people was almost terrifying—but also because he kept his hand on my arm, gently but with enough pressure that I knew the market was a place I must maintain my disguise. I had no desire to leave, but Abu must have known that under everything is the human desire to be free, that as alien as these people were to me, there was always the opportunity to disappear in the crowd.

It was our third trip to the market in Taghit. Abu had been gone for two days now, and the boy seemed restless. When I asked about future plans, he stared at me and said "it is written," the Arab answer for everything. It is written when you will be born, when you will die, when you are to do anything. It is written that I would be taken and would spend my life in the desert with these nomads. I was getting angry. I had not been alone since we arrived in this dry little town. The boy was always close by, and the rest of the caravan always looking my way the few times I was allowed to walk amid the animals. It spooked me to be among buildings and people again. It did not occur to me until that morning that perhaps they feared an escape attempt, but that was not on my mind. I did not want to be left behind in that ugly place. I wanted to be beside Abu again. I wanted to be moving through the silence of the desert, feeling the air, awaiting the evening with him.

The next day I noticed a stranger in the shadows as we passed by in the medina. He smelled of jasmine and *kif*. He was watching me. When all you can see are a person's eyes, you become attuned to every twitch, every movement; even when a person is in shadow, you know when their eyes are on you. Those eyes were hidden, but I could feel his gaze. It felt like sun blinding me. I knew to keep my own eyes downcast.

I turned to the left and gathered my robes about me, flicking the hem enough to send dust up at the one in shadow. The boy trotted up beside me and whispered.

"Where are you going? You do not know your way."

"I want to find a rug," I said.

"You do not need rug. You cannot buy rug."

I kept walking. The boy was agitated, worried.

"Please," he said. "We must not stray. We must stay where they left us."

I felt badly for him. He was being sweet, talking to me as if we were friends, when I knew the truth was he was only keeping watch over me.

"It's that one," I said and nodded towards the shadowed corner. The man stepped out; his cold eyes raked across my body.

The boy turned and stared, then turned back and took my arm.

"Yes," he said, "we must buy rug," and led me down the closest alleyway, around a corner, roughly pulling me through a throng of people.

"Do you know who that was?" I asked when he slowed his walk. I could feel a cool breeze flowing through the dark inner walls of the medina.

"Haddad," the boy said, shaking his head.

"Who is he?"

"Bad man," is all the boy would say. Then he stopped and stood in front of me.

"You did not look at him, did you?" he said.

"No," I lied.

"Good," he said, "That would be an invitation to evil."

I had bled many times, had sat under many full moons by the time we arrived at the camp. I heard the women before I saw them. Singing, waving their hips back and forth, their voices clear in the air. I was humming before I realized there was music coming over the dunes. The men pressed forward towards the children, calling and waving. Everything was waving.

The women saw us coming for days. They had prepared food and had turned out the rugs and laid herbs beneath them. They greeted the men with bowls of fresh milk and casual touches.

Abu slipped away from me, leaving the boy to tug at my robe and pull me to the side, under an acacia tree. If it was his intention to hide me, he was not quick enough. A young woman pointed and called out to the others. They were upon me instantly, smiling, laughing, touching my hand, pulling my hair out from my scarf. The boy tried to shoo them away, but he himself was shoved away and I found myself surrounded.

"*La*," I said, quietly at first, then louder. The women laughed. I thought I heard the name Abu, but they were all speaking at once and so rapidly, I could not be sure. What I was sure of was the timbre of their voices. High, soft, sometimes shrill, unmistakably female. My ears hurt. Even there, where sound was often softened by the sand or even absorbed by the wind, women's voices could pierce.

I put my hands over my ears and closed my eyes. The voices died down. A hand touched my back. Then another. And another. Then a finger wiggled into my side and a giggle erupted to the left of me. I jerked to the right and another finger found a ticklish spot. I opened my eyes and joined the women in their laughter. Two women I would come to know as Amina and Fatima took my arms and led me out from the acacia to the circle that was forming around a woman with a drum they called a *tende*. They sat me in the shade, and I looked across to see a woman with huge circles of gold hanging from her ears. I saw her straight nose, the warm skin, the regal bearing. I saw Abu greet her with a bow. She didn't return my gaze, but I knew she was watching me. I had never seen him bow to anyone before. He bowed without taking his eyes off her, and she stood quietly, her gold jewels sparking in the light, the only acknowledgement between them the delight in their eyes. She turned, her head swiveling with her robes, and Abu followed. Amina and Fatima pulled me to my feet and led me closer into the circle. My body moved, but my mind remained on the woman with the gold earrings. I wanted to think she was Abu's sister; they appeared to be cut from the same cloth, as my father would say. But I knew it wasn't so. I knew from the way they looked at each other and the way others stepped aside as they walked past. The woman never looked at me but I could feel her eyes, could feel my body aflame, as if a viper had bitten me and injected fear into my veins.

Amina took my hand and turned me around to face the circle, where an older woman began drumming and a younger one sat down with a wooden bowl with a string pulled over it in an arc. A sour tone that set my teeth on edge emanated from her fingers and lifted the women from their seats. More and more women arrived, until the circle was two deep. When I looked up from the circle, men on camels were approaching silently, some camels stepping delicately back and forth in a dance that drew approval from the women. The woman with the drum began chanting. Sometimes others would respond, sometimes the group sat in silence. I could not stand the sound and covered my ears with my hands. A while later the women stood, and I rose with them and allowed myself to be pulled along in a dance. I held on tightly and pressed my feet to the ground as if each step could add an inch to my height, as if each time I hit the earth I could stop the anger and desire from coursing through my body.

I danced until exhaustion and did not see Abu again until the caravan loaded up the next morning and the boy came for me. The women looked surprised, but no one said a word as I walked to the front of the caravan and mounted my camel. The woman with gold hoops was nowhere to be seen.

Abu did not visit me during that journey. I rode quietly beside the boy, absorbing the heat of the desert, the rocking rhythm of my camel. My time with the women had unsettled me, set me apart from the men in a different way. I saw cordial interactions in the camp, saw that the women were proud and content. The men treated them with deference—no, I searched for the word—admiration. The men admired the women in a way I had never seen before.

When we came to the outskirts of Timbuktu and Abu finally came to my tent, I questioned his absence. He raised his veil and turned aside. By now I knew this could be a sign of great respect or a sign of dismissal.

"This is not about me, is it?" I asked Abu.

He waved me aside and raised his voice. "It is about why I was put on earth and put on a path that crosses that of a white woman. Why Allah allowed the earth to mix up who is where and when."

I had heard Abu rant like this before, but not directly to me. Something was going on in the world, out beyond the Sahara. Strange people were showing up in the desert, people like me I suppose, who didn't belong here. There were the three British men long ago, and just a week or so ago there was pandemonium when an aeroplane crossed low in the sky. The camels shrieked, then hunkered down at the sandstorm that followed. Some of the men had never seen an aeroplane and remained prostrate, praying fervently until Abu eventually got them back on their feet. At the last trading post Abu kept me hidden most of the time. The boy said people were agitated and worried, and talked of the French and the Germans.

I thought of the men who had sat at our dining table in Marrakesh. The men who chased wild boars in miniature bull-fight games, the women who despaired of "good help" and could not let go of the clock.

When Abu had become agitated, I decided to look for news at Timbuktu.

"It's green," the boy had said. "And there is a river there."

I thought of Devon and the deep, dark grey of the river and flush of green beside it. When we arrived in Timbuktu, I stood beside the boy and asked where the river was. He nudged me and said, "There. Look. What do you think? Look at all the boats."

Still I stared, thinking I was watching boats on a road. A river as brown and dirty as a road. The boy laughed at me. I grabbed his arm and twisted, unaware of how much strength my body now commanded. "*LA!*" he cried.

"Where is the post?" I said.

"Post? What is Post?"

Once again I would have to take the lead. "Follow me," I said and proceeded to make my way through the crowds, my eyes and ears stretching to see and hear what, I did not know.

Up the dusty street and down, past blankets on the ground, silver, tin, leather, spices and noise, odors, men reaching out with goods for sale. And then, like an electric shock I realized I was listening again to voices speaking my old language, the King's own English. I stood in the dirt of Timbuktu and watched a white man in tight breeches supervise the unloading of a skiff. His face was florid, and his hands were stark white knobs hanging from his sleeves. He yelled, he kicked, he slapped, man and beast alike, as if the earth were about to explode. I could not imagine what each box and basket held that could exert such pressure on the poor man.

"My brother died at the front. Got the letter this week." I turned my head to see one white man speaking to another. "'Don't come home,' they wrote. 'They'll send you over there.' There will be no men left in England once this war is over. None at all, me mum wrote."

The boy touched my arm cautiously. "What is matter?" he asked.

"*LA,*" I hissed. "Be quiet." But it was too late; whoever had been speaking was lost in the crowds, and I was left once again to wonder if I could trust my own senses. War. No men left in England.

That night I asked Abu what was going on in the world.

"Whose world?" he said.

"Our world."

"The world of the desert?" he said. "The world of Allah? The world of men? Of women?"

"Stop this," I said and kicked the sand. Abu stared at my foot.

"What is this dance?" His lips curled towards a smile.

I kicked at the ground again. I would have held my breath until I turned blue if I could have.

"It is not a dance," I hissed. I knew better than to raise my voice. Hissing I had learned from the camels. Very effective. "The world. The whole world," I said. "The real world. What is happening in the world?"

"You have been listening to men's talk," Abu said.

"Yes," my voice was rising. "I have been listening. And I have heard of war. What is this talk of war?"

Suddenly Abu looked tired. He gazed at me sadly. "It will come eventually. If not this time, then the next. If not then, for our children. It is coming from the North, where they have needs they cannot satisfy."

"From England?" I asked.

"It is not our war. It is their war, but it is bleeding into our sand." Abu looked tired, more tired than I had ever seen him. "You must know your enemy. You must respect your enemy. This war that is coming. It is disrespectful."

We had been traveling for days when we came upon the buried camel. By then I was used to camel carcasses and was no longer shocked at bones lined along the route. But this was a live camel, at the least there were groans and moans from the pulled-back lips, and the eyes looked as if they were about to burst from their sockets.

"*Shouf!*" Mohammed cried, pointing his finger. When the men tapped their camels' necks, they went into the three-point bend without any of their usual hesitation. Their eyes were bulging themselves at the sight.

Within seconds the men surrounded the buried camel and began digging and tossing sand away, uncovering the saddle, the rump, the legs. The beast screeched and struggled, trying to pull itself out of its prison of sand. Abu stroked its neck with one hand, furiously digging with the other, until the back legs were free and the men instinctively jumped aside to avoid the flailing appendages. Abu kept hold of the line from its nose, trying to soothe the awkward beast as it rose from its gritty grave. The other men approached cautiously, touching the blanket still tied to its hump, examining the saddle, rocking the curve of its neck.

"*Bismallah*, it's Tahir!" one of them cried, and at once as if on a command, the men began digging again. Abu walked the camel away, taking it in a large circle, away from our herd, as the men dug like a nest of ants burrowing deeper and deeper, the sand flying about their heads and bodies like the storm of the previous day. Abu cringed when the cry went up, and I turned to see the men drop their arms and step back. He walked over to the pit they had dug and bowed his head.

We did not bury Tahir. The sandstorm had already done that. The men wrapped him in the blanket from his camel and carried him to higher ground, to the flat brown rocks, where they gathered stones and covered the body.

I watched from a distance. The boy picked at his fingers and toes, plucking as if he could get music from them. Abu was silent the rest of the day. In the evening he told me Tahir had been an honorable enemy. He had died a desert death.

Abu kept the camels hobbled at night, and we pressed farther and farther each day before stopping.

Three days after we left Timbuktu we came across tire tracks. The boy jumped up and down, panting, making grunting sounds, pointing to the lines of parallel X's. Abu halted the line of camels and dismounted, then wet his finger and touched the dirt, the sand.

"Heavy load," he said and shook his head. I kept my eyes forward and saw the truck before the others—a flash of light reflected off the windshield, and I knew the driver must have turned back towards us. I motioned to the boy and pointed ahead. He stepped up beside Abu and pulled on his robes, then pointed to the dust in the distance.

Suddenly all was motion. Abu made some imperceptible movements, and at once the men had pulled the camels into a tight line and had their hands on the swords folded within their robes. The dust kept pulling closer to us until the lorry was visible, a glinting box careening across the flat space between us.

"*Salam'alek,*" I heard Mohammed spit. *Inshallah, bismallah,* others murmured. Abu motioned to the boy, who took hold of my camel's nose rope and led me to the end of the line.

The lorry was visible now, racing towards us, and I could not believe the men and camels were not moving. The lorry was sure to drive right through them, lined up in silence. I could see the men inside, could see the driver's hands on the wheel, when Abu finally raised his arm.

The line of camels broke apart instantaneously, racing in all directions, kicking up a cloud of sand and noise as the men's voices roared above our heads. The boy held tight to my rein and kept us well back. I could not see for all the dust in the air, but heard the vehicle's gears grinding. The boy pulled sharply on the lead and my camel turned and took off.

"What are you doing?" I shouted. "I can't see!" And I threw myself forward to grab the ring myself, then had to hang on as my camel sprinted, and its jerking body tossed me about. I heard gunfire and I screamed again. "Abu," I shouted, "Abu!" holding onto my camel's neck as tightly as I could.

The dust stung my eyes, and the roar of the men and beasts drowned out my feeble cries. Then he was by my side, his foot touching my camel's neck, the two beasts racing as one, and I clung even tighter. We were in one of the circles of hell, pounding the earth into a senseless drumbeat, cauterizing our ears with a high-pitched whistle.

As suddenly as it began, it ended. The camels came to a stop. The men went silent. The dust settled. There, inside the circle we had been riding, sat a lorry with four flat tires and two dead men—one on the ground beside the vehicle, his arm stretched out towards a rifle, a rivulet of red flowing from the back of his neck, the other face down in the Sahara.

DEVON

June 9, 1970

"**D**ID YOU REALLY LIVE IN THE DESERT?" Benjamin is standing before me, a pail in one hand, a shovel in the other.

"Yes, I did."

"That was sand, like here," he says.

"Well, yes, it was sand, but not like here."

"Like where?" he says.

"Like this." I lean forward in my chair and begin pushing the sand with my feet, raising up dunes, uncovering wet ground.

Benjamin steps back and waves his little arms about. "Yes," he laughs, "yes."

I get down on my knees and reach over for his shovel. He sits down on his tiny haunches and watches intently. By midafternoon we have a respectable camp, well sheltered by our handmade dunes. We have placed the tents. "But they're flat," he says. "Yes, flat for the wind to pass over," I say. We set to work on creating camels out of sticks wrapped in beach fern.

"A camp," Benjamin says, jumping from one foot to the other. "A desert camp. In the Sahara. And here are rocks too, and an oasis," he says, pointing to the mass of gorse we have rimmed along the back side of our dunes. Benjamin points to sticks we've wrapped with pieces of the dishcloth I ripped apart. "And there's Mohammed, and Ahmed, and Nabil and ..."

"And Rashid," I say. I open my mouth, almost in a shout. "Rashid! His name is Rashid."

I grab Benjamin's hands and we do a lopsided dance across the beach. "My son's name is Rashid." I can't stop laughing and dancing.

"Your son?" Benjamin says.

"Yes," I say. "Rashid Mustafa al Akbar. Son of Great Britain and the Ahaggar, son of the Georges of Devon and the Blue Men of the Sahara. A warrior, a Westerner. A man of the desert. A man of green fields."

"Rashid," I whisper and turn to stare at the ocean. "Rashid." I lift my fingers up to my lips to feel the air pressing out as I finally say the name aloud—my first born, my only born, my son.

Edith stands up in the garden where she has been working and looks into the distance. She is not a natural gardener, not like Alice, who drops a seed and a day later it is flourishing. Edith knows phylum and genus, sets her plants out in strict rows, and follows the Sunday gardening columns.

It's always been this way, Edith thinks, watching Alice and Benjamin playing by the water. She does the right thing while Alice does what she wants, and who do people and animals and even plants turn towards? Alice. It's not jealousy that makes Edith's face fold in on her, it's bewilderment. Why are people drawn to someone so headstrong? That was the word her mother used to describe Alice. Headstrong.

Edith squints into the sun and sees Alice and Benjamin standing on the stairway with their backs to the house. Now what is she doing? Edith pulls her garden gloves off one finger at a time and slaps them against her apron to release the dirt.

"Jane," she calls. "Go get Benjamin; he's standing on the stairway."

"Isn't Aunt Alice with him?" Jane sits up from the chaise where she has been staring at the same page of *Vogue* for the past twenty minutes.

"Indeed she is," Edith says. "Go get him."

It takes a while before I can begin climbing back up the stairs from the beach. Benjamin comes up beside me and takes my hand. The sand between his fingers scratches across my palm. Such a tiny hand he has, but firm, strong for a five-year-old. Benjamin is holding tight as he reaches up to take a step. I am slow, tired, but my legs are longer and the step is not as momentous for me.

Fear, it's fear that set me on this course. Stay low. Don't upset people. Take good care of Martin. Keep quiet. Most important keep quiet. No one wants to know about the desert, the extreme world, the place where impulse can burst out and take one beyond civilized society. Civilized. What does that mean?

I put my foot up slowly, waiting for Benjamin to gain the step after me. These are steep stairs, wooden rails, splinters a possibility. I stand and turn to look back at the sea and take a deep breath.

"What are you waiting for?" Benjamin asks.

"I'm waiting to catch up with myself."

"But you are right here."

"Yes, I am here, standing beside you, but my thoughts, my feelings, are not here."

"Oh," he says. "I have to catch up too." And he turns and takes a deep breath facing the sea.

"Your son," he says. "Where is he? In the desert?"

"No," I say. "He is coming."

Benjamin smiles, turns around and places his hands on the

next step and hops himself up. "Oh good," he says. "I want to meet the desert son."

"So do I, so do I."

One foot, bare and pink and plump. Next to a weathered phalange of bone and skin. I press my weight onto the ball of my foot, slowly, and feel the pressure against the wood, the granules of sand digging into my skin.

I am hungry. All this excitement at the beach and Benjamin. He must be hungry too. This gnawing in my belly. I remember this hunger.

The boy carried a tray into the tent. The aroma was overwhelming—sweet, rank, a flood of images passed before me: the kitchen at Al Kabar, onion, tomatoes piled up, chopped, ready for the tagine. The spices in the market piled into their pyramids. Once again my body began to recoil. It was too much. The boy lifted the cover of the tagine and moistness filled the air. I opened my eyes and he nodded, then handed me a platter with pieces of flat bread. I picked one up and folded it in my fingers, then reached over and scooped up the vegetables and meat and held it to my nose. The boy was gesticulating now. Yes, I thought, I know how to eat. What I don't know is how to taste, how to savor, how to make my body accept sustenance.

Benjamin grabs my hand. "Aunt Alice," he calls from far away. "Look, Mum is coming." I turn and there is Jane, pounding down the path, her tan shoes digging into the sand and setting off miniature explosions with each footfall.

Hunger pulls at me. "Is it teatime already?" I call.

"Yes," Jane answers.

"Oh good." I take Benjamin's hand and walk him down the path to Jane.

THE SAHARA

1915

A FEW WEEKS AFTER THE MEN in the lorry were killed, we entered another trading post. This time the boy kept me cloistered in a walled garden. "You are safe here," Abu had said to me as he left. I heard him exchange words with the boy. Abu's voice dark and harsh, the boy's apologetic. The boy came to me that night with the *kif*. I had been agitated all day, asking about Abu and lingering with the animals, my discomfort obvious. He came and sat beside me with the pipe. We leaned against the wall, still warm even though the sun had passed from the horizon an hour ago. I had seen the men smoking this before, had enjoyed the aroma, had noticed how mellow their voices became. When the boy offered the pipe to me I didn't hesitate, but drew the harsh smoke in between my lips quickly, gasping and holding my breath as long as I could. The boy looked at me with alarm, then laughed when I coughed, spitting the pipe out and grasping his hand to hold myself steady.

"Is good?" he laughed. I nodded my head and leaned back hard against the building, afraid to look up at the edge of the roof, where the sky was swirling about, a kaleidoscope of stars. The boy continued to smile and chuckle and sat patiently until my breathing returned to normal and I was able to focus on his face. "Again?" he said, holding the pipe out to me. I nodded.

We sat in silence in that closed garden until the boy began scratching in the dirt with his big toe, just randomly at first, then in a syncopated pattern. I began drumming my fingers and then began to hum. He swayed a bit to the tune and then I began to sing. The Alleluia Chorus, which at a certain tempo can sound very much like the ululation we heard when we first arrived in the harbor at Tangiers. The boy and I kept up the drumming and humming and alleluia-ing I don't know for how long, but obviously long enough to have drawn unwanted attention. The door smashed back into the dirt wall, and I pressed the palms of my hands flat against the ground when Abu's dark robes slashed across my face. The boy was dragged out and the door slammed shut. The next time I saw the boy he would not, could not speak to me. His tongue had been sliced.

Does this memory surprise me? Shock me? Am I shocked by the gull plucking meat raw from the shell? By the cat licking his bloody paws? Abu was ruthless. He could kill as quickly, as easily, as he could love. He could nurse a sick calf through the night, wrap it in his own robes, hold the quivering beast to his breast and coo in its ear. He could just as easily slit its throat. Or mine. I was witness to it once or twice. It was in his eyes, the eyes that went from warm to cold in an instant. From dark pools to frozen mirrors that could shatter or reflect. I came to the point of knowing which way Abu would react, of knowing whether the creature before him was in the way of harm. In those moments Abu was like a God, a wrathful, vengeful God. His justice was swift and without recourse.

The boy became silent, his misshapen tongue a vestige of that justice. Like siblings we maintained our connection. With time, our edges softened and we returned to our familiar ways with a wariness, even, I assumed, with affection.

I never spoke of Abu's vengeance. I was as guilty of the assault as Abu. I had put the boy in harm's way by treating him as a brother, by encouraging his familiarity. By then I knew the pecking order of the caravan. I knew the boy's life depended on protecting me. I sometimes wondered if the boy would seek his own revenge, never thinking I would be his source of retribution.

DEVON

June 9, 1970

WE SIT ON THE PORCH FOR OUR TEA, Benjamin peppering me with questions about the desert. Edith pinches her lips together and carries a general air of dissatisfaction into the room along with a tray of scones.

"What have you been telling this boy?" she says.

"We built a caravan," Benjamin says. "And there were camels and men and Aunt Alice danced and called her son's name over and over." He giggles and sways his hips in his seat.

"Alice." Edith rakes her eyes back and forth. "He's too young for such talk."

"Too young for what?" I whisper. "For the truth?"

"What truth?" Edith asks. "What are you talking about?"

"I'm talking about the fact that there is a world beyond this island, beyond this family." And then, once again, I have taken the air out of the room. With one large inhale Edith and I look at each other, and I can see the decision to remain silent take hold. I should take a deep breath too, I should wrap myself in the same silence. But I don't.

"Is he too young to know who he is? Where he came from? Who his tribe is?"

"Alice!" Edith scrapes her chair. She grabs Benjamin from

the table, jam dripping off his plate, and walks him out of the room. "Alice, this is unseemly," she says as she passes my chair.

I bow my head.

The room is empty now. The table has been cleared, and I am sitting with my hands holding my face firmly as I stare into the past. There are things you can't reach inside yourself. Things buried so deeply they will never pierce the surface. My son was one of them, buried in the aperture of my heart step by step as I left the desert, each grain of sand filling the place where the life of me beat.

Who did I think I was? Bringing a child into a world I never really understood? A babe I could not protect from the elements, much less from his own heritage. And where did I think I was going? Back to the world of tea dances and public schools? I was right to leave him with the tribe. What mother leaves her son with strangers? They were not strangers. They are his people. What mother abandons her child?

This is what I cannot reach. Morning to night I can feel the scar tissue growing. Sometimes I wake in shock to feel the blood beat in my body. Didn't I look for him? Didn't I try to find him? Yes. I wrote to the Sisters of Blessed Mercy. Sister Margaret wrote back: "God forgives you." No other words. I suppose in Sister Margaret's world God forgives Mary, a mother who gives up her child to him, to the world he ordained. And look what happened to her child. Sacrilege!

And now I will tell myself the truth. It is possible to live with things out of reach. A limited life, to be sure, but it is living. Breath goes in and out of the lungs. Blood sweeps through the body. Muscles expand and contract. It can keep one very busy, this eating and breathing. It's the mind, it's the thinking, it's the synapses firing wildly in the brain and skipping the heartbeats that trips things up. This is why I left my son in the desert, why I made the choice to walk away. Afraid of who he would become—a man of violence, a man without boundaries or borders, a man like his father. But really, was I more afraid of who he would become if I took him out of the desert? A man with no tribe, with tight boundaries and borders, a man constrained by false expectations? Fear—*my* fear—that is what set *him* free.

THE SAHARA

1915

I REMEMBER BLUE. The day I put on Abu's *tagelmust*. The shock in his eyes. Then the laughter, and then the relief I saw as he pointed at me and said, "Yes—you are Abu now, you were born with no choices, only burdens. You must protect your people—you must live or die for them. You must marry for them. You must lead for them. You must provide."

I put my hand up to my throat, thinking the scarf was wound too tightly, but it was my own constrictions I was feeling. The scarf was loose about my shoulders.

"You have no choice?"

Abu looked at me for so long I thought he had forgotten my question.

"I have made one choice in my life," he said. "I chose you."

"Me?"

"The driver wanted a buyer."

"You did not buy me."

"No, no exchange. Not necessary," Abu said, lowering his eyes, and it was only then that I realized the driver had been killed. *Of course.* I was rolled in the rug. By the time I was released, the driver was gone. *Of course.*

"The driver was a fool," Abu said. "It is necessary to rid the world of fools."

"You are wrong," I said.

Abu's eyes flashed. I knew I was in dangerous territory. I pulled the scarf tighter around my head. "I am Abu," I said, raising my shoulders. "I do not choose to rid the world of fools. I do not choose to kill."

"You are foolish," Abu said, reaching out for my arm.

"*LA*," I said, stepping back. "You do not touch Abu."

"Game ends," Abu said, standing, turning his arrogant bare head back and forth.

I took a deep breath. "This is not a game," I said. *He's the wrong man, I think.*

I see his eyes soften. I relax my breath.

"I fail you," he said softly.

"What?"

"It is written, I am of the desert. You are not."

"And what am I of? What is written for me? Was it written that I would walk into the desert? Into your life?"

"You are here," Abu said, smiling.

"Where is it written?" I shouted.

"It is written on your body. I saw when you struck the driver. You are not a Western woman. I think you are not woman. You are animal. You are not afraid of death."

"I am afraid of death. Everyone is afraid of death."

"You do not let that fear run through your body," Abu said, and ran his hand gently down my arm.

I curled into Abu's side and rested my head against the leather pouch that hangs around every Tuareg man's neck, the pouch that never leaves their bodies.

I ran my fingers through the leather fringe.

"What is in this?" I asked.

"My life," Abu said, and pulled it out of my hand.

"Your life?" I turned to see if he was being silly. He was smiling, the sly grin hard to read.

"You have a small life," I said, "if it fits in this." I reached for the brown leather, the turquoise and yellow design faded. "You wear your life outside your clothes?" I laughed.

"It is how we are made," he said. "A man carries his life outside his body. A woman carries hers within."

I was not sure if he was speaking of anatomy or of the pouch. I laughed again and put my hand on the warm leather. He put his hand on mine and smiled.

"It's good to laugh at life," he said, putting his fingers through mine and pulling them away from the pouch.

Abu was not a true Muslim. The Tuareg were considered unconverted. When the Arabs swept out of the East, across the continent, the Tuaregs made the motions, the five times bowing and praying each day, the *bismallah* the *inshallah*, not as true believers but as those who knew in which direction the sun rises and falls, when the sands will shift. They adopted the creed as they adopted the need for flat tents, the need for wrappings of light cloth. If you were going to survive in this world, you needed such things. Who was Allah to Abu? The force that drew Mohammed. The force that kept men together.

"These ideas," Abu said one night, under the cascade of clear stars. "This need to believe in order. I understand. We do not control. As with your God, your songs, your prayers, they are the same. Sing your songs, Aleece."

I do not have a good voice. Sometimes I can follow along

when others sing, but alone, I waver and lose the tune. "I cannot stay in key," I say.

"Stay in key? What is stay in key?"

"My voice, it does not sound good."

"I think it is good. Sing your song."

"The song," he pressed. "I love you in the song."

I began "Amazing Grace," faltering immediately. He looked hurt, as if I had done it on purpose. I put my hand on my navel and turned my head up to the sequined sky. The notes made their way into the cold air with a strength I did not know I had. Each one clear and clean. I forgot the words. I sang sounds, an aria to the night. Abu took my hand and stood beside me, looking above. His voice joined mine, offering the words in perfect English, stunning me into silence. Until he put his arm around me and lifted my shoulders in a gesture to open my heart. We completed the song and stood wrapped in each other, a human tree in the center of the Sahara.

I ignored the number of times I bled. It didn't seem to come as regularly. I ignored the number of moons and the lack of blood. Until the time came when I could not ignore the nausea or my swelling body.

For weeks we had been softer with each other. I caught Abu looking at me amidst the men, found him waiting for me more often during the day. At some point he began to ride beside me and his eyes sometimes smiled, sometimes carried caution. One day we came across the remains of a lion kill. Abu watched me stifle the nausea that arose at the smell of the carcass. That night he put his hand on my abdomen and smiled, and when my tears began, he told me all would be well. He would take me to the women.

This time the earth bumped in its rotation and I felt myself trying to straighten my head on my neck.

"The women of your tribe?"

The woman with the gold hoops.

"We can be there in four days' time," Abu said. "You will be well cared for."

At the age of twenty my knowledge of childbirth was woefully inadequate. I knew storks were no longer involved, and that women, including Mother, went to "lie in" somewhere. But what went on there was not definite. I knew how lambs entered the world, and kittens, and even horses, and so had some residual idea that women, being mammals, provided similar portals. But how one managed the process I did not really know. For the first time since I joined with Abu, I wished I were back in England, in a stiff corset, seated at the tea table, my only discomfort the wisps falling out of my hair knot.

As happened the first time, the women were well prepared for our arrival. Amina was the first to greet me at the camp. The woman with the gold earrings did not appear. They led me by the hand, one on each side of me, to a tent at the edge of the camp, well situated under an acacia tree. "It is quiet here," Amina said. "You will be rested here," Fatima said. The boy disappeared, as did Abu.

I had no idea how tired I had become. For days I slept long hours, walked a bit with Amina and Fatima, drank cool tea and watched the women work with leather, played with the babes. When I asked for Abu, Amina said, "He will return." "You must rest and prepare," Fatima said. Days passed in this fashion. I dreamed of the green hills of Devon, the grey skies of England and the blue water; then I awoke to the overwhelming blue of the sky above and rambled about the browns and greys and rough reds of the camp until night took me back home.

Nature protects mothers. I know this now. There is a semi-permeable membrane that allows a woman to accept the fact another body is within her. At the same time it keeps her from anticipating what is to come, except perhaps in her dreams. In my dreams I gave birth by the sea and watched as the waves came up the beach and took my child. I gave birth to an animal, covered with fur. I chased the waves, I nurtured the beast. And I woke to the calm of Amina and Fatima.

This is how it was. I was not sleeping. I had been feverish for days. The women kept me comfortable, cool and comfortable. Sips of mint tea now and then, a bit of meat or vegetable. I was never alone. They sang or hummed and treated me with the care they had for the infant strapped to their backs or slung over their breasts as they went about their work. I had stopped sleeping three days before. Stopped dreaming weeks before.

"Soon," they smiled, "he will come soon." They knew the sex of the baby from watching me move. I drifted during the day, in and out of a feverish state; but like a cat with its eyes not quite shut, I was aware of every sound, every smell, every breeze. Still, I was not ready for what came. The pain went up behind my back and knocked me to my knees. "Now," Amina called out the tent flap. "Now!" She put her arm around me and cooed to me, pulling me back onto the cushions. "Now it begins," she said and kissed my forehead. The tent filled with women, smiling, laughing, eager. "Like this," they said, as I gasped for air, and I followed their breaths, and managed to bring light back into my vision. They sat me up the next time, one leaning her back against mine, the others holding my hands. "Now," they said, and pushed against my back as I leaned over, spreading my legs apart. Many times, like a lever going back and forth, my body pressed forward, my breath pushed downward, and the pain shot through the tent like thunderclaps.

I looked down in terror as my legs began to shake uncontrollably and the women began singing, wailing, or making some sound I'd never heard. Or was it me? Shrieking?

"Now!" Amina cried out. When her back pressed into mine again, I raised up with an energy I didn't have and watched my body eject another body. I have no other word for it. I ejected this manchild into the world.

All was motion. I heard an unknown cry, a cord was cut, he was at my breast, and I was now a mother.

Amina fed me, washed me, kept me and the babe secluded for days. I asked for Abu. "He is coming, he is coming," they said. "The name is coming."

I sat with the women of the camp, watching as they carried their children, as they untied their bundles and slid them from back to breast. I watched the easy animal movements of their bodies, the child an appendage, an extension, a moving part of their own body. It was not as natural for me.

At birth, he was perfect. "A man already," the women said. I saw Abu in his eyes and my sister in his sweet cheeks, and an intensity that I never expected in a being so new to this world. A week later Abu entered the tent, looked first to me, then to the babe in my arms, and then let out a long sigh, such as I once heard in the passing of a night owl's wings. He bowed and sat down before me, then reached out his arms to embrace us. With three hearts beating together, I looked from the face of the father to the face of my child and the unbidden thought arose: *Will my son kill? Will he slice a tongue? Will he betray his own?* The fear that had subsided in Abu's arms was now taking seed—I had opened myself to a wildness I did not understand. A power I could not control. The force that drew this child from my body was the force that pulled this tribe through the desert, that kept them alive in treacherous terrain, a force beyond mother and child.

Abu turned my face to his and bent his forehead to mine. Although I was tired, and the babe suckled often, I could not wait to mount my camel and leave the camp. There is a desert saying that Allah had removed all the excess human and animal life from the desert so there would be space for him to walk in peace. I now understood why the Sahara was called the Garden of Allah. I needed that space, that peace, now more than ever.

The desert is a palace of winds. A palace of space. We traveled well after the birth of our son. The pace felt almost leisurely, the men more relaxed. How did I manage alone with a babe amidst the men and camels? A caravan is its own oasis. One must remain calm in the desert—fear, anxiety, anger, strong feelings are irrelevant in such spaciousness. Just the moment exists.

Our child was born into this calm space, rocking through the heat of day and playing in the cool of the evening, enveloped in our tent. We returned to the camp more often then, spending time amidst the women. Amina always greeted me with smiles and coos and arms open for our child. When thoughts of home intruded, I pushed them aside. This was home now. These were my people.

"Abu, help!" I cried. The wind was whipping my robes, the baby was swaying. "Abu," I called, "*Help!*"

He turned sharply at my call, his nostril flared and I saw his palm open ready to defend; then he saw the baby and instantly he was beside me, wrapping our son in the blue cloak, so swaddled I began to laugh.

"He is a bundle of laundry," I said.

"No washing today," Abu said and gathered the child in his arms and rocked back and forth.

The fire of a wild white sun had eaten up the arm of our child. His skin was red and raw. How did that happen? He was strapped to my body as I walked. Suddenly I was seized with the image of his arm hanging out of the *cheche*. Could that be? Could he have been exposed for more than a minute?

"His skin is delicate," Abu said, smearing a white paste on it. "More water," he called. When the boy brought the bag, I leaned over to wash the baby's lips.

"*LA*," Abu said, a bit harshly. "For you. You must drink the water. He will take from you. You must be well watered for the baby to be well watered."

I lifted the jug to my lips and watched as Abu stroked the arm of his tiny pale son. From the earliest days our son had been in the presence of his father. I sensed this was unusual, but the tribe did not interfere. I saw in the looks around us that the force of Abu's role kept them from protesting.

"I'm worried," I said.

"Worry. What is your word worry?"

"I fear," I said.

"Fear, what do you fear?"

"I fear he will be sick, the burn will make him sick."

"Fear," Abu said. "Fear is useless. *Bismallah*, the child will live or die without your fear. We put ourselves to God's hand."

"In God's hands?" I said.

"No, *to* God's hands."

I did not understand.

"We put ourselves to work for God. We put our hands to the work of Allah." Abu looked up at me, took my hand and held it over the blistered skin on our child's arm.

"Here," he said. "Let Allah touch him."

I held my hand above the greased red skin.

"Let God do the work," Abu whispered. *Inshallah, bismallah.*

I held my hand over the yellowing ooze, closed my eyes and waited.

"Do not stop your breath," Abu said.

"No," I said. "I will not stop my breath."

"*Rocketday baaa beeeee raocketing baaaaabeeeee,*" Abu began to croon.

I felt a tremor in my arm, but kept my hand an inch above the skin of our child.

"Rock-a-bye baby," I began to sing softly.

"*Robkeekapoty bagaaa beeee,*" Abu continued.

We kept up our fractured nursery song, attracting the camels, who raised their heads from foraging and began to shuffle closer.

"Enough," Abu said. "We rest now."

I opened my eyes and smiled at this rocketing *babbbaeeee* man.

"*Bismallah,*" he whispered.

"*Bismallah,*" I answered.

The camels settled again.

Our son slept soundly. The next day the blisters were gone and the skin on his arm was a bit redder than the pink of him, but nothing I needed to fear.

DEVON

June 9, 1970

W HEN I HEAR THE ICE CUBES TINKLING I salivate for the gin and tonic Edith is making. Two years after I returned from the desert, the world began celebrating, dancing on the graves of the dead. It was an amnesia I gladly partook of. The war was over, the landscape would never be the same. They call it the "Roaring Twenties" now, but I remember it as tinkling and tap dancing, not roaring. That's when I met Martin, in the early days, the heady days, when the amnesia was falling like a light mist over the countryside. Men walked the streets with missing arms, legs, patches over their eyes, walking reminders of the war. Perhaps it was guilt that kept us dancing and drinking. If we kept moving, we wouldn't have to really look at the devastation. If we kept drinking and dancing, we could fashion new lives out of the shame of the old.

There is no word for virgin in the Tuareg language. There is no shame in having sex with a friend. It is not done in secret, in disgrace. Neither is it done in public. In some ways it was like those country weekends, except the British never managed to let go of the shame if caught. At Lady Hammersmith's weekend party, we all settled into our rooms after the cocktails and dinner and interminable bridge or silly games. After people had managed to make assignations—I so enjoyed watching the cocked ear, the tilted eyebrow, the brush of an arm against a shoulder—my game was guessing who would switch bedrooms during the night, then sitting at breakfast the next morning and watching the eyes, the blush, of each one who entered the dining room. I never missed a cue.

It was essentially the same in the desert. All the music, the dancing, the prancing, and then the arrival at the back of the tent. And the lovemaking, secret but under the very nose of the parents. And the lift of the tent flap before dawn, the teasing and laughter if the young man was caught. But no shame, no horror.

Amina was the one who told me of the code among the adults. "Do you have stories to tell?" the man calls through the tent flap. If a woman is alone—and women were often alone when the caravans were crossing the Sahara—a woman could say "Yes, I have many stories," and thus the night was spent together. What stories they told, I never asked. Amina crinkled her eyes at me and we laughed together.

When I asked Abu about this habit of men checking for an available tent, his eyes flared.

"That is not our way," he said.

"But it is, I have seen and heard it," I said.

"It is not our way," he said pointing his finger back and forth between us.

Of course he was right. Did I not wonder then why I was allowed to travel with the caravan, why I was so rarely in the camp with the women? I sit here, fifty years later, the heat and dust of the desert in my head, and I gasp. I had thought I was so free in that world of Abu, but I was never as free as the women in their tents with their night stories.

We are on the porch with our gin and tonics. Edith is asking questions, and I am trying to answer.

"It had something to do with touch," I tell her. "He was essentially a gentle person. I felt safe with him. That is hard to believe, I know."

"But he captured you," Edith says. "How could you live with that?"

"He *saved* me," I say.

"It just doesn't make sense." Edith waves her hands in the air. "The man captures you, rapes you, and you say he was your lover?"

I know I should keep my mouth shut. Edith is agitated. She will not hear anything I say. I try to keep my lips pressed together, but fifty years of secrets are pushing from the back of my throat.

"No," I say firmly. "He did not capture me. He rescued me. From the driver."

"Well, he raped you."

"He did not rape me."

"You fell in love with your captor? That's a romance novel, not a life."

"Edith, please. My life was no more a romance novel than yours was. I don't expect you to understand." I am in dangerous territory now.

"I don't expect anyone to understand," I say. "I can't say I actually understand."

I do not tell her the truth. The truth is reserved for me. I was the one who seduced Abu. I stalked him. I watched him constantly, could not keep my eyes from seeking him. A fearful fascination.

"Where is Abu?" I said. The boy was pouring tea. He jumped back, spilling tea on my robe.

"Abu?" he said, reaching out pointing, but not daring to touch the stain that was spreading down the front of my garment. The boy put down the pot and then shuffled backwards out of the tent as if he were in the presence of the king.

"Jaysus, Mary and Joseph," I said aloud, brushing my hands down the front of my robe the way Kate did when the bread wouldn't rise or the soup boiled over.

"Jaysus, Mary and—," I said louder. The tent flap sent light onto my hands. "Joseph," I said, and stepped backwards. Abu was standing in front of me, the boy cowering behind him.

Abu turned his body slightly and the boy scurried out of the tent. I looked up at Abu's eyes, which were laughing despite the tightness of his mouth. He reached out and took my hand, and I found myself stepping forward, as if a waltz had begun, gliding my arm up to his shoulder. If he was startled he didn't show it, but gathered me up and we twirled around in a spastic movement that broke us both into laughter. He smelled good to me. Like fresh mint and wood smoke. I stumbled, and my hand tangled up in the blue fabric, falling across his shoulder. The scarf unwound from his head, and we both lost balance and tumbled into the cushions.

How can I tell Edith? I did not lose my virginity. I offered it.

"Jaysus, Mary and Joseph," I whisper.

"Why do you have to swear like that?" Edith stands up and leaves the porch.

I look out to the horizon, to the long thin line of blue, and feel my breath deepen.

This time next week I will be standing in front of my son. I can barely say the word. *Son* like the sun in the sky—it makes me squint and blink and even sweat. I was so jealous of the word *son*. When I saw Father look down at James and say, "Come here,

Son," it sounded like a term of endearment. He never called me "Daughter," for which I was thankful. No soft endearment in that noun. Daughter. Hard, guttural, demanding obeisance.

But at this time next week I will be a mother. Again. For the first time.

How could I tell anyone I abandoned a child? Allowed the tribe to claim its own? "The desert is his destiny," they said. And I let go of him, handed over a part of my soul, believed them when they said he was not of me, told myself it was the right thing to do, then turned my back and promised God I would never bring another child into this world. And God concurred.

But God is good. God is great. God will torment the true believer. Edith wants to know. Why this telegram? What does it mean? What do they want? And I know Martin has the same questions. And deserves the answers.

Fear will set you free.

"I thought it was 'the truth will set you free.'" Edith has returned. She wipes her hands on the dishcloth and puts them on her hips.

Have I been talking aloud again?

"It's the same thing," I say.

"Oh, Alice," Edith's voice drops. "I don't have time for your philosophies today. I mean, you're probably right and that must make sense on some level, but you know, I didn't live my life playing with paint and entertaining with words. I had family and husband and laundry and cooking."

"I smell onions," I say, trying to deflect the anger rising in Edith's voice.

"Yes, Jane is cooking," Edith says and wrinkles her nose.

"I'll help her," I say and take the tea towel from Edith. "You can sit for a while."

She looks at me, distrust on her face, then relaxes her jaw and sits down.

In the kitchen I find Benjamin up on a stool watching and asking questions. "Tell me about the camels," he says when he sees me. I laugh. God love this young boy. Inquisitiveness will take him far from the shores of this family. I watch Jane wipe his dripping lips and I laugh again, thinking of my camel.

"For its own sake, the camel keeps a nasty disposition. The spit is really just the aftereffect of being a cud-chewing animal. The snorting and stamping, well wouldn't you snort and stamp if you were loaded up with all the ribbons and bows and jangling jewels they draped over you?

"The truth is camels are sweet creatures. They're soft and kind and will give you shelter in sand storms and will walk straight into a blinding empty landscape carrying other people's burdens. So they get out of sorts once in a while. Who doesn't?"

All this I am saying to Benjamin while Jane and I cut up the onions. I watch her eyes get tighter as she tries not to show her concern. Is Aunt Alice losing her marbles? Camels? Desert? This is the horror of the British family. Or perhaps it is the strength of this British family. That we could stay connected, polite to each other, take care of each other, be there on the other end of the telephone, on the other side of the door. That we could be present in each other's lives for days, years, decades, and never ask of each anything more than the daily necessities of life. As in the marriage vows we declare, we are there in sickness and health with no mention of being there for pain, or confusion, or secrets, or despair, or joy—all that lies beneath the sickness and health.

"Aunt Alice," Jane says softly. "You can go relax on the porch.

I am happy to do the cooking." I remonstrate. She shakes her head and points to the porch. "Please, go relax." It is an order rather than an offer.

When I return to the porch Edith holds up her empty glass and says it's time for a refresher. I refresh us both, then settle into the rocker, lift my half-filled glass, and return to my blue horizon, the smell of onions still with me.

"In Morocco we had onions at every meal, do you remember? Onions for breakfast, lunch, dinner. Moroccan onions. Cooked until they melted, their sweet stickiness as close to toffee as we were going to get a thousand miles from England. Alif brought the small spring onions into the kitchen and I watched as he bit into one, sinking his teeth in as if it were an apple or a plum."

Edith laughs, and smiles at me. I'm happy to think I've struck a chord that can connect us. I lean closer to her and listen as she speaks into the breeze.

"You spent so much time in the kitchen courtyard. Mother was in despair, but you've always been a dramatic cook, you must have learned well out there."

I ignore the dramatic comment and eagerly push the conversation forward. "I did, I really did. I remember watching Alif peel a small onion—a quick flash of the knife around the root end and the stem, then a twist in the palm of his hand. He tossed it from one hand to the other a couple of times, then offered me the perfect white sphere. I lifted it to my mouth, sank my teeth into it, and began crying, stinging red tears." I turn to the sea and go silent.

Alif laughed and pointed, unintelligible words coming between his laughs, as I wiped my eyes, smearing the juice from the onion across my face, making me cry. I wrung my hands and dropped the onion on the floor. One of the kittens ran over and batted the mangled onion, pouncing on it and knocking it about the tiled floor. My eyes were streaming then, and anger and humiliation ready to take over. I heard more laughter in the courtyard, but could not see anyone through my tears. "Dammit," I said and wrung my hands. "Dammit." Alif reached out and touched my arm.

Real tears were washing out the remembered ones now, tears as I remembered standing in the middle of the courtyard, my arms loose at my sides, my face a sodden mess, my nose full of the first spring air in a Devon garden, the lambs in the pasture, the cows lumbering by and the sweet scent of onion on my fingertips.

The wind has picked up. I rub my arms and look over to see that Edith has left the porch. I pick up my shawl and walk through the front room but stop when I hear the voices in the kitchen. Edith and Jane are standing at the sink, side by side with their backs to me.

"Alice was always strange," Edith says. "Even as a child I knew she was odd. She made up stories all the time. Talked to the animals, as if they knew her. She was fun though, and sharp. I couldn't wait to follow her out of the room and up the stairs after one of Mother's friends had come for tea. She could size a person up in two minutes. And she was a brilliant mimic. Once we trotted upstairs and collapsed in laugher over some particularly offensive grand dame, and when Alice began mimicking the woman's strident voice, Mother burst into the room practically apoplectic. She actually thought the woman had come upstairs and was talking with us! I always said Alice should have been on stage. She got a character so thoroughly it was spooky sometimes.

"The year she returned, when she kept going on about the

desert...I don't know...And after her first year at home...after that, not once in fifty years did I hear of any of these people she now talks about. I just don't know what to think."

I am standing between the sound of the waves and the sound of my sister's voice, thinking *What Alice is this? We don't know that many people with my name.* It's not until the word "desert" that I realize she is talking about me. I hold still and listen harder.

"She is not really to be trusted. I'll never forget the day she returned. I don't know what I expected. But there was Alice. Thinner, and I have to admit, despite the evidence of some sort of suffering, more beautiful than she had been." *Beautiful? She thought I was beautiful?* "What was strange was that she didn't look like someone who had been through the gates of hell. She looked different, but she didn't look tormented. Relieved, perhaps, which would be understandable, once you've been reunited with your family after all those years. But still, there was something unsettling in the way she looked at me. I wish I could describe it, but there probably wasn't anything specific, just a feeling I had. She was like a feral cat."

Jane makes a muffled sound. "That's a good description of Aunt Alice," she says.

"But I don't know, all this desert talk, I just don't know what to think. No one asks about us, about the ones who were left behind, a father dead, a sister missing and given up for dead. I suppose that's not the dramatic story, is it? But it was just as scary, I can tell you. Can you imagine being told someone has returned from the dead? Being told, at the age of twenty, to meet someone you long ago buried in your heart?

"I had no choice. I was the only one who could go. And it was terrifying. There was the excitement of seeing her alive, but then when I saw her, I realized this was someone different, totally different. Same face, same body, but not the Alice I knew."

I hear Edith sigh deeply, almost gasp for breath. "But my story isn't the one anyone wants to hear."

I step across the kitchen threshold. Edith looks around, her mouth a silent "O."

"I want to hear your story," I say.

She stares at me a moment. "After dinner," she says.

THE SAHARA

1917

WE RETURNED TO THE CAMP MANY TIMES after our son was born. Each time, Amina and Fatima greeted me with joy, and our son was enveloped with attention and care that allowed me to relax in a way I had not expected. Once Rashid began to walk, Abu told me I should spend more time in the camp with the women. I missed Abu greatly but it was a comfort to be among the women and to watch our son grow strong and happy amidst them and to listen to the women's poem-stories. Until the time of celebration, when the poetess began to speak of the kite and the island just before Abu's last return.

We were sitting in a circle around the drum, the *tende*, under the protection of the largest acacia. Indolent is how we were. Relaxed and comfortable, the children running about in and out of the circle, then collapsing on their mothers' laps. It felt like a game of musical chairs, with a dry breeze and the admonition to return to the proper lap at some silent signal. I did not realize we were gathered for a celebration until the poetess began to speak. What were we celebrating? By then I thought I knew the ways of the Tuareg, knew the importance of a *tende* and the power of the stories the women recited. Would I ever understand the spontaneous gatherings, the way these people celebrated their lives?

"He was a kite," the poetess said. "She was an island. Together they were a world. He billowed through the desert sand, his robes waving over the dunes. She created an alien space in the Ahaggar." The poetess told the story of the blue man and the white woman. "He flew too high and far from his own people; she furrowed through their space, disturbing the fabric of their life."

The poetess spoke for hours, describing the camels, the silver, the blocks of salt, the number of oases traversed, the battles won. The kite and the island were part of her story, slipped in when the listeners were tired and only a few would hear the words of treason. Even fewer would know what a kite and an island were. Only two or three would know *who* the kite and island were.

Others drifted in and out of the circle but I remained still, listening to my fate.

Two or three was all who needed to hear; two or three can become a multitude. The poetess repeated her story throughout the day, each time adding a more telling detail to the kite and the island. By the end of the feast the decision must have been made. The kite must no longer fly. The island must no longer float.

A week later the women came to my tent. Abu was not there when they came. I held my son within the folds of my robes, stroking his cheek, singing a nursery rhyme under my breath. Handsome boy. My blood went quiet when I heard them approach. The women took him from me. The men must have known I'd kill them if they touched me. The women sat beside me, the same women who sat beside me when he entered the world. I could feel the pulse of his body quicken when they entered the tent.

"*La*," I said, quietly at first.

"The child is not yours," Layla whispered. "He was born to us, he will stay with us."

"*La,*" I said again.

No one spoke. They sat quietly, respectfully. We all knew there was no choice. They could wait patiently or they could grasp quickly. That choice was mine.

"No," I said calmly. "I will not leave him." The women bowed before me; no one said a word. "You cannot make me," I said between my gritted teeth.

"It is God's will," Amina said, so softly I barely heard her. "He is a man of the desert."

"No," I said. "He is my son."

"We are only the mothers. The desert is his life. You cannot deny him his life."

I stood, opened my mouth, another "No" about to erupt, when the boy appeared at the tent flap. He opened his mouth revealing the misshapen tongue, then put his finger to his lips.

"No," I whispered and sank to my knees. Amina put her arm around me, and Layla took my son from my arms.

The next morning everything was burning. The sun, the sky, the sand. All was ablaze. My eyelids were flaming. I could not open them. I could not see. What is this? Then I remembered the women taking my son and I did not try to open them. I did not want to see. I walked in circles, exposing my body to the burning world. I pressed my feet into the scorched sand. I held my arms out to the flames above.

"Aleece." It was Amina calling me. I ignored her and kept walking. She too will burn in this fresh hell. I walked, awaiting the flash or the melt, listening for the sizzle of flesh. My nostrils flared for the reek of my own combustion.

The earth began thrumming. I could feel a wind at my feet; the vibration of a *tende* was coming. The women had set out their drums. A *tende* for the ailing spirit. The drumming began, the relentless beat making the earth hit back at my burning feet. I could feel the women sitting in a circle, corralling my spirit. The men, I knew, would be keeping a respectful distance. And where was Abu?

The drums continued; the beat quickened. I twirled, I ran the circumference of the circle, the heat ran up my legs, up my spine, around the top of my head, out through my arms. I was setting fire to the camp. I was burning these heathens, I was the sun, a destructive flame. Amina, Layla—the woman with the gold earrings—I was incinerating all of them. I continued running. Around and around the circle. The earth throbbed. I pounded it with my feet, my legs, my super-heated body. I didn't look at the women, didn't acknowledge them. I moved faster and faster, willing my body to leave this world, to release me from this hell. Faster and faster. My heart was drumming. Faster and faster. I could hardly feel the earth.

Amina stepped in front of me. "The spirit is loose," she cried. "Catch her!"

The heat evaporated instantly and I was overtaken by cold. I could not feel, my skin was numb. I could not see. My eyelids were fused.

"You have been released," Amina whispered.

I did not tell Abu I was leaving. I had not seen him since the women took my son. He did not return to my tent that night. You could say he was a coward. Certainly that was my first thought, in my rage, but now, I think he was being kind. My last image of him was of the three of us, Abu and his son, laughing, tickling, chanting. Our child completely at ease in his father's arms. I held onto that image for ages, even as I seethed and raged, the sight of our son gazing at his father's face, then reaching out and patting his cheeks.

Once my child was taken, the desert was a barren land that could not sustain me. Abu knew that. He told me as much. As usual, I would not listen. In many ways he prepared me for my escape. He made sure the boy was aligned with me. He made sure I knew how the tribes operated—in the city and in the sand. I set off the next morning. The boy seemed ready. I thought he was eager for his own liberation, to leave slavery behind. But who knows; Abu knew me better than I knew myself sometimes. The boy was there before dawn. He understood what I wanted and packed our things quietly. We left without anyone's notice. Then again, maybe they noticed and didn't interfere. See how I move back and forth? It's how I've kept myself from blaming Abu, how I've kept myself from being a victim. The mind can rationalize anything, even the loss of a child.

I dressed in male garb, covered myself so well even my blue eyes went dark under the slashes of kohl. The boy was agitated. We set off on foot. No camel, no goat. Fortunately we were only a few days' walk from the town. I cried most of the first day. The boy nodded at me, as if encouraging this release. He himself made no sound. When I began to sing on the second day, I saw his shoulders shake and I almost bit my own tongue off remembering how he lost his. I touched his arm and put my hand to my mouth, then to my heart. He bowed and smiled, and pointed to my mouth, nodding and motioning. I began to sing again, and he smiled broadly and swayed his body as we moved off into the desert like some drastically distorted hurdy-gurdy show.

I became a "man" for that trip with the boy, not just in

disguise, but in desperation. Once I became a man, my body didn't move so well through the world. It was upright, tense, even in those flowing robes. My toes were cracked and brittle. The blood seemed sluggish. My woman's body was so much more comfortable, but of course so much more vulnerable. Now that the boy and I were on our own in the desert, it was better to adopt the whole male persona, not just the costume. The boy shook his head at me, pointing to my body. He motioned to his own, gesturing to me to hold the ground between my legs. I did, and immediately the force of the rock beneath shot up my hips. I stood taller, I breathed louder. I could feel myself taking up more space in the world. It was amusing at first, the swagger, feeling like my body was being controlled by my shoulders, but it was tiring too. I watched the boy and saw he lived in between the hips and shoulders—not yet fully a man.

I closed my eyes and saw Abu and wondered that I never registered how like a tree he was, solid, tall, arms that grew out of shoulders and neck. Then I saw my son taking his first steps, the knees jerking up and out, and I began again to lose all balance, then fell forward on the ground and cried out. The boy was beside me immediately, motioning to me to get up. I rubbed my hands in the dirt, then covered my face to hide the tears. The boy pulled at me from behind, raising me from my upper arms. I stretched out my arms and rose like a beast, flinging him off with a roar that echoed across the expanse in front of us. I could not stop myself. The roar came from deep within me, reverberated through my breasts, made my hands shake. The boy was laughing now. "Yes," he nodded. "Yes," his gestures said, holding his arms wide and tapering them down to the ground. I turned and slapped him across the face, hard. He continued to nod. Then he bowed to me and gestured for us to proceed.

When I became a man I did not speak to the boy. I grunted and poked and was surprised to realize this was a familiar language to him. I tried to remember how Abu spoke to the boy and could not come up with a scene. They seemed to not need words. Abu turned his head and the boy knew what to do. He lifted a hand and the boy moved faster.

When we arrived in the town I looked for the doorway where the jeweler traded, but nothing was familiar. I turned to the boy and pointed to my bracelet and unwrapped my scarf to reveal the necklaces beneath. He understood immediately and took my hand, leading me deeper into the medina.

A short time later we came upon a tiny market along a narrow sidewalk, with scarcely room to maneuver. I wondered why it was not within the main area of the medina, but I didn't ask the boy. I had pulled out my jewelry early on our journey and spread it before him.

"Can I sell this?" I asked, and he fingered each piece, his dirty nails outlining the luster of the silverwork. The gold he shoved aside. I pulled it back. "La," he said, the one word he could make. "La"—"No"—a useful word, a dangerous word for a slave.

I touched the gold bracelet. "LA," he said, shaking his head. And then I remembered. Gold. I had only seen one person in the tribe wear gold. The woman who took my son. I grabbed the gold and tied it around my waist when the boy was not looking. *Keep one's enemies close.*

The boy tapped a stick on the ground and pointed deeper into the medina. We squeezed between the wall and the tables, stepping sideways until we came to an opening. The boy pushed me in front of him, through the passageway, which was even darker than the lane we stepped in from. My eyes could not focus. I put my hand out to touch the wall. Air rushed past my face. I stepped backwards into the boy, then turned to see his arm waving in silhouette against the light coming into the passageway. He was waving energetically, ushering me forward. It's okay, he signed, and I turned back around to see a tall figure before me—something familiar in the stance.

"Salam'alek." He bowed, put his hand to his heart and led me into a large room. The boy stood close beside me as the man leaned forward and bared his teeth in a smile.

Show him, the boy pantomimed.

"Show me," the man said.

I put my hand inside my robes and felt for the bag, hesitant to pull it out. The boy nudged my side. If I was going to make it out of the desert, back to England, I would have to get money. The silver jewelry was all I had. But this man. There was something familiar about this man. The boy's shoulders twitched and he folded one lip over the other, as if the lack of a tongue could be made up for by the smack of his mouth. I pulled the pouch out from the folds of my robe and the man stepped back respectfully, shaking his head.

"First we have tea," he said, and clapped his hands. A short fellow scurried out from behind a screen and nodded his head before the man even looked at him.

"Tea."

The short one bowed and disappeared as quickly as he had appeared.

The boy folded his legs onto the floor, deflated. The man offered me a large pillow and the three of us sat in silence until a brass tray appeared from behind the screen, followed by the short fellow and the tea, whose fragrance filled the room with mint. I felt myself relax watching the familiar lift of the teapot, the steady stream of tea flowing from the pot to the cup growing

thinner and thicker like pulled taffy as the hand that held the
pot made sure the tea was well aerated. The three of us drank
quietly, smiling and nodding to each other. I opened my mouth
to speak, then went silent when the boy shot me a look. He held
out his hand, and I passed the pouch to him. The man spread
out a cloth, the boy opened the pouch, and I watched as the
mute negotiated the best price for the earrings, necklaces, and
bracelets that Abu had first held out before me in the light of a
full moon over the Sahara.

I placed my left hand on the boy's shoulder and he smiled.
He had done well. The money was more than enough to get me
back home. Or so I thought.

"Where are we?" I was speaking to the boy's back. He did not
turn. I knew he heard me, but he didn't respond. We had left the
jeweler and were moving even deeper into the medina.

"Where are we?" I asked again.

This time the boy swirled around and motioned to me to be
silent. I laughed and repeated in English, "Where are we?"

The boy grabbed my wrist with such force I stumbled into
him. He pushed me away, then put his hand over my mouth. I
could not believe he had touched me so intimately. Then I saw
his eyes and I knew the gesture was not the least bit intimate. I
beseeched him again, this time with my eyes, and he tightened
his grip on my arm. No, I thought, this cannot be happening.
This cannot be. Then I remembered the man who had bought
the jewels. The figure of the man the boy had warned me away
from on my last visit to this medina, years before. At the same
time I knew that this moment had been a long time coming.

"*La,*" I said slowly, softly. "No, *LA.*"

He was pulling me then; despite my resistance, my body

was being pulled through the medina and I could see we were leaving the jewelers' alley. We were turning down a dark passageway. Do not struggle I thought. *Force will invite force.* I tried to keep pace, to lessen the pain in my wrist. I could see light ahead; we were coming into a square where the medina opens up, a space of light and air. Perhaps the boy was just spooked, or tired, perhaps my fear was unfounded.

I tapped his shoulder. "Where are we?" I said quietly. He stopped in the middle of the square, which was oddly deserted. I saw ornate doors, I saw filigreed walls. The boy stood in front of one of them and I saw something flutter. I saw movement behind the stillness.

"Where—" Before I could get the sentence out, a door opened and the boy pulled me into the darkness. I smelled jasmine and *kif*. The boy dropped my arm just as another pair of hands reached around from behind me and pulled both my arms back. I began kicking and screaming, and once again a hand covered my mouth, but this time it was not the boy's. I tried to scream louder and was answered by laughter. The door opened again and I saw the boy's back as he stepped out, holding a sack tight to his body. I bit the hand over my mouth and the laughter stopped; then my head hit the wall and I stopped.

DEVON

June 9, 1970

W̲E̲ ̲M̲A̲D̲E̲ ̲I̲T̲ ̲T̲H̲R̲O̲U̲G̲H̲ ̲D̲I̲N̲N̲E̲R̲ with small talk and Benjamin talk. Jane is putting him to bed, and Edith is pouring another glass of wine.

"You were reported missing, of course," Edith says, looking out to sea. "But we had no real hope. The Home Office told us they could do nothing. And there was no actual law enforcement in Morocco. The *Caliph* sent word to Mother, and the house servants talked about *djinn* and some of them actually cried. But really, there was nothing to be done. No way anyone was going to go looking for you. Then the house servants began to leave, *djinn* again or something. And the Home Office said we should return. Mother never said you were dead, but she began speaking of you in the past tense. Eventually, once we were home and the mourning period for Father was over, she stopped speaking of you. I didn't dare speak your name." Now she turns and faces me.

I try to calculate at what point my name left the family vocabulary. Where was I then? Edith said they left Morocco two months after the accident. Mother wore black for six months. Six months. Where was I? My flesh is cold. I am shivering. Six months into the desert—is that the time the British men

159

appeared? When I turned my back on the possibility of escape? When I chose the world of Abu and his men?

I sit silent in my chair. Edith looks embarrassed.

I can believe there is more to heaven and earth than we will ever grasp. I can believe I knew the family gave me up for dead. I have heard people say they stopped in their tracks a continent away, at the exact moment a family member died. We've all heard such stories. The clock stops. The dog gets up and leaves the room. Who can explain such actions? Such intuitions? The family stopped speaking of me. They gave me up for dead. And I sensed it, a thousand miles away, I sensed their release. I knew I was alone. No one was coming for me. All these years I have not spoken of my own son. Has he sensed it? Has he lived with the belief his mother is not in this world? Did I abandon my son the way the family abandoned me? I am shaking now, unable to control the shivering. Edith stands up.

"Are you ill?" she says.

"I'm cold."

"A shawl," she says, and picks up the afghan she knitted last summer and wraps it around my shoulders.

"Here," she says. "It is chilly tonight, the wind is onshore."

"It is not the wind," I say.

She sits down and looks out to sea again. "Let's not talk anymore," she says. "It's not good going over the past like this."

PARIS

June 9, 1970

A YOUNG GIRL IS STANDING in front of 49 Rue du Bac, posing for a photo beside the ghoulish carving in the center of the oversized door. Martin waits respectfully while she giggles and mimes fear at the sight of what must be an interpretation of one of the residents of Dante's seventh level of purgatory. The photographer does not seem bothered that Martin is waiting, and takes his time clicking away. Is this a fashion shoot? In front of a nunnery? Well, this is Paris. This is 1970. Martin finds himself with a catch in his throat. He never feels like an old man, not physically, despite his years and a slight stiffness in his left knee. It's only in situations like this that he realizes the world has moved on in a direction he had not expected. These two, the girl and the camera fellow, they are young enough to be his children—no, his grandchildren. For the first time in ages, Martin feels old. Childless. Untethered to the next generation.

"Sorry to hold you up," the young man says. American. They are everywhere these days. He nods at Martin as he takes the girl's arm and moves along the sidewalk. Martin smiles, then turns to push the buzzer before wiping the wet from his eye.

Inside the Mother House Martin sits on a spindly chair and

regards the Madonna and Child on the wall before him. All is hushed. Sepulchral. The tones of blue on the wall, in the drapery, and in the carpeting remind him of his nursery at Holland Park. This is a house of women, he tells himself. A house of holier-than-thou women, Alice would say. Why would they be telegramming Alice?

"*Bonjour, Monsieur.*" Martin pulls himself to his feet and unconsciously turns Gallic in manner and tone, French flowing fluently from his lips as he makes an imperceptible bow before the formidable woman encased in white, the gold cross hanging from her belt glinting as it rocks back and forth.

When they are seated in the office, he declines the offer of coffee, compliments the Reverend Mother on the *maison,* and waits for her to press her lips together in the French signal that pleasantries had been addressed and accepted and business can now be attended to.

Mother Chlotilde leans forward and speaks softly. "M. Witherspoon was most gentle in his demand," she says.

Martin smiles and waits.

"We understand who you are and why you would inquire about this telegram. It is only because I believe in the sanctity of marriage that I agreed to meet. We were most happy when Alice married and were relieved when we learned she had found pleasure in painting."

Painting? Martin remembers the first painting. A wide expanse of yellow and mauve. He thought it was abstract—long sweeps of color across the canvas. It made no sense to him. He wanted to compliment Alice, to encourage her, to tell her how good her painting was. He wanted it to be good, for her sake, for her health, for their well-being. But he couldn't find anything to say. He stood dumbly in front of it until she said, "How does it make you feel?"

"Feel?"

"Yes, how do you feel when you look at this?"

"Bewildered," he blurted.

"Yes," she said quietly and put down her brushes. "I will wash these up and we can go to dinner."

The Reverend Mother is smiling at him. "How do you know about her painting?" he asks. Alice had never shown her works, even when galleries pressed her to. By then he understood that her vision, as they called it, was unique, and that her painting was of value. But she refused to release any of them. "How could you know about her painting?" Martin is not used to asking questions he does not know the answers to. He feels as lost as he had been in front of that first painting.

"Alice stayed with us when she came out of the desert," Reverend Mother says. She folds her hands and gazes impassively at Martin. He is confused. Alice painted for years in the studio they bought after she left Vincent Grove, then decided to sell it when her eyes began to bother her. Alice never said she stayed with the Sisters. In Paris? Or—no—the mission in the desert? Alice painted in the desert?

Martin allows silence to fill the air. Then he asks, "Do you know the name Abu?" Reverend Mother averts her gaze. Her skin is a youthful pink against the tight white of her wimple. Martin remembers that pink—in one of Alice's paintings. Pink against white surrounded by yellow. He had thought it was an abstract flower, a faded peony perhaps. Now he sees it was the woman sitting before him.

"Yes, I know the name Abu." Martin is aware Reverend Mother is choosing her words carefully, watching him as she speaks. He could almost believe her tongue was tip-toeing inside her mouth.

"He was the Amenokal of the Kel Ahaggar, the leader of the Tuareg tribe. He brought Alice to us, wrapped in a rug."

Martin tries not to react. *Wrapped in a rug.* The words Alice spoke as she entered Vincent Grove. "I should be wrapped in a rug," she had said.

Mother Chotilde pauses, looking directly at Martin.

"Abu saved her life. They would have killed her. An eye for an eye, of course."

Martin waits. The two of them sit across from each other like the last two pieces on a chessboard. He waits for her move.

"We came to an agreement. We would shelter Alice, and when she was strong enough we would find safe passage for her to return home." Martin calculates—Alice returned home in 1917, safe passage through the end of the war, home to England. That could not have been easy. His respect for Reverend Mother increases.

"And the bargain? The—the agreement, I mean?" Martin knows this is a delicate subject for a woman of the cloth.

"Abu has donated to our cause quite generously over the years and has made sure our mission was protected."

A generous agreement, Martin thinks. Money and protection. Essential to survival in the unbounded desert.

"And for that you—" He sees the Reverend Mother wince a bit. She's clearly a practical woman and knows how to adjust her vows to accommodate the necessities of life.

"Abu asked us to keep him informed of Alice's whereabouts at all times."

"At all times," Martin echoes.

"Yes." The Reverend Mother lowers her eyes. "We almost lost her when you visited to New York—America is so wide open. And we were concerned about Vincent Grove, but that seemed to be of great help—her painting is proof of that."

Martin takes in the fact that this quiet, grandmotherly presence before him has the wherewithal to track someone across continents.

"And why—" Martin stops himself. He has always had a sixth sense that tells him when a question might elicit an answer that could shut down a negotiation.

"Indeed," Reverend Mother says. "Why the telegram? Abu has died." Martin nods. "His instructions were for us to send a telegram when he died. Then to send his pouch. Then to expect the son."

"The son?"

Reverend Mother opens her hands as if in benediction.

"Yes, Alice and Abu's son," she says.

Martin does not react. He waits to see what assumption the Reverend Mother will make.

Reverend Mother waits a moment. "This is a lot to take in, I'm sure."

Martin does not know how to read her beatific smile. He wants to trust her. She is a woman of the church. But a woman who made a pact with a tribal leader.

"An eye for an eye," he says. "Is that a reference to the son?"

Reverend Mother shifts in her seat. Martin is surprised by her discomfort. "You said Abu saved her life. They would have killed her."

Mother Chotilde rakes her eyes across the room. Martin knows that signals duplicity. He knows to verify whatever she says next.

"There was a death," she says carefully. "Alice was involved. These things can be confusing among the natives."

"Death is confusing?" He is parrying with her now, playing the cat and mouse game. She has been complicit in something, that's clear to him now.

"Well, given your position, Monsieur, you may not want to—this was all so long ago—it was another time and place, another age, another country. The world has changed. We live in a different world now." She is speaking calmly, her voice modulated, but he can see a flush beginning at the edge of her wimple.

Martin is exactly where he likes to be. He thanks the Reverend Mother for her information and for the care and concern the Sisters of Blessed Mercy have had for Alice all these years. He knows to leave now, before the Reverend Mother tries to make an agreement with him.

DEVON

June 10, 1970

I WAKE UP THINKING OF THE 1918 influenza epidemic—the best catastrophe. It brought about the end of the stalemate we call the First World War. Men dug into trenches for years, unimaginable numbers of dead, James among them, no end in sight—until nature said enough and the influenza erupted and they dropped in their tracks. Can't have a standing army if the army can't stand.

We didn't know that's what was going on. Not in the desert. Disease doesn't take root so easily in dry desiccated areas. People in the desert are remarkably healthy. No sweat, no real grime. When I first returned to England it didn't look green to me, it looked brown. All I could see was the mulch, the deep squishy dirt that stuck to my shoes, that caked up on the wheels, that stained the floors and carpets. We had mud in the oases, glorious chocolate water, but mud did not follow us home into the tent, onto the rugs and discolor our fabrics. We had dirt and dust and the foul smell of goat leather cured with urine, but the air was clear; such odors only arose when you put your nose close to the source.

My first day back on British soil I was blinded by the fog. Claustrophobia hit me hard. I felt as if I had been dropped into the sea—I reached my arms out to swim, to push aside the mist, to wade through the coal stink, but it was useless. Edith grabbed my arm. "What are you doing?" she said, not for the first time. How many times had I embarrassed her on that journey home? It was like traveling with a circus person, Edith later said. Did she know how cruel her remarks were? "You were deaf, dumb and blind," she said.

I know she spoke the truth. I was deaf to my own language. Mute in society, and blind to what had become of us all. In seven years the human body grows a whole new skin. Not a single cell covering my body when I left England made the return trip with me. In seven years my skin had shed all knowledge of damp, dark, dense air. My soul remembered it, but my body remained in alien territory for years. And now? Now I have the pale skin, the white on white skin of someone who lives sheltered by clouds and convention. I'm almost as white as I was in the Sisters of Blessed Mercy.

I step into the breakfast room. Edith and Jane look up, and I register the fear on their faces. Apprehension. Expectation. What I saw when I first returned to this island. Everyone was afraid of me. Afraid of what I had survived, what I was bringing back into their well-protected lives. Mother and Edith looked up, as Edith and Jane do now, ready to quiet me, to settle me. It's not that I was behaving wildly. I didn't chatter away for hours. Neither did I wander the room in silence. I didn't fidget and fuss with things. I was not melancholy. But in some indecipherable way I was different. And it scared them.

And I was loath to confront them. With their fears and expectations. Was it anger? That I was once again in the land of tea and crumpets? I should have been grateful. That I was rescued. That they took me in despite all that had changed between us. In the wild, if a cub is removed from its mother, from its siblings, from its lair, it is not welcomed back. Once removed, it is forever estranged. I should have been glad to have been accepted.

But I was not. I was confused. I was burdened. I was lost among my people.

"Good morning, dear," my mother said brightly, reaching to pour me a cup of tea and never looking above my nose. "How are you feeling this morning?"

I answered with the expected platitudes and settled myself on the cushioned chair, still slightly stunned to be sitting so high above the ground.

"The fog is temporary today," she said. "We can go for a walk later. The doctor said you should be as mobile as possible."

"Yes, Mother," I said, wondering why anyone would refer to a person as mobile, like a ship, a car, a vehicle of motion.

I marveled at the words in the room, how they fluttered back and forth across the table—"dinner . . . tea . . . the pasture . . . butter, please"—how meaning remains solid but empties of sense, how a bitter old woman gripped the handle of a teapot so tightly her fingernails turned as white as the bread on her plate. The woman who now looked directly at me and called my name.

"Alice, Alice," Mother said. "You really must try to stay focused. You are among civilized people now. You must learn to listen when someone speaks to you."

"Alice, I'm speaking to you," Edith says.

I look up from my coffee. Jane has left the room; Edith is sitting across from me.

"Please tell me," I say.

Edith looks like she's eaten something rotten. Her mouth is distorted and her face is pink. She twists the rings on her fingers.

"It is fine," I say. "I really want to know. Where were you?"

"Where was I?"

"The accident. In Morocco. After the car flipped over. Where were you?"

Edith fidgets in her chair. She looks to the window, then sighs deeply and lowers her head. I wait for her to speak.

"Under the car," she says. "People always asked me if I saw you leave. I couldn't. I was underneath the car, the shelter of the upended seat, lying in the sand. Perhaps I fell asleep," Edith says. "I know that sounds strange, impossible even, but I remember Father putting his arm out to touch the driver, and I remember screaming. Then I remember waking up and it was dark and warm, and for some reason I thought it was the middle of the night and I was home in bed, and I just rolled on my side a bit to get more comfortable and fell back asleep. The next time I woke, I heard voices. Someone was calling me, and I realized I wasn't in bed. I was lying on sand. I began to scream. And that's when they turned the car over.

"Who is 'they'?"

"Some men. Mother had sent some men out to see why we hadn't returned. It was dark. They had a cart and horse and managed to lift the car without touching me."

I take a deep breath before I ask, "Where was Father?"

"I don't know. I didn't know. I thought you had gone home somehow, although I didn't ask, just got into the cart next to all the blankets and bundles. When we arrived at the compound and they got me out of the cart and Mother started crying, that's when I realized one of the bundles was Father's body."

I reach across the table to touch Edith's hand. She looks down and smiles, then pulls her hand away gently.

"Everyone wanted to know where you were, and of course I didn't know. They put me to bed and Mother came and sat by my side during the night. The Colonel came the next day to ask who the driver was, but after that they told me to rest, and then we had to decide where to have Father's funeral, and it was all about you, every day for ages it seemed. And then all foreigners were told to leave and we had to return to England."

She sighs deeply and drops her shoulders. Sun strikes the glass sugar bowl and blinds me. I close my eyes and we sit in silence. When I hear her draw in a deep breath, I look up and ask about the accident again. I see her nose twitch.

"Really, Alice, it was so long ago, how am I to remember? I don't dwell on such things. Some people rub their wounds constantly, going over and over the past. But I don't. I move on. The past is past. Particularly when you've lived as long as we have. I live in the present. It's healthier."

"Yes, Edith, you're right." I speak softly. "It's healthier. But given the circumstances this week, the past is here. In our present, isn't it?"

"I suppose it is," she says and pats her knee, smoothing her skirt by rolling her index finger back and forth over the seam. It's a while before she speaks again. "I remember it was quiet," she finally says. "A quiet I'd never heard before or since. And hot. My skirt was wrapped around my legs. I could barely move."

Edith shivers a bit, then rubs her nose. I wait for her to continue.

"At first I thought I was back here. At the seaside. There was sand on my face and under my fingernails. I thought I was at the beach, but I had heavy shoes on, and we never wore heavy shoes at the beach."

I laugh, which startles Edith.

"It's not funny, Alice," she says.

"No," I say, "it's not. I'm sure it was terrifying."

"What is it?" I ask. "What's the matter? Are you all right?"

She begins to cry.

"I wasn't terrified, but I knew I was alone." The tears are small and don't go beyond her cheekbones, hanging there like glass pearls set on her pink cheeks.

"Yes, alone," I say. "Those times when you wake up in the house and you know from the feel of things that there is no one else there. You knew there was not another person in the world at that moment." She is nodding.

I dare to reach my hand out again and hold hers. She allows me to.

"I had so many stories in my head," Edith finally says. "People questioned me for days. Did I see you leave? What happened to the driver? It got to the point where I couldn't remember what I had remembered. Then we had to return to England, and at that point I guess we decided to believe you were truly lost. 'Lost' was the term we used. Then we stopped mentioning it. I kept expecting you to turn up at the door one day, like a lost dog, even though I knew that was impossible. People looked at me strangely for so long. As if I knew something and wasn't telling anyone the truth. Or maybe I was imagining that."

Edith pulls her hand away.

"When the Colonel called five years later and said you had been found, it was hard to understand. The war was on. James was gone—that's when we truly lost Mother. Father, she buried. You she seemed to pass over." Edith looks at me. "I don't mean that in a cruel way, just that she no longer referred to you as lost or anything. Your photo remained on the mantle and she would say 'my daughter Alice' if anyone asked, but at some point people stopped asking.

"When James died, that's when we truly lost her. She dressed herself, and maintained her toilette, and came down to tea, but other than a dim smile and nod of the head, there was no real communication. She managed to be a widow and even managed being the mother of a missing child, but when the War Department arrived with the news of James's death, she just became so far away all the time. I was lonely.

"When the Colonel called, Mother couldn't understand at first. 'Sisters of Blessed Mercy . . . Sisters . . . Daughter.' She was confused for days. Uncle Horace took me to tea at the Savoy and said he could arrange things. It was still wartime. He said he could get you home."

I look at Edith wringing her hands as she talks. I watch the sparkles from her diamonds flash as she twists one hand inside the other. I see the broken light on the desert floor, the sun burning into the crystals of sand, the heat, the pressure of that light against my eyeballs.

"Keep walking." The driver pulls my arm. The heat is loud in my ears, the wind is stinging my eyelids, thunder and lightning are inside my body.

I pull my arm away from the driver, pull myself backward from the force of the heat. He turns, reaches out for my hat, and in the swirl of dust kicked up by his movement, I see Edith reach out.

"Jane," she calls. "Jane, come quickly."

I am on the floor. My face is in the carpet. A carpet that does not move, that does not scratch across my face with every swing of the camel's hip, a carpet that lies still and flat. I feel my bones on the tightly woven fibers. I turn at the sound of Edith's voice.

Jane's head appears above Edith's. "What? What are you doing on the floor? What happened?" She leans over Edith, who loses her balance and comes crashing towards me. I cringe at the thud as Edith crumples beside me.

"Mother!" Jane is on her knees, ministering to Edith.

Light flashes across the room as Jane lifts Edith's arm and helps her to sit up.

Gold fills my eyes. Gold in the flap of the tent. Gold attached to those ears, pulling the lobes with their weight. "Is this Aleeze?" The woman with the gold earrings asks. Amina nods. I see the woman's lips curl and I want to run my fingernails across her perfect skin, I want to gouge her eyes out. I pull myself up to standing and am thrilled to see I stand taller than she does. She holds her shoulders back. I can feel myself vibrate with the tension between us.

"Alice, Aunt Alice." Jane takes hold of my arm, gently, firmly. "Alice, it's all right now. It's me, Jane. And Edith. It's all right now."

I reach out and touch the gold on Jane's ear. She recoils.

THE SAHARA

1917

WHEN THE DOOR OPENED, no one looked up. None of the figures seemed to notice my entrance, although light was thrown into the dim room and noise must have crossed the threshold into the quiet space. I was pushed forward and stood as the door closed silently behind me. Then it came to me. This was a room full of women. Sitting on cushions, leaning against the wall. In the light of the candles I could see they were all beautiful, all uncovered, their faces and hair unhidden, their ankles jutting out from the folds of luxurious fabrics. Not a single one of them looked at me or acknowledged my presence.

After a few moments my tired feet told me to take a seat. I moved forward into the room, unwrapping my headdress, when suddenly all eyes were upon me. Until I uncovered my face, these women must have assumed I was a man. I continued to unwind my wraps and even leaned over and undressed my feet. The energy in the room had changed, but still no one spoke to me. I was among my own sex, but there was no comfort here. I looked around at the dark faces, the almond eyes, the magnificent hair and became totally self-conscious. These women were pampered in some way I could not understand. Their skin was smooth and soft, not seared by sun. They wore jewelry such as I had never seen. And they sat or lay back with a boredom I could feel.

The women allowed me to sit for a few minutes, then, like a rush of wings when a flock of birds leave a particular tree, all at once they were on their feet, surrounding me, touching my garments, my face, talking to me. I sat dumbly, like a beast. When it became clear I wouldn't respond, one of them sat down in front of me and took my hands in hers. The others stayed gathered around me while she continued to inspect me, turning my hand over in hers to look at the fingers, the nails. Pulling at my hair, stroking the skin on my legs. After a few minutes she led me to an inner room with a steaming bath, undressed me, and walked me to a tub where I soaked in water that relaxed and revived me at the same time. A young black girl took direction from the woman and scrubbed my back and washed my hair. Then a smooth lotion was rubbed over my entire body. I was given a warm drink, then wrapped in tight towels and blankets and left in a dark room, where I slept a sleep I have never had in my whole life, before or since.

At last I had come out into night, myself the center of darkness. My skin was alive, my hair soft and fragrant, and I was a wonder to myself, leaning back against the pillows of an opulent settee. The room was lit by one single candle and I was aware it was evening, even though I had not seen the day's light since I entered those rooms. Vanity is the strongest drug. I was quiet, at peace, not on alert. Despite the boy's treachery, despite the dislocation of time and place I then inhabited, my mind was as relaxed as my body.

I drifted in and out of a lovely dream, visions of Abu on the edge of my consciousness, when I was brought back into the room by the rustle of fabric as a curtain drew back, carrying the cold of night into the room. I sat up, about to speak, when I saw that the man crossing the room so swiftly was not Abu, but a stranger, who leaned towards me and put a rough hand on my arm, a murmur of pleasure escaping from his lips. All sense left me and I stood up from the settee, yelling in English, "Who are you? What are you doing here?" The man tightened his grip on my arm and laughed loudly, answering me in rapid Arabic.

I could hardly think this was happening. All the fears that crawled around the edge of our existence in Marrakesh were burnt away as I crossed the desert with Abu. All those fears returned in the shape before me. The man was determined, and sexually excited. This was why I had been pampered and prepared, allowed to luxuriate in sleep. I watched myself as he pulled at my arm, and I slapped him, kicking the cushions and struggling to get away. He was laughing, happy with the hunt, and I knew that no matter how much I struggled, how much I screamed, it would all be part of the anticipation that had brought the two of us to this meeting place.

I cannot tell the rest. It is something my mind has blessedly colored over. If I wanted, I could recall every ugly touch, every shoot of pain through my body, but my mind has translated the entire intercourse to one black moment, after which I was left bruised and breathless, grasping for the sense of myself that had allowed me to follow Abu and then the boy, silently and whole-heartedly into this labyrinth.

Then came the last night. I knew it was Haddad. I recognized the slope of his shoulders, the heavy tread of his lame left foot, the smell of his foul mouth. I watched as he crossed the room, pulling off his sash, and took note of exactly where he laid his dagger. This I know now. This I can see clearly, almost in slow motion, clearer to me fifty years later than it was the night I finally did pass through those walls, an insensible woman with the blood of another on my body.

Haddad never looked at me, just began pulling at my garments, guttural noises accompanying the febrile touch of his dirty hands. I sank back, and he pulled me closer, scratching my face with ragged nails as he tore the necklace over my head.

I can watch it all now. I see my hand shoot up in front of my face. See Haddad rear up like a beast on his hind feet and strike my hand away, see myself recoil and see him laugh as he lifts my body and tosses me against the pillows.

The dagger is on the table to my right. It glints in the light, like a beacon, like a shell reflecting a bitter moon on a cold night by the sea. I moan, a tiny bit of sound to appease a man who wants to hear how he can overpower a woman. I lift my hips, twist my body and moan again, then reach my hand up to caress the back of his neck. This is what he wants, a struggle and a surrender. I open my eyes and smile into the filthy depths of his black eyes and wait for him to enter me, and as the pain sears through my body I reach out, my arm curving through the air in a final surrender, loose, limp, my fingers determined in their reach.

Haddad shivers, raises his head, bares his neck, and my hand passes in front of my eyes, the silver flash one quick stroke, silver and wet red splashing before me, the weight of Haddad like a casket above me and I laugh, a short high laugh that takes all my breath away from me and leaves me alone in the blackness.

If I told you I was capable of murder, that I had the strength and the presence of mind to take hold of a knife, his own knife, and slash his neck. If I told you I did all that, aware of my actions, and yet shocked at the blood and the raspy breath. If I told you I wasn't in the room when they finally came with the police or what passes for police in that territory. I was in the rafters, hovering like a lost soul above the body below, watching as they rolled the dead weight off the young woman, watching as they pushed her aside to inspect the wound on the neck and to wrap Haddad's body. I watched silently as the young girl pushed herself along the wall toward the door, watched as the man reached out one arm to block her exit, watched as she slid to the floor and gathered her skirts about her legs, folded her head over and like a slowly melting piece of ice slipped under her garments, then slithered naked out the door. If I told you I then watched as she ran through the dark hallways, no sound, no rustling robes announcing her escape. She found a door through which the world of the harem gave way to the world of the medina, and I watched as she grabbed a rug from a stall, wrapped herself and continued, stumbling along the walls for hours, and if I told you she collapsed in the darkest corner of the maze, only to awaken to the soft brown eyes of a Sister of Blessed Mercy. If I told you then and only then did I descend from the rafters, coward that I am, and rejoin my body, it would be the truth.

PARIS

June 9, 1970

*A*LL THE DISTRESS IN THE WORLD *comes from other people's secrets.* The words run through Martin's head as he walks to meet the staff before the Peace Talks. Who said that? The fellow in the trench at Argonne. It whistled out of his lips as the life left him. Martin always wondered if it was a last cosmic comment on the war or if there was something he should know, should have known, when he wrote the letter to the parents telling them their son had died a valiant death. The secret all officers kept from the grieving. Would the next disastrous war be averted if parents received letters bearing the truth: your son died in agony, taking ground we gave up the next day?

Martin stands still, listening to the sounds of Paris 1970, the sounds of Paris 1915 echoing in his head. The war was so close to the city then. When it began people would drive out for a day's entertainment, sitting one hill over from the front lines, listening. He shakes out his hand and feels the missing digit. Something is missing in the Reverend Mother's story. What is her secret?

Martin returns to 42 Rue Bac and rings the bell again. When the novice answers, this time he bows deeply and apologizes profusely, telling her he thinks he left his pen in the room. A very special pen. The pen he signed the Armistice with.

She is sweet and cordial and leads him back a different way through the blue walls to the Reverend Mother's office. Martin notices packing boxes and files and paintings leaning against the walls. The novice checks the room but does not find anything.

Martin claps his hand to his forehead in mock shock and exasperation. "*Ici*, it is here!" He pulls a pen from inside his jacket. "*Je suis désolé*, so sorry to disturb you."

She laughs and puts her hands together in prayer pose. "*Merveilleux*," she whispers. He walks back down the blue hall and points to the boxes. "You are moving out?"

"Oh no," she says they are moving in. "Our Africa mission is closing."

"*Pourquoi?*" he asks.

"The situation is unsafe . . . Algeria . . ." She bows her head.

He nods, then thanks her again and stands quietly after the door closes behind him.

The mission is closing. Unsafe. Abu's protection has ended with his death. Questions flood him and he knows what to do. He walks to the closest café, pulls out his pad and pen, and begins listing questions:

—where is the son?

—why does he not continue the protection?

—why is he coming here? To stay?

—where is the money? Always look for the money.

And the question he underlines twice with a thick line:

—Why did the Reverend Mother not tell him the mission was closing?

Martin takes a long sip of the strong Parisian coffee and wonders if his instincts had been right when he decided not to discuss Alice with the Reverend Mother, not to ask for her memories of the woman who arrived wrapped in a rug.

"Richard," Martin barks into the phone in the Gare du Nord. "Algeria 1917. The Sisters of Blessed Mercy and Reverend Mother Chlotilde. I'm taking the Night Ferry back and coming straight to the office. You can brief me at the elevenses." He starts to hang up the phone. "Oh, and Richard. Thank you."

ALGERIA

1917

"Miss George? Can you hear me, Miss George?" A hand touched my arm gently. I reached up to my face and felt the gauze, wound around in layers, across my forehead and my eyes, except for one tiny slit. A nun stood beside me.

"She's responding, Doctor. Look, she's touching her bandages."

"Yes." A deep, brusque voice came from the far side of the room.

I could not move my lips; the bandages were pressed against them. When I took a breath to speak, pain shot across my chest.

"She appears agitated." The voice was soft, female.

"There is no more morphine left," the male voice said.

The bed was covered with a big white sheet as if it were a smooth table. The Sisters of Blessed Mercy moved quietly along the corridors like human statues, evidence of legs and the mechanics of motion never visible. I lay in the bed and watched them glide by, wondering if they were some form of angels, brought softly close to the earth. The time in their Algiers hospital was a world between worlds for me. From the desert to the green fields of home. From the Sahara to Britain. Without the hospital and the big white bed and the Sisters of Blessed Mercy, I doubt I could have survived the transition. In many ways it was more traumatic, more painful than the initial remove to the desert.

The monotony of each day with the Sisters kept me anesthetized even when the drugs ran out. Five a.m. bells calling the sisters to matins, six a.m. *petit déjeuner*, coffee in a bowl, stale bread on the side. Seven a.m. a bath, sponged down in the bed, all my skin revealed to the world, the sister in charge revealing only face and hands, her skin as white as her scapular.

During the first month, sunny, coughless and serene, I observed with astonishment the waste of my constitution. Bruised, battered, worn thin from days and nights with no exercise, no air, no light, I lay like a babe in the nursery. I ate, I slept, I stared at the light, I listened to the sounds of the sisters and the wind. I did not move. I had more volition wrapped in the rug, those first days in the desert. Here, among kind souls, I was empty. Then came the day the Mother Superior came to my bedside and asked, "Where is home?"

Home? I have no answer. The fields of Devon pass before my eyes. Green. The ocean racing to meet the rocks ashore. Gray. Home? When she speaks the word I see Abu, I see the folds of his robe, the reach of his hand, his head blotting out the sun. I see his eyes turn blue to black, and I see my son.

I blink. "Home?" I say.

"Yes," she answers. "Where do you want to go from here?"

I look at her, unable to speak. I close my eyes and feel her light touch on my hand.

"Don't worry," she says. "It's too soon. Rest a while longer and we will sort it out."

Naked and alone I arrived at the Sisters of Blessed Mercy. A body in need of repair, a mind deranged, a spirit lost to this world. Kindness and patience. Food, rest and those white sheets were what brought me back. I became aware of all I had to keep silent about.

The war wasn't real to me until I arrived at the Sisters of Blessed Mercy. They had painted a huge red cross on the side of their pristine white wall and kept a map of the Mediterranean in the refectory. When I was conscious long enough to absorb my surroundings, I asked Sister Natalie why the blankets had HMS embroidered on them. She put her finger to her lips and smiled. "C'est la guerre," she said.

"You mustn't stay here much longer," Sister Natalie said one day, when I was strong enough to sit in the garden. "The world is not what it was. There is war, you know."

Abu was right. Five years before, Father had been jittery, Britain was meeting with France. I heard slices of conversation in the hallway between Mother and Father the day we were separated, but I walked by, uninterested in such things. Now, at the word war, the sight of three British men alone in the desert comes back to me. And the overheard conversation in Timbuktu. And the time the caravan changed course at the sight of a line of lorries in the distance. And Abu's disgust.

"It rumbles around us," he had said. "The desert is the only safe place in the world." At the time it sounded like one of his Tuareg proverbs, but sitting there with Sister Natalie, the past five years took on a different color, as if a haze, a beautiful haze, was beginning to lift.

Sister Natalie was the only "native" in the Sisters of Blessed Mercy. She too had come out of the harem, but not in the way I did. She had dropped rose petals from the roof each time she saw the sisters passing on market day. For weeks, she told me, she dropped rose petals. The sisters looked up and smiled, but Natalie did not dare to call to them and of course she did not speak French at that time, so the sisters smiled and waved and walked on past each week. Until the day Natalie dropped olive pits with the rose petals, pits she had stored in her garment after each meal. The clatter echoed in front of the sisters and one, Sister Gertrude, stopped and looked up at Natalie with a question in her eye. Natalie began crying and flapping her arms in and out from her breast. She looked like a stricken bird, Gertrude later told her, as if she were tied to the trellis and kept flapping her wings, but couldn't rise. Gertrude waved, but she didn't smile. She pantomimed, some sort of eternal gesture, to say "Do you need help?" Natalie kept nodding and waving her arms in and out until each woman, at the same moment, put her hands together in prayer position and bowed.

Natalie said she never knew what the sisters did, whether they "bought" her, or if there was some other form of trade, but the next week when the sisters came to market, Natalie was summoned, presented at the door, and had been with the Sisters of Blessed Mercy ever since. She told me this story the week I left the Sisters. We stared at each other a long time.

"God forgives you," she said, and pressed a Tuareg cross into my hand.

DEVON

June 10, 1970

I CAN HEAR JANE CALLING TO BENJAMIN. I lift myself from the bed, groggy from a mid-day sleep. Why am I back in bed? I feel the bruise on my elbow and remember the morning conversation with Edith and sigh. At the window I see Benjamin jumping in and out of tiny waves. I stare at the sea and try to remember the last time I saw my child. I can remember the feel of him, sitting astride my hip, his legs flapping against me as I walked. I can remember the sweet smell of him, the top of his head, soft with fuzzy blond hair. I can remember the sound of his cry as the women carried him away, almost drowned out by my own cries, but I cannot remember the face of my boy, the beautiful, beautiful face of my boy. The memory of young Benjamin comes to me, waddling across the floor, and smiling and raising his arms to me, and Jane poring over her nursery books. Edith's children, her grandchildren, they come to me, but my boy, the face of my own son, has faded out of memory, the worst penance.

My eyes are watering again. Double vision. The flashes of lightning at the perimeter, to the left of my vision. I need to rest my eyes, protect them from the reflection of the sea. A *tagelmust*. I need a *tagelmust*.

I turn gingerly toward the hallway and wait for my eyes to adjust to the light. Then I find my way to the chest. I dig to the bottom and see the bright blue cloth. I reach out and pull it from the pile, letting the pillowcases and towels flop onto the floor. It's long, but not long enough. I take a thread from the edge and bite hard, then pull the thread slowly, releasing the weave, pulling straight and tight until it comes out of the cloth and I can take hold of the material in both hands ,and with one quick pull the material comes apart into two long pieces, a perfect *tagelmust*.

I step out into the garden and wait for a sign. Fatima always said that was the way to begin a journey. Wait for a sign. Stand in stillness, like the animals. Wait and the sign will come. Fatima had stood beside me in silence the day they took my son. I didn't struggle against her hand on my wrist. Just a light grasp of my wrist, hardly a touch. Just enough to keep me standing still.

"Wait," she had whispered. "You have done the right thing. There is no struggle. There is only surrender. You have surrendered."

My wrist twitched. "Wait," she said again. "Wait for your sign. You will know when to leave."

Then she let go of my wrist and my whole body let go at the word "leave."

My sign appeared a day later when the boy spilled the morning tea. Mint leaves spread across the sand, a perfect pattern of footprints going northwest.

My eyes hurt. My hand hurts. I stand in the garden and wait. A breeze takes the end of my *tagelmust* and blows it up in front of my face. I wipe the water from the edges of my eyes and let go of the fabric. A seagull swoops down and takes the edge of the *tagelmust*. I stand still.

"A bird, Fatima," I whisper. "It's a bird. The sacred symbol. A bird is revealing me, unraveling me." And I hear Fatima begin to sing, I hear the dissonant tones of her song, calling me home.

My son is flying, I think. Gull was the name given to him at the *isnawen*, the naming ceremony seven days after his birth. The *marabout* and Abu held a goat firmly. The marabout sliced the goat's throat and called out "GULL." Abu repeated the name Gull. Thus was our son acknowledged as a member of society as we prepared to feast on the sacrifice.

"Our son will fly," Abu had said, and smiled at me.

I gather the material from the ground and rewind it over my head, covering my eyes.

"Alice," Edith calls. "What are you wearing?" She walks up beside me and stands like a sentry.

"A *tagelmust*," I say.

"What is *tagelmust*?" Edith asks.

"It's what I wore in the desert. It filters the light and sand. Sometimes I miss it; being swathed in cloth is entrancing."

"Certainly you don't want to go back to corsets and linen?" Edith looks me up and down as if she can see through my garments.

"No. But free-flowing clothes, that's what I miss."

Such is the nature of a long life. Conversations roam through decades, through labyrinths, through strange memories. A conversation between two aging women in a garden by the sea in the last quarter of the century has almost all the elements of a pinball game. There is no way to know what bells will ring, what lights will be lit up, how the thoughts will ricochet.

This is what she remembers: my silence. My strange manners. I should be more compassionate. I know it. She cares, she's stayed around all these years. Why did she never ask? Why did I never tell? She remembers an older sister full of life, tramping the fields and tossing her shoes to run in the sea. What do I remember? An eager little girl trailing behind me, watching me, telling on me. And the pressed lips, the light shake of the head, the turned shoulder. No longer eager to follow me or listen to me. Frightened of me. That's what happened. She became frightened of me. "We don't need to talk of that," she'd said. "That was so long ago. I live in the present." She crinkles up her eyes and crosses her arms.

"I'm sorry, Edith," I say impulsively.

"No you're not." The tone is spiteful.

And we're not seventy, we're seven. And our parents are in the next room and if I don't calm her down, she'll start screaming and Mother will come in and send me to my room without tea. "You are the older one, Alice," Mother will say. "You must be responsible." And I'll catch that smug look on Edith's dimpled face. Smug for a few seconds until she sees me leaving the room, and then the loss registers in her eyes as she realizes she'll be alone in the nursery the rest of the day, and the dimples deflate and her face goes slack.

"Yes, I am, Edith, I truly am sorry. I've missed you."

"Missed me?" Her voice is rising, but I keep my eyes on the cheeks beside her lips, looking for the dimples. "Missed me? I've been right here in Kensington Place all these years. Missed me? I'm always here. You just don't see me."

And then I see it again, the faintest indentation in her soft left cheek and I reach out to touch it, but she draws away and slaps my hand down with shocking strength.

"What are you doing?" she cries.

And I pull back, heat rising up the sides of my neck, and look to the gate, sure that any moment now Mother will step through calling my name before her foot even steps through.

This is what Edith doesn't know. The sun in the desert. The look in Abu's eyes. The yards and yards of cloth unwrapped and wrapped each day. The five years we were apart. This is what I cannot know. The move from Morocco back to London. Her transformation from little sister to young woman. The anger subsides in me and I find myself looking at the ground.

"Thank you," I say.

"Thank you? What are you talking about now? Thank you? What is Miss High and Mighty thanking *me* for?"

"For getting me home."

Edith stares at me, and for a split second I wonder if I've slipped and spoken Arabic instead of English. I wait while she takes a deep breath and steps back against the railing above the beach.

"I never thought I'd hear you say those words," she says.

I wait for her anger, but when I look up she is looking out to sea.

"All your talk of the desert and the God of sand and heat and survival. You hardly spoke when I met you at the dock. I was terrified. You were still so weak, and so strange, sometimes speaking English, sometimes French, sometimes Arabic. When we got in the car you began trembling."

"I was not used to cars. The last time I was in a car—"

"Oh, yes, of course—that day—with Father—and you and the abduction."

"Is that what the papers said? Abduction?"

"What papers?"

"The newspapers."

She turns to look at me. "Alice, that was never in the newspapers. Father's death was announced in the Sunday *Times*. 'Motor accident' it said. But I'm sure it didn't mention your disappearance."

"It didn't?"

"No, too sensitive, too disturbing. There were conversations about whether to post signs, rewards for your return."

"Signs? For my return? Or for my capture?"

"Capture? You'd already been captured. Why would they want to capture you?"

"Because of the murder."

"Murder?" she gasps. Her face is ashen. "Murder?" she whispers. "How do you know about the murders?" What is she saying? We stand staring at each other, our hands stopped in mid-air as if we are speaking different languages and even hand signals no longer suffice.

She wipes her hands across her apron and points to the garden bench. "Sit down."

We both sit down and face forward, towards the sea. I welcome the horizon and the momentary silence. Then Edith whispers:

"I will tell you about murder."

I sit up and wrap the cloth tighter around my beating heart.

"Those men were at the compound, the day we left Morocco," Edith says.

"What men?"

"Those blue men."

"The day you left?" I ask.

"Yes, August 11, 1912."

"August. Two months after the accident?"

"We got word that all foreigners should make their way to

Bab Doukkala, the Western Gate. From there we were offered safe passage to Safi.

"We had no choice," Edith says. "They were murdering foreigners. Mother was distraught. She couldn't make a decision. James was carrying a sword around, ready to attack anyone in a robe. I had to restrain him a number of times. Don't look at me that way. Father was dead. You were gone. Mother couldn't cope. I got us to Bab Doukkala and to Safi. I got us home. There was nothing we could do in Marrakesh. The Colonel had told us to assume you were dead."

"How would he know?" I burst out.

"He said no white woman could survive an abduction. No white woman had ever returned from the Sahara."

We stare at each other for a moment. Then I turn my head back to the blue horizon.

"What were the Tuaregs doing?"

"What Tuaregs?"

"The blue men you said were at the compound."

"They arrived on horseback, with swords drawn. They just sat there, inside our gate, lined up on their horses. Fierce men. The horses barely under control. None of them spoke. Not even to each other. Not to the servants. They just watched as Omar and Alif carried our suitcases out."

"Omar and Alif," I murmur. "They were so kind to us."

"Yes," Edith sighs. "I wonder what happened to them." She goes silent.

"And the Tuaregs?" I say.

She shudders. "They watched us. Mother was weeping, James waving a cane about. Omar put his arm around James's shoulders and walked him past the line of men. We took a cart to the medina. Mother didn't want to get in a car after the accident."

Edith draws her breath in sharply, then puts her hand over her mouth.

"I know," I say. "It's unspeakable."

Edith chokes, pulls her hand away. "NO, you don't know what's unspeakable. You were not there. What's unspeakable is what we saw on the way." Edith puts her hand to her mouth again and chokes.

"What did you see?" I whisper.

She opens her fingers wide and speaks through them. "Heads," she whispers.

"Heads?"

"Yes. Heads. On spikes. Along the walls of the medina."

I hold my breath.

"And you know whose heads they were?" Edith says, clipping each word as it leaves her mouth.

I don't answer.

"Do you?" Edith is shaking her head now. Her voice is shaking as well.

"No," I say, as calmly as I can. "Whose heads?"

"They were friends. People we knew." Edith takes a deep breath and looks away from me. "As we approached the gate, James looked up and laughed, 'Look,' he called out, 'they made masks of us.' Mother looked up just as we passed by the head of Dr. Patterson. She raised her arm as if to greet him, then cried out and grabbed her own throat. Omar put his arm around James's shoulders again and pulled his head away from the sight."

Edith lowers her eyes and I can hear her labored breathing. A minute later she raises her eyes and glares at me. "It was the blue men," she says. "I know it was."

I stare at Edith, and then it comes, a faint memory, one I could never reconcile. The kitchen courtyard in Marrakesh was oddly quiet. I stepped out from the passageway and Omar looked up, a warning in his eye. I did not speak but sent a question with my expression. He cast his eyes sideways and I saw the figure in the doorway, a tall blue streak, standing still; a young boy in front took a heavy bag from the cook, then they were gone. No one moved until some signal invisible to me, at which they all released their taut muscles, their held breath, and moved back to the positions they must have been in before the two appeared at the doorway.

I stepped up to Omar. He shook his head. Alif shook his shoulders at me and turned away. Omar lifted his hand and drew his finger silently across his throat.

I stare at Edith. She is rigid, staring out to sea. I bow my head and feel tears wetting my *tagelmust*.

LONDON

June 10,1970

MARTIN STANDS IN THE HOUSE in Mayfair, tired but unable to sleep. He can feel the absence of Alice. Without her he has no desire for dinner, for a gin and tonic. He thinks of calling Devon, of checking in with Edith and talking with Alice, but cannot bring himself to engage with people. He walks to the piano and sits, looking down at his hands. The room is silent, light from the street filtering shadows of leaves across the walls.

I'll never play again was his first thought when they had unwrapped the bandages. Nine fingers, no 'little piggy' finger. No way to reach an octave. Then daylight opened his eyes and he had to press his hands into the coverlet to stop them from playing. The nurse had noticed. She walked him down to a room off the main hall of the makeshift hospital. "I don't think it's too badly out of tune," she said, and left him there in front of the Bosendorfer.

It was, of course, but his fingers sought the keys anyway. He didn't press hard enough to make a sound, just enough for the muscles to remember, and to grieve when the missing finger left a gap in the song.

Now Martin takes a deep breath and places his hands on the keyboard. Nine fingers have learned to do the work of ten. The brain is exquisite. It can compensate, recalibrate, make sense of the insensible. He lets go of the news about Alice. He closes his eyes and lets Schumann direct his world for the next thirty minutes.

DEVON

June 10, 1970

"**S**HE IS HALLUCINATING," Edith says. Her voice comes from far away.

At the fork in the road we went west. Ha! They don't think there are forks in the road. They don't know there are no roads, much less forks in them, when the world is made up of ground-up rocks, decimated by the pressure of millennia of travel by the heat of a volatile entity. The world is hot and spicy, and there is no center. There is no fork, no spoon, no plate. Just fingers and teeth and hunger and thirst.

I climb that mountain of dust every day and slide down it every night. The grit is under my nails, in my eyes, inside every crack and crevasse of my body. You think there is a way through the world. Well, you're wrong, there's no path, no trail, not for women. There's only breath and blood and you only know time because the new moon makes that breath labor and blood comes from that hidden crevasse and then comes the time when the new moon doesn't bring the blood and then you're really lost, when all direction is gone.

That's when a woman lifts her head and has to believe in herself no matter what fork they use at the table—the fish fork the salad fork the dessert fork the forceps the triceps the lock step and the lockjaw.

"She is ranting, it makes no sense. We must get her to bed. Don't let Benjamin see this."

I am in my bed again. That is where they want me. "Rest," Jane had said, sending Edith and me to our rooms, as Mother used to do. "Rest, you both need rest," she said when she found us sitting stricken on the garden bench. Me wrapped in wet cloth, Edith folded over holding her stomach. As if getting us to lie prone will keep the past from invading the present. I have closed and barred the door to my room, but I can no longer close and bar the door to my heart. I brought him into this world, from a tribe that unleashed horrors upon my own family. I have engendered a monster. All these years thinking I was the one who survived the war, I was the one who suffered the misunderstanding family. Thank God the family went silent, never asked for the truth. Who would harbor an enemy among their own?

"Shhh, she is sleeping," Jane calls to Benjamin. "Let her sleep. We all need a rest."

Yes, they all need a rest. I must meet him. I must keep my son away from the family. I lie quietly and see the light from the shutters lay stripes across the bedspread.

Mustapha is pacing. With my eyes closed I see him, dressed in long black-and-white stripes, head bowed, hand behind his back, a tall whip of licorice crossing the floor from left to right, then from right to left. When he gets to the center of the doorway I squint my eyes and see him as the pendulum on a clock, his back-and-forth movements counting out the hours the two of us spend inside this tomb.

Mustapha continues pacing. Up one side of the wall and down the other. Or rather, along one wall and back along the other. But, truly, sometimes I think he does go up one wall and down another.

Mustapha doesn't talk. Mustapha is a eunuch. They removed his sex, but somehow it seems as though they removed his tongue, the other sex organ. My mind goes to such forbidden places in here. Well, not forbidden, not by Abu, not in my life with Abu. Mustapha paces. I count. The diamond tiles on the wall and on the floor. I count until I can't keep up with it and either fall asleep or begin again. Is this meditation? Or is this madness? Mustapha is wearing black-and-white stripes and walking on the black-and-white tiles. Thank God the walls are gold. I should certainly lose my mind if the walls were white. I hate Mustapha's pacing.

Mustapha the eunuch. In the harem. The only man allowed among the women during the day. We washed in front of him, talked in front of him. In some way he wasn't human to us. Mustapha brought our towels, scrubbed our backs, Mustapha was always there. When there was nothing else to do he paced the walls. I look up at the shutters and blink.

"Open your eyes and don't blink," the eye doctor had said.

I was under water. The walls of the exam room were sliding down in sheets. The doctor looked like a Modigliani.

"Don't blink, Mrs. Hightower. It's important to let the drops settle in."

"Am I hallucinating? I haven't seen a room like this since Vincent Grove."

"Were you in Vincent Grove?"

"Oh, a few decades ago."

I could hear the doctor's breathing—short, spastic.

"No need to be embarrassed, Dr. Black, many women spent time at Vincent Grove. It was almost a spa."

"Yes, I've heard it was posh."

"Not as posh as the harem—"

"The harem?"

"Another time I stepped out of life. May I blink now?"

"You've already blinked, Mrs. Hightower. We need to do the exam now."

He gently guided my chin into the cradle of the machine and then moved his monstrous lens into my eye socket.

The spirals began then. At the edge of my vision, twirling up and away to the right, then around and around. Blues and oranges and red flashes.

I sink back into the pillows and blink. A white wall. Blue spirals. A white wall. Orange. Red. Blue. White. I rub my eyes, then keep them closed. Sister Natalie was the first to pass the doorway. Call to prayer had begun. I could see her feet clearly. The rest of her spiraled away to the right.

"Did you ever have an injury to this eye, Mrs. Hightower?"

"An injury?"

"Were you ever hit in the head, did you have a hard fall?"

"I fell from a camel once."

The doctor pulled away from his instrument and rolled his seat around to face me. "You fell from a camel?"

"Did I say camel? I meant a horse. When I was a young woman. Before my thirtieth birthday."

"I see," he said.

"You see what?"

"Hmmmmm . . ."

"What do you see Doctor?"

"Mrs. Hightower, you have macular degeneration. Your eyesight

is fragile. You may remain stable in this condition for quite a while, or it may go at any time."

"Go?"

"Your peripheral vision is still strong, but your ability to focus directly in front of you is compromised."

"I've been compromised before."

Again the spastic breathing.

"I mean, I'm able to look at things from the side. I'm a side-winder if I need to be."

Dr. Black stood up and opened the door.

Light blasted at me and the tent flaps snapped back with the force of his entrance.

"Where is the boy?" Abu was angry, his face a mask, his hands stretched open at his sides.

"He is not here."

"This I can see." He switched his hand back to grab the tent flap.

"The nurse will finish up here, Mrs. Hightower, you can meet me in my office."

The door closed and my eyes followed.

I used to see fear in people's eyes. I saw it when I entered a room and looked directly at them, challenging their apprehensions. Now I see differently. From the side, like a camel. I must move through life like a camel now, sliding my feet silently forth, my eyes to the side. I must relieve the family of this burden, of my history. I close my eyes and wait for dawn.

DEVON

June 11, 1970

LORD WHAT I'D GIVE FOR A NEW FACE. This one is a road map of my life. Cheeks flushed with all the dairy of my childhood: custards, bread puddings. Eyes trained by the desert to still focus on the horizon first, before anything else can come into view. Now I have a face that scares little children. The hair wildly flying about, earlobes stretched almost to the chin. I was a beauty. An unnatural beauty, some would say, but a beauty nevertheless. Men eyed me as I passed by, the same eyes I saw at the county auction when a particularly striking mare was led around the ring and no one wanted to drive the price up by letting on that that was the one they really wanted to take by the reins and lead home to their own paddock.

The past is inscribed and the future defined as thoroughly on my flesh as on my soul. I lift my foot and turn the bottom towards myself. I can see where I have walked on this earth. The smallest toe is curved under the next toe, folded under a bit, not enough to be painful, but enough to tell me I have been forcing it into shoes that are too tight. The toes are pink, despite the desert dirt—or perhaps because of it—the red dirt flushing the sole of my foot. There is an arch, a curve to my foot, and the heel is tight and callused but holds me up well. I am a fortunate woman.

I dress carefully. One must always prepare the mask for the journey. Today I must look normal, British, I must not draw attention to myself. The pearls will work.

And a hat. I must find the right hat. A lady always wears a hat, Mother said. When I left England every head wore a hat, every woman covered her ankles. And now—now the body is erupting everywhere, people walk the streets in the most amazing outfits. Women leave their heads uncovered, their hands exposed, their feet poking out of open shoes. But still, no color anywhere. Dull browns, navy blue, black or gray are the outdoor coverings of choice, making any bit of skin all the more shocking. Except on the young. They have taken on color with a vengeance. And the hair—they are letting it grow everywhere—boys, girls, men, women, they've let their hair loose in the world. Maybe I don't actually look all that different now. I take off the pearls and put on Sister Natalie's Tuareg cross.

The year I first returned, I felt the world had turned inside out, or that I had stepped into the negative of a photo. It was weeks before I stopped staring at people in the streets. Sunday, Hyde Park, the crowds gathered for the soap box speeches and everyone stared at the dark Moor in a long robe. I was staring at the belted and buttoned Britons stepping around the pigeons, politely making their way around and among their fellow men. Saturday, Camden Town. I closed my eyes and listened to the medina noises, the clatter of copper and brass, the slap and smack of leather, the muffled call of the muezzin. And Monday. In Piccadilly Square. I looked up and there, standing quite demurely by the lady in the maroon hat, was a large brown bear, looking for all the world like her pleasant shopping companion. That was the London I once loved, the city so drab it lulled you into believing nothing is extraordinary, the city that didn't blink at a well-dressed woman walking a brown bear in Piccadilly Square on a Monday morning.

The house is quiet. The sky is rosy, promising warmth for the day. While the others sleep, I prepare for my journey, for my wander, for the nomad miles that will unravel my confusion. My straw hat, my blue linen jacket, my comfortable russet skirt (the hem a modest mid-calf length), and my best walking shoes. I take out my pen and paper and make my goodbye, then place it carefully on the breakfast table.

> *Dear Edith,*
> *Thank you*
> *For offering me a place to rest*
> *For telling me your truth*
> *For listening to the past as it returned to me*
> *For being the strongest member of the family*
> *I am sorry*
> *To bring distress into the lives of Jane, Benjamin, and you.*
> *Forgive me*
> *I must face this myself.*
> *Love to all of you,*
> *Alice*

How good this is, to walk in the early morning. The birds have finished alerting us to the day, there is a shift in the air; it's almost as quiet as the desert. The privet is sweet. I touch the leaves to release the fragrance. At the station I take a seat on the bench and feel my whole body sigh.

My name is Alice. Like the girl who fell down the rabbit hole. The one who kept growing too large for the house, then too small to reach the table. I sit here waiting for the train to London, waiting for Edith to come around the corner of the building waving a crook like the Red Queen, yelling, "Off with its head." Or the rabbit to bound along the track calling out, "It's late, it's late." Or the Mad Hatter to sit beside me and yell, "No room! There's no room!" Why should the family care about me and my son? About a life they never knew existed? The train is coming, the rush of air pushing leaves aside; the throbbing of the ground comes up through my shoes. I can feel my life rushing forward, the days and hours and seconds allotted to me in this body beginning to tick away. Two days. My past is coming to meet me in two days. Can I do the right thing this time? I stand and step forward as the hiss of the train slides into the station, then bustle up the step and into the carriage.

I fall back into the seat and into the fact that I was a young woman, alone in the desert among strange men. What more perilous situation exists for a woman? I know people can't believe I was free to choose Abu. Edith's first reaction was to call him a rapist. There is no question he could have overpowered me at any point, any of the men could. But that was not their way. Abu's men were not desperate. Desperation is what drives people to force themselves on others.

Women held power in Tuareg society. This I understood later, much later. After I had returned to a society in which women essentially hold none. A Tuareg woman owns property, lives without a veil, chooses to divorce if she wants. I had no power in my Devon family—marriage was definitely the only "career" on the horizon, and Mother would have moved heaven and earth to see me get to the altar.

But I was not a Tuareg woman. I was a white woman, and when it came to property and family, when it came to my child, I had no power among the women in the camps. Is that why Abu kept me with the caravan? I shiver. Of course it was.

Was it the hardest decision I ever had to make? The decision not to fight the tribe, to let them take my son? It should have been. I should have agonized over it, I should have screamed and scratched and fought and kicked them. Why didn't I? *It is written.* The day he was born, and lifted into the hands of Fatima, caressed and soothed by the women of the tribe, that was the day I knew what was written. On the wind, on the sand, on the back of a camel, it was written that he was born to the desert and he would stay in the desert. And it was written that I was not, and could not stay. Abu had told me that. But I did not want to hear. How does one take in the truth of life? We think we make decisions. Weigh the pros and cons, figure out the best path to take.

Not true. We follow our instincts. We may think we have higher resources, a brain, an intellect, but when it comes to which road to take, which turn to make, it's the inner compass that guides us, directs us. I want to think I did what was best for my son, but I know I did what was best for me. Once Rashid entered the world, my place was redefined. No longer the exotic, the pride of Abu. It's the natural order of things. I've watched it often enough in my many decades. The beautiful bride, chosen for what she appears to be on the day of the wedding. Disappointment awaits every man who somehow thinks what he sees is what he will get. Men are myopic. Or maybe it's that their bodies don't change on them. How could they believe the beautiful woman before them would tire, wither, lose the clear skin, the radiant eyes? How could they imagine the rage that could course through her blood? The grief that could erupt unannounced? The blood that could spill?

I have walked away from life as I knew it twice. Once into the desert and once out of it. The Valley of the Shadow of Death walks. Both times I moved with a companion by my side. Once with a stranger. Then with the boy. Each time I walked towards an unknown future with an unbroken stride, a positive, foot-for-ward motion that seems to occur when you least want it. Each time I did not know where I was going or why, only that I was going. This time I will walk alone. To meet my son.

"I want to know why Auntie Alice left," Benjamin says.

"She had to meet Uncle Martin," Jane says.

Benjamin makes circles on the kitchen floor with his foot. "I don't think so," he says. Edith raises her eyebrows at Jane. Five years old and he thinks he's an adult. She had told her daughter that she must disabuse him of this or her life would be a nightmare.

Jane ignores the directed eyebrow and tries to appease the wiggling child in front of her. "Why don't you think so?" she asks him. Edith wrings her hands and lets a loud sigh escape.

"Because her son is coming."

"What?" Jane looks at Edith, who puts her hand over her eyes. "Aunt Alice doesn't have a son," Jane says.

"Yes she does. In the desert." Benjamin stops jamming his foot against the groove in the floor and looks at his mother as if she is stupid.

"What?" Jane is speaking to Edith, who has lowered her head and is now shaking it. Jane can't tell if she is laughing or crying. "Mother, what is he talking about? What is going on here!"

Edith raises her head and sighs deeply. "I'll call Martin," she says.

The train rocks back, that disquieting nudge before it moves forward, all the carriages aligned, swaying gently as the line of iron beasts gathers enough strength to drag us through the countryside. I lean back into the movement, close my eyes, and feel myself tumble down the blissfully calm expanse of travel.

The man on the seat across from me has been eyeing the cross that Sister Natalie gave me. He is impeccably dressed in a three-piece suit, Italian shoes, silk tie. Not a hair out of place. Sitting on the northbound train to London on a Thursday morning, I am guessing he is an antique dealer. And I wonder what he thinks of my cross. But he is obviously too well-mannered to interrupt an old woman on a train journey.

I pull the cross over my head, run my hands over the fine leather strap, finger the hammered silver. The man looks at the cross, then looks up directly into my eyes. I smile. He nods, embarrassed at his boldness, surprised at my reaction.

"It's Tuareg, isn't it?" he finally asks.

"Yes," I say.

"From the central Sahara," he says.

I stare at him dumbly. Then I notice his hands. Deeply tanned. And his face. Finely lined.

"You've been there," I say. Not a question.

"Yes," he answers. And we speak no more, but bow to each other and sit in comfortable silence.

After a few minutes I hand him the cross and watch as he spreads his fingers across it like a blind man examining a newborn. He closes his eyes and inhales deeply, and I know he is in the desert now, amid the caravan. I watch as the well-groomed form in front of me relaxes, as his arms lengthen from his suit cuffs and his legs spread out, his feet flatten on the floor between us. I can see his face, open to the wind and the horizon. A slight shiver passes over him, the brow creases, and he looks directly at me again with a countenance of fear or astonishment, I can't tell which.

"But you"—he stutters—"a woman of your"—he swallows the word 'age'—"But how did you—"

I cannot pretend I bought this in a jumble sale. He knows the world where this was created, was worn to keep one aware of the four directions of the earth, unaware in which direction death may lie. He knows the world in which this was a metaphysical and spiritual compass for people who were always on the move. He stares at me, the first person this week to recognize my world. I close my eyes. From which direction did Abu's death come?

Everything is swinging. Heaven, earth, water, fire, the curtains are swirling around me, I am soaking wet, it is black, blacker than a desert night without stars. I am cold. When I touch my face it is wet. When I touch my body it is naked. I sit up and stare wide-eyed into the blackness. The wet is sticky. I bring my finger to my mouth and touch my tongue. The liquid is salty. Blood, I am sitting in blood. All is black.

I see light but no fire. The room has been solid black for hours. There must be a chink, a small hole in the stucco. I sit mesmerized, staring at it, wondering if that means there is daylight on the other side. There is no odor, no sound. That rules out a flame. But the light is not white, not clean as I remember daylight to be. It has a yellow cast. I sit for hours watching, but the color of the light does not change, as sunlight would as it passes overhead. For a while I imagine it is paint on the wall but finally realize paint would not show up in this black unless light were reflecting on it. All this time and I do nothing but stare at the light. I make no attempt to investigate beyond what my eyes and ears can tell me. Then the light goes, and I am sitting in blackness again.

"Miss? Miss? Are you unwell? Shall I call the porter?" It's the man across from me. He is standing over me, his hand on my upper left arm. When I am stressed, my skin breaks out in a rough patch at that exact spot.

"No, thank you very much. I am fine. No need to call the porter. Just a touch of fatigue . . . I'm no longer used to travel." The man releases his hand and sits down again.

I smile at him. "Thank you for your concern. It's a shock, I mean such a surprise, to meet someone from the desert."

He nods. I keep talking.

"The desert is getting closer. The heat, the red morning sky, the quiet fierce faces on the train. Life is getting harder, closer to the bone, our cushioning is wearing out. I can feel the desert, the elements in our face."

The man is still holding my cross. He nods his head as I talk.

"It's getting closer all the time. And then the doorbell rings and there it is. My past has returned. Will return. Any day now. Am I strong enough to get there?"

Still the man is nodding, as if these are not strange words, not odd ramblings, as if British women always reveal their lives to strangers on a train. He is back in the desert with me, he knows the urgent need to release, he respects the words of a traveler. He nods to me, and I know my words are safe. We bow our heads to each other. I lean back in the seat and turn my head to the window. The train starts up again and the rocking motion moves up my legs, up my spine, and I remember sitting across from Edith when she brought me home from Dover. She waited until this same station before she told me James had died. I didn't understand. "At the Somme. His first day out."

"On holidays?" I asked, thinking she meant he drowned.

Her eyes watching me were slightly crazed.

"At the front," she said.

"Of the boat?"

"He was infantry."

My mind was scrambling then. He was not an infant. We had tea together in Marrakesh. We chased cows in Dartmoor. What on earth was Edith talking about? My body went cold as the words scooped up her meaning.

"The war," I said.

"Yes," she sighed.

"The disrespectful war," I said.

Edith shook her head.

"Who is the enemy?" I asked.

"You don't know? Germany."

Germany was James's enemy?

Edith turned her face to the window.

One must know one's enemy, Abu had said. One must respect one's enemy. James. Dead. Killed by Germany. James in Dartmoor saying "Look at Taymoor—like a foot stretching out of the earth." Like a leftover battlefield, I think. Edith and I sat in silence through the rest of the journey.

It was right there, inside the door when Edith brought me home and I finally crossed the threshold. My sun umbrella. The pale blue Fortnum and Mason umbrella with the bamboo handle. I stood on the doorsill staring at it as Mother came down the hallway, Kate came out from the kitchen, Mother's eyes went wide, Edith talking and brushing her skirt, Kate hooting and hollering. I could not take my eyes off the pale blue umbrella that stood in the holder, its handle leaning against the ceramic urn, just as it did years before in Marrakesh when I casually dropped it in before crossing the threshold to the waiting car.

"Alice, we're late," Father had called.

Edith had rushed past me in the doorway, and I looked down as my hand released the bamboo and heard the delicate clink as it hit the edge of the urn, then ran out to drive off with Father and Edith.

Miracle was all I could think. Miracle to be reunited, not with Mother and Kate and the house I grew up in. Miracle to be reunited with the last piece of my wardrobe I touched on the day I was taken.

"Alice." I looked up, and Mother looked away. Kate enveloped me in her arms and began calling on the saints. Something inside me dislodged. Tears erupted.

Edith led me upstairs to a lovely room overlooking a garden. "You can wash for tea," she said. Some things are ingrained. Five years in the desert, months with the Sisters of Blessed Mercy, the steamer passage and rail and donkey cart, and yet, with the words "wash for tea" I automatically rolled my sleeves up, filled the bowl with warm water, and dipped my fingers in, wet the washcloth and tapped my forehead, behind my ears and the nape of my neck. I raised my eyes to the glass above the sink and gasped.

Before me stood a thin, pale woman with wild hair and eyes that threatened to shatter the mirror. I stepped back in horror, raised my hand to my lips, and only then, at the sight of my fingers, recognized the person before me as myself. I reached out and touched the glass, patted the reflection of my ears, my nose, my eyebrows. The glass was cool to my touch. My fingers left prints, smudges that softened the face reflected. Is this *me*? Did I look like this with Abu? And then I slapped my own face. What nonsense. Why think of Abu here? Without mirrors I knew myself through the actions and reactions of others. Abu had looked at me as if he were seeing the best thing on earth.

Was this what he was looking at? The Sisters of Blessed Mercy smiled at me, as if it were a pleasure to see me. Even Edith, after her first quiet gasp, looked at me cheerfully. But this, this was frightening. No wonder Mother looked away.

"Alice, tea is ready."

I took the linen towel and draped it over the glass.

"I'll be right there," I called.

I look up. The man is no longer sitting across from me. My cross is lying in the middle of the seat.

I look out the train window. Now comes the rain. Intermittent in Southwest England. Not heavy, not dripping, just a thick mist. My hair was often damp on my return, my feet snug in their Wellies. I don't remember mold, although I do remember an odor of rot, so slight, rot is a nasty word for it. Just the quiet decay of leaf, flower, bark. Life settling down and layering itself into the earth. One footstep in the woods and the squish of the boot released years of growth, earth disturbed in its ageless sleep. The opposite of rain in the desert. The metallic taste of the air that put every muscle of the body on high alert. The dust flying up with the first jackhammer drops of moisture, the faces turned to the sky, the tongues sticking out for a taste of the elixir. Then the quick search for shelter, as the earth, overwhelmed by such a feast, fails to absorb the shock and water runs in crazy rivers, following a map charted by ancient footsteps, long forgotten trails.

The train rocks to a stop as the public address announces Waterloo and I am on my feet and out of the car into the station before my body realizes it. I tap my umbrella along the floor, as much to warn the bodies moving so madly about, as to announce my own arrival in this locomotive greenhouse.

"Pardon me, ma'am, this is not the best place to stand." I look up at the tall young woman beside me. "Are you lost?" she asks.

"Lost in memories, not in space," I say, and ask directions to the cab stand. I set myself a course straight on from her pointed finger and tap my umbrella across to the exit, where I am blinded by light and deafened by noise. I raise my umbrella into the air, just missing a group of young people in saffron robes with pigeon droppings on their foreheads, swaying back and forth on the sidewalk. "This way, ma'am." An arm reaches out and leads me to the open door of England's gift to the world: the black cab. I settle into the seat and say "The Savoy, please" as if this were 1952 and Martin were waiting for me to join him.

I recently saw a collage from a French artist of a figure stepping forward in one of those full-skirted 1950s dresses. The artist told me she made her work with illustrations from old-fashioned magazines pressed onto paper by "found objects." The piece I was holding had been pressed onto paper by a squashed tin can. When I turned the piece over, it was titled "Alice." That could be me, I thought, stepping out from the confines of my smashed life, a comely ankle, whittled waist and voluminous skirts.

In 1952 women wore pearls. Women wore furs. I did not. I wrapped myself in flowing shawls and silver beads. My niece Jane thought I was exotic. Martin did too, at first, but as the decade moved on and the world was put back in order, he needed a wife who didn't draw attention. I began declining invitations and spending more time with my books and only ventured out to visit relatives. Until Martin drove me to Vincent Grove.

LONDON

June 11, 1970

MISS PATCHETT POURS THE TEA and walks out of the room, her ample hips just barely brushing the doorknob. Martin waits for her to put down the tray and return to close the door. He nods as she backs out with the doorknob in her hand.

"What do you have?" Martin asks, a bit too cheerfully. He can see Richard is uncomfortable.

"1917 Algeria is not the problem," Richard says. "1971 Algeria is our problem." Martin takes a sip of his tea, holding the cup with both hands. "Shall we begin at the beginning?" he asks.

Richard pulls a photo out of a file and hands it to Martin.

"The Amenokal," he says. "Also known as Abu."

The eyes strike out at him. Directed at the camera, challenging the viewer to look anywhere but at that direct gaze. The figure tall, erect, the robes adrift, the head covered, except for those eyes. Martin slowly raises his eyes to Richard, and they nod at the same time.

"Yes," Richard says, "the file was pretty full. The Reverend Mother is in there."

"And Alice?" Martin asks.

Richard looks away for a second.

"Was Abu a murderer?" Martin asks.

"No—well yes, of course, I'm sure there were deaths in the desert—he was a Tuareg and they were—and are—warriors some would say—pirates others called them."

"Reverend Mother said there was a death—was Abu the murderer?"

"No," Richard says. He waits a beat, then says, "It was Alice."

Martin puts his tea cup down slightly off center of the saucer.

"Alice?" he whispers.

"There's not a lot of detail. A white woman in a harem killed a man, a visitor. Sliced his neck open during intercourse. She escaped when the enforcers arrived. Left her clothes behind. You'd think a naked white woman in a medina would be noticed, but there is no evidence of who the woman was, how she got out of there. We made the connection through the Sisters of Blessed Mercy. Again, nothing official anywhere. Just the fact that a white woman stayed with the Sisters for a few months and then the fact that the Sisters remained comfortable and safe for years while Algeria struggled. It was not hard to connect the dots."

"Alice," Martin whispers.

Richard looks out the window. "There's no evidence," he said. He shifts in his seat, then says, "It's the son that is the problem."

Martin takes a deep breath as Richard passes another photo across the table. The eyes again. This time not dark—more translucent. The same tall stance, the robes, but something definitely different beneath them.

"He's Rashid, of the Kel Ahaggar."

"Kel Ahaggar?"

"Some mountain where the Tuareg tribe lives."

"And you have reason to believe he is Alice's son?"

Richard hands another piece of paper to Martin. It's a photo

of the contents of a box, the wrappings carefully unfolded and
set to the side.

"What is this?"

"It's the father's pouch. Abu's pouch. The son delivered it to
the Sisters."

Martin flips his briefcase shut and wraps his three fingers
over the handle.

"Is that all, Richard?"

"No, there's more." Martin loosens his fingers and waits.

"The son," Richard looks away. "He's been on our radar for
a while now."

"Why is that?" Martin asks.

Richard looks directly at Martin. "Petrol attacks," he says.

Richard knows Martin is a consultant for the board of
British Oil. He knows the subsidiary is drilling in Algeria. The
Sahara is promising, that's what they are saying. Promising.

"Yes," Martin says, "I know about the attacks, the explosions."

"We have reason to believe it's his tribe," Richard says. "The
Tuaregs. It was their territory at one time, correct?"

Martin puts his briefcase down. "The tribes have always
crossed the Sahara, yes."

"Yes," Richard says.

"And now there are borders."

Richard nods. Neither man speaks.

"Evidence?" Martin asks.

"No, just talk at the moment, from informants."

"And where is the son now?"

"We've lost track of him."

Martin stops himself from saying "good." No doubt the son
is on his way. The telegram said so. Reverend Mother said as
much. What day is it now? Thursday? No time to go down to

Devon. No time to check in on Alice. He hopes she is enjoying the seaside.

"Thank you, Richard," Martin says. He will have to handle the rest of this himself.

MAYFAIR

June 11, 1970

MARTIN SITS AT THE KITCHEN TABLE with a cup of bitter tea in his hand. Not the way Alice makes it. How does she do it? He never thinks of her as domestic, but somehow the house is always in order, the tea ready for him exactly as he prefers it. Martin does not think of himself as a demanding person; he prides himself on being able to adjust, to accommodate. The war taught him that. Which war? Both wars.

He rubs his missing digit and ponders the fact that he does not know the woman he married. He had read of children abducted by Indians on the American frontier, about how those who were rescued rarely readjusted. They always wanted to return to their adopted families. And here is Alice, who has never really re-embraced this island. And now a child, her child is returning from the desert. And Alice, did he himself adopt her? Did he take her from her natural world? Is she no longer a person of one place or another? Martin has seen this at the negotiating table. All the peoples of the world, hungry for the place they first came alive, first drew breath, first stood upright on the soil. It's never enough to settle elsewhere; they always hunger for the place they call home. Alice. Where is her home?

Martin startles when he hears the post drop through the

slot. Without volition he stands up, walks to the door, and cannot help but feel a small satisfaction in finding the letters in the holder, not on the floor. Another heavy envelope. This one with the imprint,

The Private Secretary to Her Majesty the Queen
Buckingham Palace
London SW1A 1AA

The phone rings as Martin slices through the Palace envelope. He pulls out the heavy paper and reads The Queen's State Birthday Honors List. He sees his name and registers the fact that he is the recipient of an OBE, Order of the British Empire for valued service to the country for such and such, ceremony details attached. A laugh escapes from his lips. Valued service to the country, such a sham. He turns to call to Alice, then realizes the phone is still ringing.

"Martin, Alice has left," Edith speaks loudly.

"Where did she go?"

"Home, I presume."

"She's not here—"

"She left a note, a strange note—"

Martin breathes deeply, waiting for Edith to finish her sentence.

"She wasn't making much sense yesterday. We were worried. She was talking of a son, a son she had in the desert, and she told this to Benjamin, if you can imagine—" Edith sputters.

"Can you read me the note?"

Edith clears her throat and recites Alice's words. She pauses, awaiting a response.

"Martin?"

"Right. Thank you." Martin places the receiver gently down.

He stands still, his hand still on the phone. Where would Alice go? What does one do when the past comes careening back at you? When a world you thought was forever closed suddenly opens before you? Where would Alice go? He doesn't believe she's coming to Mayfair. Martin removes his hand from the phone, drops the heavy envelope, picks up his coat, and steps out to the street.

LONDON

I LOOK OUT THE WINDOW OF THE CAB at all the people in the world, all the busy people. I looked for you, Rashid, when the children in the street all began to look like you. When every face was upturned, open, eyes blue, skin dark, hair fair. I remember once, a year or so after we married, the sight of such a child holding a mother's hand made me gasp in the middle of Harrod's Food Hall. The closest thing to a *souk* I could find in Kensington. There in front of the spice counter I stopped and waited for the vision of you. I waited for the memory of your face. And when I couldn't call it forth, I wailed. The man in checkered bib and white apron looked up, then stepped to the side and pushed a button on the wall. I continued to wail, deep, labored gushes that parted the crowds before me. I had barely taken a second breath when a hand took my elbow and a voice spoke into my ear. "Come with me, Miss, it will be all right."

I did not resist. They took me through a side door, sat me down, and handed me a glass of water. One tall fellow, lean and crisp. One squat fellow, sweating at the brow. I knew they were afraid. A woman wailing in the middle of Harrod's on a major shopping day.

"Is there someone we can call, Miss?" The tall one's voice was neutral, calm, ready to write down the phone number.

Is there someone I can call? I asked when I was leaving the Sisters of Blessed Mercy.

I'm afraid not, they replied. You're on your own now.

I heard their words. I remained untamed. Every day since returning, I closed my eyes and saw my son, the upturned face, the blue eyes, the dark skin, the fair hair. When the day came that I could no longer see that face, I stopped and waited, and wailed.

"No one to call," I said. "I'm afraid not. I'm on my own now."

The men heard something in my voice. The tall one put his pen back in his pocket and stood back from my chair. The squat fellow reached out his hand. I took it, lifted myself up and nodded to each of them, then walked out the door. I have rarely set foot in Harrod's since.

Maybe a year after that there was Russell Square. The sign on the post by the British Museum, "Reward for lost cat." It caught me sideways. "Reward for . . ." and I saw myself staring at the sign in the medina, "Reward for English Woman." How curious. I couldn't imagine an English woman lost in the desert. It couldn't have been me. I was not lost. I called the boy over and showed him. Even read him the text. There I stood in Russell Square years later reading "Reward for" and seeing the boy's face, the look in his eyes, and finally I understood why the boy betrayed me. It should not have been a surprise. Once Abu sliced his tongue, there was no life for him beyond the camels and me. No words, no favors, no young woman to impress and delight. I hope he got good reward money. I hope Haddad gave him enough for his losses.

Ah, the Savoy. They have seated me by the window, at the far end of the cavernous room, just where Martin used to hold court. Could they remember me? Possibly.

"Gin and tonic, please," I say.

This is why God made alcohol. To soften the edges of grief and fear. It's been five days since the news of Abu's death and the impending arrival of progeny. Five days of incessant memories, and only a tall glass of gin could loosen the grip of the past enough to face the family at the end of each day. I'm an old woman. Alcohol is an old friend. I know the smell of it, medicinal. I know the feel of it, cool as it goes across the palate, hot as it descends the inner organs. I know the taste of it. And I know the fear of it.

Each night of the past fifty years, when evening arrives and I lift that blessed blend of gin and tonic, I feel my body relax like a cat sliding its long leg out in the sun that warms it through the window. I settle back, put my hand around the glass, and sense myself in three worlds at once—the land of my virginity, when we drank quinine daily to avoid the vicissitudes of a strange culture; the land of my marriage, where in drawing room and garden I savored the tart taste of our evening libations, the way we moved into the world of husband and wife, just a bit of a buzz to loosen our limbs and let our tongues speak the language of our intimate world. And the land of my solitude where I sit today, eyes at the horizon, able to enjoy the scene before me. It's like living inside a prism as I watch the gulls swoop back and forth outside the windows of the Savoy. I hear the voice of my mother, dead decades ago, as she pours the quinine. I see the release of my husband's shoulders as he settles into the chair beside me and takes his first sip of the gin and tonic, unaware I have made mine twice as strong as his.

It is at the cocktail hour that I am most removed from my

life in the desert and yet so close to the feeling of that life. It's a curious thing. I never drank anything stronger than tea in the desert. And that remains the clearest, most vivid part of my life, despite the fact that I have lived ten times as many years away from that world. Gin is my lifeline now. A way of leaving the desert as much as a way of staying here in Lilliputian London. Gin is the drug that kept me in the world I was born to, the world I was brought back to, the world I accepted as my due. I shiver.

I was cold all the time when I first returned from Africa. Layers and layers of clothes covered my body, but still I shivered. Where was the sun? Did it not reach this part of the earth? All day we were inside the body of the house, sitting by the fire, sipping hot tea, trying to warm up our hearts. Mother's had gone cold long ago, I could see that. Edith's sputtered now and again. Mine was not working properly. It sent warm blood through my body when I spent time in the kitchen with Kate, or when I walked through the fields and stopped to watch the cows, but inside, in the drawing room, in the tepid light of the dining room, my heart was too weak to overcome the grief that separated us.

The end of the war should have been a joyous occasion. In our house it was a door that closed on hope. War was something to strive against, to overcome, to keep the family united. When I returned, and the war ended, the reality of who we were set in like a thud. A widowed mother, a son beneath the ground of another continent, two daughters to marry off and no men in sight. Mother sighed from morning to night.

Her suffering was a vile thing that altered the air in any room she entered. The oblivion of home seeped out into the surrounding fields. My daily tramps through the woods and fields began to feel like desperate attempts to keep the feet at the end of my body moving, each step a possible sinkhole, each lift of the leg a superhuman effort. I thought of my camel, of her fully padded foot, and wondered if it could keep her from sinking into mud as well as it kept her from sinking into sand. Edith found Frederick again, and I began to accept any and every invitation that came to the house. A tea dance, a library meeting, a weekend in Bournemouth.

I didn't know I had become an unspoken celebrity. No one ever said a word to me, but when I entered a room a path would open, a hush would fall on those gathered there, and although no one was ever rude enough to stare at me, I felt the pull of every pair of eyes as tight as the lead line on my camel. At Lady Hallowell's tea dance, I could barely get across the floor; the eyes were paralyzing me, leaving me as lost on the parquet as I had been on the desert sand. Once again, I found myself being taken by the hand of a stranger and pulled into alien territory.

"May I have this dance?"

I looked down at a pale hand and watched as four fingers curled over my five. He stood a foot away from me and moved one heavy shoe, then the other. My camel was more graceful. I stepped forward, held his hand tightly, and began swaying. He looked me straight in the eye, another question mark in front of me, but I just laughed and let my hips follow the music, bending and swaying until Edith was standing beside me saying, "Excuse us, Martin, my sister is really overtired. Do forgive us."

Another week, another tea dance.

"I know you."

My heart stopped.

"You're Alice, the one who escaped the desert." It was Martin again, standing in front of me with a gin and tonic, the ice clinking back and forth. He was tall and good-looking, a fact I had not quite noted before.

"Escaped the desert?" I said, and stared harder. "I lived in the desert for five years," I said.

"You *lived* in the desert." He took a long sip of the gin and tonic, and I took a long look at his body. Good structure. Skin rather pale, but that's to be expected. Good amount of hair. Good teeth. Stop this. He's not an animal. Well, yes, all men are animals, but this was not the marketplace. Well, yes, English tea dances were definitely marketplaces. And then I saw the missing digit again and the squint in his left eye, and I didn't have to ask if he was a veteran.

"Would you care to dance?" he asked, and I smiled. He had a relatively whole body, quite an accomplishment in 1919. And he was the first person since my return to mention my name and the desert in the same sentence. We both opened our arms. I placed my left hand demurely on his surprisingly high shoulder, he placed four fingers on my back and we glided out onto the dance floor with our hands still clutching our gin and tonics, ice melting as we dipped and flowed through what was left of British society.

I take a sip of my drink. My joints are lubricated by this elixir. I hum to myself as I look about the room. Then I remember. "Progeny." A word from Martin's world—progeny, an offspring of person, animal, plant, something that develops or results from something else. I feel the strength drain from my arms and I place the glass on the table before it can fall from my hands. Martin will know what this means. He will know what to do. Martin will understand. Or will he?

London is crowded despite the heat. Martin tries not to think of the villa outside Paris where the latest peace talks are being conducted in secret, without him. Peace can't be negotiated, he mutters to himself. His stride lengthens, his pace quickens, as he makes his way through Hyde Park towards a crowd gathered at the Speaker's Corner. He tries not to think of what has been jettisoned this week—his career possibly, not showing up for consultations, not checking in with Miss Patchett, not being direct with Richard. He snorts as he remembers the heavy envelope from Buckingham Palace.

There is a speaker standing on a fold-away stepstool. A woman, with a long scarf tossed around her shoulders. Martin gasps, then pushes his way through the crowd to stand directly in front of her. Give Peace a Chance is hand-painted on a sign leaning against the stepstool. She's singing and swaying back and forth in a see-through nightgown. The crowd begins to chant loudly and Martin turns away, shaking his head. Someone pokes him. "Why are you shaking your 'ead, man? Don't you believe in peace?" Martin stops, raises his four fingers to the young man and speaks directly to the flowered bandana wrapped around his head, trying not to squint at the reflection from the man's wire-rimmed glasses.

"I believe in peace," he says quietly. "I fought for peace," he says, his voice gathering an edge. He waves all four fingers wildly in the man's face. "I work for peace." The man is stepping back, murmuring to himself.

"Please. Leave me in peace," Martin is shouting now.

"Hey man, no problem, go in peace," the fellow says, smiling and ushering him through the crowd, which is parting quickly to let him pass. Martin smells incense and sweat. He gasps for air as he turns away, surprised by his pounding heart. He clasps his umbrella and continues walking, returning to the questions of yesterday.

How old is Alice's son? If he's actually her son. Old enough to become the Amenokal, old enough to have seen the devastation of his tribe, to have seen the Sahara divided by borders. To have seen how the oil companies are digging up those shifting sands. Tuareg. Nomad. What nationality would they be? What nation now claims them as citizens? Martin keeps walking until he reaches Round Pond. He sits by the water, watching a swan glide by in the midst of pedestrian ducks.

He hadn't wanted to go to the tea dance at Lady Hallowell's. He knew Edith would be there, and he had no desire to see her again after telling her his feelings had changed. Before the war she had seemed like the perfect choice—a proper British woman, someone who would do well beside a statesman. To think he once wanted to become a statesman. Edith was kind. She understood, and was quick to find Frederick.

Something made him shake off his lethargy and join the crowd even after Edith had pulled her sister away from the first dance. The next time he went to Lady Hallowell's he looked across the room at Alice and he knew. "There you are," he whispered. When he asked for a dance she looked directly at him, clearly assessing him. No dissembling, no coy smile. It felt like a meeting of the minds if not the bodies. She accepted the dance and that was that. Alice fit perfectly in his arms and into his fractured life. Undemanding, she clearly saw life as more than parties, tea, and so-called society. They settled into such an easy companionship he didn't notice that they had failed to discuss family, children, or the usual marital expectations.

Two world wars had dampened his enthusiasm for offspring. There were moments when he noticed children in the park or saw the excitement in the faces of Edith's children and grandchildren, and he had a fleeting sense that he might have missed something important. But he let it pass. He didn't trust the world anymore. He knew it would eat its young again. He enjoyed his quiet home, his music, his books, and the energy of Alice. Then came the crack-up, as some would call it. The disruption was how he saw it. Alice needed to find an outlet for her energy, and Vincent Grove helped her do that. He was amazed by her art. Impressed. Stunned.

But what does she need now? What can he do now? A child. An adult child with possible terrorist ties. He watches a large crow strut along the path, its beak pressing forward and its splayed claws tapping the gravel with determination. The sheen on its dark feathers sparkles with green and violet. Martin watches in fascination as it walks among the strollers and prams, its eyes dark jewels embedded in its ebony cloak, never veering from its path, unperturbed by the crowds. He watches as it hops off the walkway to join a cackling group of its black-suited friends. A murder of crows. Martin shivers, staring at them. That's what a flock of crows is called. A murder.

Alice needs protection. The Sisters of Blessed Mercy knew how to get their protection. But Alice, she has always lived by her wits, lived in the present without care for others' potentially malicious thoughts. That will not help her now. The son is tilting at windmills. Oil is becoming the next flashpoint. OPEC will no doubt hold the West hostage. Not the time for the tribes to interfere. They may have ruled the desert for centuries, but they can't survive against the ravenous greed for oil.

Protection. Talcott. The man who hunted Nazis after the war, the man who could run a rat to ground. He will call upon Talcott.

THE SAVOY

"**H**OW ARE YOU, MY DEAR?" I look up to see the Savoy waiter, smiling deferentially.

"*How are you, my dear?*" *Martin asked.*

"*Outward,*" *I whispered.* "*I am outward.*"

"*What?*" *Martin leaned down and put his hand under my elbow.*

"*Outward,*" *I said.* "*I am outward. I would do it again.*"

"*Do what?*" *Martin looked into my eyes but I could not see him.*

"*I would do it again,*" *I repeated.* "*Sever the cord, cut the connection. I would suffer the splash of his blood on my body, rip the clothes that covered me and face the world in my own skin. I would do it again.*"

Martin put his arms around me. "*Sweetheart,*" *he said.* "*What is going on? The neighbors tell me you were cooking a leg of lamb over an open fire on the patio. And singing. And dancing.*"

"*Yes,*" *I said loudly.* "*I cook, I sing, I dance.*"

He winced. "*Please lower your voice.*"

I pushed at him then, shoving, kicking his shins, all my energy directed to my hands and feet instead of my voice. "*I can't live this way! I am drowning!*"

He grabbed my wrists and held them away from my body,

239

immediately paralyzing me. I kicked even more fiercely, striking at the air.

"I can't live this way!" I began to wail, my chest heaving with rapid gasps of air I took in and spit out.

"What way?" he asked. His voice was gentle but there was steel in it. "What way? As a woman of privilege?"

There it was again. Martin and Abu were the only people who ever spoke to me in the third person. Bile rose in my throat. I could feel the pressure building in my ears. I pulled my head back, drew in my cheeks and spat a most foul wad of spittle directly across the room. I think he could have recovered from a gunshot more easily.

I look around the Savoy at the other diners and try to establish what year this is.

Martin drove me to Vincent Grove himself. He did not go to the office that day, did not send a driver for me. That day we had breakfast together for the first time in ten years.

"This will be good for you, Alice. A complete rest. That's what you need."

Apparently my behavior had become alarming. That's the word I overheard Martin use on the phone the night before. Then he put something in my drink. Wormwood perhaps. I recognized the musty edge of it and welcomed the sleep.

In the car. The windows closed. The radio off. Martin's hands gripped the wheel.

"Martin?"

"Yes, Alice?"

"This is more than just a rest, isn't it?"

Martin's lips pressed tightly against each other.

"Martin?"

"Yes, Alice?"
"I always knew you would drive me crazy."
We both laughed aloud.

I shiver at the memory and look again at the waiter. "Check please," I say.

Vincent Grove is still a respectable place to house the deviant—women who make no sense, men who've tipped over the edge, youngsters who won't adapt. A genteel looney bin.

When we drove through the gates in 1953 I pressed my hand against the door handle. The building was red brick with crenelated roofs. Straight out of Henry James. The grounds of green rolled off from the sides of the gravel drive for acres. I listened to the crunch of the tires spit out pebbles as we passed by blooming fruit trees and empty benches sitting beneath broad chestnuts. I wanted to roll down the window to take in the scent, but I stopped myself. Martin reached over and took my hand. I wanted to slap it away but found myself clenching it tightly and bowed my head to look at his whitened fingers.

We made the turn and stopped in front of the colonnaded front door, where a woman in a white nursing outfit stepped lightly down the stairs, a large smile on her face.

"Welcome to Vincent Grove," she sang out as she took hold of the door handle.

She looked like a clown. The mouth showing too much teeth, the eyes open much too wide. I held onto the handle from my side of the door and shouted "NO."

I sat in the chair in front of Dr. Omer at Vincent Grove, listening to him breathe. It was a stand-off of silence. I had no desire to speak; he seemed to think it was a game.

"Why do you think you are here?"

I did not answer him. There were no words for why I was sitting in front of this paunchy fellow with the wire-rim glasses. There was no way to explain the betrayal of men. My life had been a straight line, an arrow, headed there to the leather chair, to the dead-air room, to that bitter April day in 1953.

The arm, the driver's arm—flailing at my father, my father's arm, under the car, Abu's arm reaching out to hold me, Haddad's arm. The straightness of arms, the bend of an arm, the arm that held me as I crossed the threshold to that institution. I kept my arms crossed. I kept my eyes unfocused. I kept my silence.

"Alice?"

I did not answer.

"Alice, can you tell me why you are here?"

I did not answer. Why was I there? Ask Samuel Johnson: *Nature has given women so much natural power, the law has rightfully given her little.* Ask Mr. Shakespeare: *Vanity, thy name is woman.* Ask Martin: *Really Alice, you simply cannot say those things to the prime minister.* Ask Abu: *It is our way. He is a child of the desert. You are the mother. The desert is his destiny.*

I remained silent. I did not hate men. I brought a man into this world. I did not hate men. A man released my soul. I do not hate men. I do not hate men. I do not want to hate men.

"Our time is up, Alice."

ST. JAMES PARK

"TALCOTT HERE." THE VOICE GRATES on Martin's nerves, but he doesn't let on.

"Good afternoon, Charles," he says. "Hightower here. Have you got a minute for a weary traveler?"

"Of course, of course, where are you?"

"Close by," Martin says. Don't reveal need, don't say I walked across the city for you. I am in a phone booth around the corner.

"Perfect timing," Talcott laughs. "I'm heading for my club in St. James Park. Meet me there."

"Perfect," Martin says, and means it. Talcott may exemplify all that Martin disdains—social climbing wife, ravenous appetite for luxury goods, all of which he gained by doing the work others wanted to avoid. But Martin can't forget the rascal who lied about his age to join the troops and managed to survive the worst of the trenches.

Minutes later the men are seated in folds of leather in a quiet corner of Talcott's club. Martin breathes in the rarified funk of tobacco, wet wool, and decades of male perspiration gently overlaid with bay rum. He looks at Talcott and takes in the black suit, the dark tie, the beady eyes set deep in his florid face. It doesn't take long to make a connection. Unlike with the Reverend Mother, Martin knows exactly what motivates Talcott. Oil is the best investment these days.

"What news of Algeria?" Martin asks.

Talcott grunts. "The usual muddle. Oil is a messy business. And Africa is a disordered place. You can imagine. The French are not the ones to organize things, we've always known that."

"But the business, it's managing?"

"Yes, we're managing," Talcott says. "Those blue fellows keep coming out of the desert, like flies to a picnic, but we've managed to pick them off."

"The Tuareg? I heard of them, during the war."

"Yes, those tribes in the desert—they ride camels, cover their heads in blue cloths, ridiculous really. It's 1970 for God's sake, and these people still come galloping out of the dust as if the apocalypse were upon us. Bribes worked for years—they understand that—but now, now, we're dealing with a different kind."

"What do you mean?" Martin leans back in his seat, waiting for the opening.

"It's just like here, I suppose." Talcott gestures to the window. "This younger generation has to do things differently, in love with the earth. Back to the land, although what the tribes want with that pile of dust, who can say."

Martin nods, then places his glass on the tiny table beside his chair. He leans forward and holds Talcott's gaze.

"Strange times we live in," Martin says quietly.

Talcott shakes his head, his flushed jowls quivering like an aged beast. "Two wars and now the chance to put our house in order and what do we have, blasted oil fields and children dancing in the streets." He shakes his head again and sighs deeply.

"Did you ever come across a tribesman they called Abu?" Martin asks.

Talcott sputters, "Dead, died recently. Thank the good lord for that. Cost us millions."

Martin waits.

"There's supposed to be a son, a new leader, but he hasn't come forth with his hand out."

The two men sit in silence for a minute. Talcott drinks deeply, then looks directly at Martin. "What do you know?"

"Nothing known. Just questions."

"What do you want to know?"

"Is the son alive? Where is he?"

"We're looking for him. We're pretty sure he's behind the gas line explosions. Not someone you would want to be asking questions about."

The two men lock eyes again. *Cui bono.* Talcott burps. *Who benefits?*

Martin tips his head imperceptibly.

"Right," Talcott says. "I'll get on it. Check in later this afternoon."

Talcott stands and offers his hand. There is a crack in the sky as Martin takes it. Both men turn to the window and watch the sheets of rain. They clasp hands and let go without shaking.

TRAFALGAR SQUARE

S T. MARTIN'S IN THE FIELDS. My favorite church. A concert.
They are singing. I walk up the steps and decide to stop in
for a listen, to join the congregation.

"See that you join with the congregation as frequently as
you can." These were Mother Superior's words of advice to
me as I left to rejoin my family. She was a skilled nurse and
beatific nun. And it was quite generous of her to counsel me
in what she thought was my own faith, rather than to attempt
to save my scarred soul for the Holy Roman Catholic Church.
I did as she counseled and joined with the congregation at
the White Horse Pub and the congregation of shoppers at
Harrod's and the congregation of my family at Whitsuntide.
But the church was not a draw for me at that time. Reverend
Gilmore's God was so peaked compared to what I had wit-
nessed of Allah and his power to make a caravan stop dead in
its tracks, turn around, fall to its knees, and bow to the unseen.

It was Martin who finally got me under those Gothic arches
again. "Well, a church wedding is in order, don't you think?" he
had said. And, really, it seemed so sensible, or maybe it was desperation, but I went off with him to meet with the Reverend and
we chose all sorts of lusty hymns and I sang more loudly on my
wedding day than I have before or since.

"Sing modestly," Martin would wink from beside me. I never could sing modestly. It was my only outlet when I returned. Still is, to tell the truth. I cannot carry a tune, but every Sunday I trot off to stand among the other doddering leftovers of the Church of England and raise my immodest voice to caterwaul level. I know it upsets the other parishioners, the ones who aren't deaf that is. Looks are exchanged, and I can tell discussions have been held, but I have as much right to raise my voice in song as the fools who walk around with radios attached to their ears raising their voices to absent faces.

I grab the iron railing at St. Martin's in the Fields. The walk from the Savoy was longer than I remembered. Or perhaps the gin and tonics were stronger than I remembered. At the door I stand to gather my breath, and a young man dressed in a tight suit pushes past me, then turns and holds the door for me. I smell bay rum.

When I dressed for the parties Martin's career demanded, I sang to myself. An old habit. I sang as a child, long involved ballads of my life. I sang in the desert, calling back my language, my home, trying to remember nursery rhymes, singing to the camels, and that one time to the boy.

I settle myself into a pew, adjust my backside, and smile. My life has always been off-key. I have lived at the whim of my instincts for too long. *Impulsive. Willful.* They served me well in some respects, led me astray in many others. It was impulsive and willful for the family to move to Morocco. It was impulsive for James to enlist in the war. The war itself was impulsive and willful. So there it is: I was a child of my times.

That may have worked when we were young, but it doesn't hold water now. It was Martin, sitting across from me again, the gin in the glass, the logs on the fire. "Impulse is useful when we have time to recover from it, when one can backtrack or move sideways or change course and there's plenty of time to catch up or find the right path. We don't have that kind of luxury at this age."

"The path before us is short?" I said.

"Indeed it is."

"Why do I not feel this? I have lost friends, family, more and more left this world in the last few years. And yet I do not feel old. I don't have a sense of foreshortening. My eyesight is foreshortening, my heart is out of sync, but I don't feel old."

Martin smiled. "You will never age, my dear. You are a changeling."

I almost told him then. Almost opened up my life in the desert to him. Changeling, the one who was taken. As I was taken. As my son was taken. But I was not taken. I left. My son was not taken. I left him. The truth is somewhere in between those two acts.

I sat in the chair across from Martin and raised my hand for another gin and tonic. And did not tell him.

I bang my shin against the kneeler in St. Martin's. Stupid Henry the Eighth. When he created the Church of England he could have dispensed with the kneeling. This is just too uncomfortable. And the music is lugubrious. I think of Mohammed, five times a day turning to the East and bowing deeply, lowering his tired limbs to the ground, his forehead on the sand. His God was demanding. No cushions, no music, no bells, although the cascading tones of the muezzins could fool you more often than not.

So here I sit. I made my bargain with you, God. After I left a child in the desert I did not bring another into this world. And when I tried to reverse that bargain, you kept your side of it. What do you want of me now, God? How cruel can you be to bring him back to me fifty years later? I abandoned a boy, a child, barely able to stand, speaking which language still unclear. And now, you dare to return him to me? Now! He is not a son, he's a stranger. What do I do now?

The concert is over. St. Martin's is emptying. People are looking sideways at me with my notebook as they pass down the aisle. I lift myself up and walk slowly into the vestibule, where my eye catches a poster with the iconic image of the Madonna, the mother and child. I see the woman with the gold earrings. When I asked Abu about her, he did not answer. Amina and Fatima tried to explain things to me, but it was confusing. Maybe there was no way to explain the fact that women held power in Abu's culture. All property was theirs. I saw it in the demeanor of the men when we entered the camps. Like a dog who raises the hairs on its back at the sight of an enemy but twirls and rolls playfully at the sight of a friend, I watched the men's anticipation play across the muscles of their shoulders as we approached. It was sometimes difficult to tell where home was for the men—in the camps or on the caravan.

In the camp I watched as Abu became a stranger to me in the presence of the woman with the gold earrings. Amina never referred to her by name, and he did not speak it. I didn't learn her name until the day they came to take my son. "Layla," they whispered.

She stood at the entrance to the tent and smiled, her gold earrings glinting in the sun. She smiled, not at me, but at my son. A smile of satisfaction.

"You have been a good mother," Layla said. I noted the use of the past tense.

"He is a strong boy," she said. "He is a smart boy."

"He is his father's son," I said, and she winced. Amina was still

young, was pregnant, but I had never seen Layla, the woman with the gold earrings, with a child.

The others had watched from afar the first time I left the tent with Abu and my child. They had stood apart whenever we returned from the caravan. I saw the betrayal, the threat to their way of life. I saw it again in my own family when I returned to a mother whose son had been torn from her life. I lost my child to the tribe, a blessing I eventually came to believe. They could have turned us both out. Banished us to the heat and dust that swallowed the out-of-place travelers. Instead they chose to ignore the bloodline of mother and child, they chose to keep a foreigner among them. While at home my mother lay murmuring, prostrate before the forces that took her own son and buried him in foreign soil.

I turn and walk back to the sanctuary. Take a seat to the side behind a pillar and bow my head. *God forgives you*, Natalie had said. Can I forgive myself? Can I forgive myself for all that I ignored in my search for survival? For falling in love with Abu? Do I need church for this? Maybe. I was young. Eighteen years at that time was much younger than what I see in eighteen-year-olds today. And innocent? Naïve? Sheltered? Yes, all that too.

Alone on the breast of the world, I used every wit I had, every sense I was born with. I ignored my family, did not stop to grieve the loss of the father, did not question the fate of the sister. How can I forgive myself? Begin with others, that's always easier. I fold my hands together and bow my head as I had been taught, and I begin.

I forgive my mother for taking me to a strange land without explaining the strange terrain of my own body. I forgive my father for taking us to live in an alien culture as if we were on a short holiday from our own. I forgive my family. For not asking, then not listening.

Can I forgive myself? Can I forgive myself for trussing up everything I learned in the desert and ignoring the truth? The truth is the tribe did not take my child from me. I never truly believed he was mine. I knew he was of me, but he never would be mine. The truth is the tribe did not need to take him from me, I would have given him to them. How can a mother admit such a thing? Did Mary feel this way when she gave birth? Did she know the child she carried was not hers? Sacrilege to even think such a thing. But there it is. A woman is born to carry and deliver, and sometimes that is all she can do. Can that be true? It felt true to me. He was a child of the desert. I knew it from the instant he was born. He cleaved to Abu. He cried for Abu. He recognized my smell, he suckled at my breast, but from day one he was turned away from me and mine.

And yet I cannot forgive. It is not mine to forgive. It doesn't matter how it was done. I remonstrated, pushed and pulled, screamed and cried. Then I let him go. Even so, we were never completely separated. A mother and child can never be separated. That cord, that umbilicus, it does not rupture at birth—it has to be cut. It never heals. On one end it twirls inward and gathers dust. On the other, it throbs silently the rest of one's life. It doesn't matter that I let him go. A mother and child can never be separated.

But Martin. How can I forgive that? I left my son in the desert, locked up my heart, and then, with a stone where the heart should be, entered into marriage with less than my whole self. I left my better self in the desert. Is that forgivable? Violence took me into the desert and violence delivered me from it, but what is more violent—to act upon your feelings or to act without them?

ST. JAMES PARK

I WALK A FEW BLOCKS TO THE PARK and sit with my note-book. St. James Park. Not named for my brother. Nothing is named for my brother, one of those who never returned. Not even the pin. No name, only a number. A metal safety pin with the number 359 engraved on it. Still attached to the duffle that contained his "kit." Mother burned the kit, but the pin remained. Kate gave it to me a week after I returned. I kept it in my jewelry box, the number 359 the only way I could think of my brother, not having seen him for five years, not having known the young man who lied about his age and signed up to help change the face of Europe in 1915.

"James was so eager to go," Edith said. "He was too young, of course, and even if he had been of age, he could have been exempt, being the only man in the house. But nothing could have stopped him." In Marrakesh he spent day after day arranging his soldiers in the dirt in the courtyard. Whole armies set up for days, ready to do battle.

The years 1914 to 1918 changed the face of Europe but hardly rippled the desert. The French were still manning out-posts, storing *Chateauneuf-du-Pape* under the battlements. The tribes laughed. Only the French would try to build a railroad across the desert. Their own soil was being stained with blood, troops digging across the drowning fields one meter a month, and a continent away they were laying tracks on shifting sands. But I did not know this. I did not know the French were commanding the water holes, widening them, fouling them with too many animals and men, demanding money for the use of them.

I cannot put a face to my brother. I cannot put a face to my father. Too much that was once my whole world. And even now I see the car, always going, always leaving. The car that should never have been in Morocco, should never have been in such a country at such a time. I see the car, an open casket burying my father, tearing my sister from me and launching me into the world of sky and sand.

I smell the damp here in St. James Park. I see the mold. I feel the weight of wet tunnels when I think of my brother James, unknown uncle to my son. A cloud passes and sun hits my notebook. I shiver at the thought of Layla, at the smile that opened her face when she lifted my son from my arms. The smile that appeared to me on church wall after church wall in the warm countries of the Mediterranean, the smile of Madonna and child.

I keep walking. Here is another park. The corner of Hyde Park. The wilderness in the middle of London Town.

In the *souk* the ancient mariner approached me one hobbled foot at a time. "You," he pointed. "You must listen. You must hear." In Hyde Park the berobed man turns and points at me. "You," he says, "You."

Is it written on my face? Is the past always pushing through the present? Why do these madmen point at me? What do they recognize in me? I turn away, as if the back of my body can protect me, can hide what I have experienced. Not from the madmen. Not from those who have altered vision.

It is written. It is written on the body. The past and the present and the future, as clearly as tattoos spread ink beneath the surface, seep into the layers of the body. No one speaks this language of the past within the present but the madmen. It is written, not spoken. It is silence. It is stealth. It is ancient. It is reserved for those who open themselves, like a flower, opening innocently to the light.

I turn away and see children.

I sat with my son for the last time that afternoon. I touched his golden head so often he turned to me, brushed my hand away, then giggled and swept my hair with his small paw. I drank him in with my eyes, the flawless skin, the eyes already reaching for the horizon, the determined legs. Standing steady under his tiny body. That is what I tell myself, that I touched him, I held him, I told him I loved him. That's the story I wrote in my head as the boy and I set out into the infinite black of a desert dawn. The truth would not have let me leave. The truth would have kept me as captive as the boy, desperate for any glimpse of the child I allowed them to take from me. He had a golden head, and sturdy legs and keen eyes. I think that is true. The truth is I didn't know, when I was sitting with him laughing and admiring him, that it would be the last time, and that I had not said I love you nearly as often as I could have.

The speaker steps down from his box. The crowd is dispersing. Where is Martin? Where is Abu? I need to stop this. This pounding in my chest. I want the pills that calm the heart, but I know this time it's not the vicissitudes of age I'm feeling; it's the distant drum of time catching up with me. This isn't narrow arteries and heavy blood flow. This is my own blood and another's blood unleashed on the world. I should not be surprised. I saw what pent-up need can do. I watched the parched earth give way when rain finally arrived. When all that it wanted and needed finally was given, the earth submitted, gave ground, gave over, and what was essential to survival became the means of destruction. Thus one could listen, with no sense of irony, to the news that someone had drowned in the desert.

I must keep walking. The desert walk. One foot in front of the other.

There is a crack in the sky, followed by the thick, muffled boom of thunder. I look up and feel the water, a blessing. A storm in the desert is hard to imagine. Like a circle of Dante's hell. The air swirled, water cascaded from the sky, light and sound ricocheted around us. There was no shelter. No barn to run to for cover, no trees to hang their branches and leaves over us like an umbrella. The animals had long before sat themselves down, turned their hides from the direction of the storm. The men followed suit and tied down the loads, fastened things together, and sat on the lee side of the cargo.

I sat against my camel and turned my face upward. There was no use cowering before the face of the storm. The cool wet brought back home, brought back years of Aprils in the garden and woods, brought back mud and tea and Cook at the door, and the taste of wet air fetid with the force of green nature. I reached out my arms and laughed at the lashing rain and the pounding thunder and the deafening cracks of lightning, and my camel turned his head and that deep dark pool of a brown eye stared at me in bewilderment. The men began to look at one another and mutter to themselves. But no one approached me. No one stopped me as I stood up and swayed in my clinging wet robes, my wet hair splashing my back and my tears streaming down my face, the salt washed away by the rain, and my toes kneading the wet sand as I used to do at low tide so long ago and so far away. No one came near me, no one touched me, until I awoke in a heap, my body enveloped by wet fabric covered in a crust of sand.

MAYFAIR

H ERE I AM. One foot in front of the other and I am standing, soaking wet, at home on Green Street. There is a package at the door. I take it inside, and I can smell it before I open it. I reach out my hand and stroke the brown paper covering.

"*Salam'alek,*" I say, bowing my head as I carry it to the kitchen table. The paper wrinkles when I unfold the flap of the box and I pull my breath in.

The smell is overpowering. Sweat, salt, the end of a long journey.

"It's the humidity," I tell myself, putting my hand out. "It doesn't smell in the desert." I take a deep breath. Abu.

I lift the pouch to my breast. This is the closest I will ever be to the life I once lived. This is what is left of Abu. A foul piece of leather that hung from his neck since the time the tribe declared him a man. A work of art fashioned by the most talented woman in the camp. Colors that faded under the desert sun, a hide that softened and curled in the folds of his frame. It had become, as it became for every Tuareg man, an appendage of his body.

I pull the pouch from my breast and lay it on the table, surprised at the size of it, the length and width of a man's forearm; it looks like the carcass of a small beast. The image of heads along a wall flashes before me and I feel my hands shaking. *LA*. That was not the life Abu and I lived. *LA*.

I close my eyes and breathe in the scent of Abu, then reach out for the pouch again.

A short fringe hangs from the bottom of the pouch in a mound, chewed and softened with age. I laugh at what I am stroking. *Man carries his life outside his body*, Abu had said. And here it is, in turquoise and gold and magenta and layer upon layer of finely tooled leather.

I lay the pouch out on the table, holding the neck string taut, and draw the top up from the bottom. It pulls away like an envelope slit on its short end, the release as smooth as the release of one open palm from another in the Tuareg salutation.

The inside pocket is smooth leather, the color still vibrant, with two worn stripes where the leather had been pulled along the neck string, back and forth, inside and out, for decades, for a lifetime. I flip the fold open, and there on the underside of the hide is Abu's mark.

I shiver and close my eyes. I squeeze the pouch, then reach into the inner pocket with two fingers and pull out a piece of paper, ragged and faded. Two gold earrings clatter to the table.

When I lay the paper open I do not recognize the letters.

And then I see it, the child-like letters as Abu worked his fingers with the ink to put my name on paper

"A—*like a tent*," *I had said.*
"L—*an open arrow*," *Abu said.*
I—upright, a staff
C—the crescent moon
E—the crown has fallen sideways
A L I C E   G E O R G E

The letters filled the page, the *O* in George cut in half by the fold of the paper.

I am a long way from that home. From the center of my world, where the sand flows away from my feet and the sky is wide above me. I can close my eyes and taste it now, the grit between my teeth, the sweet lingering skin of a date. I can close my eyes and all the years and all the miles and the lost friends and family, the blood I shed, the animals I rode, the men I knew, it's all a kaleidoscope that leaves me dizzy and gasping for breath, in shock at the wonder of my own life.

I never forgot you, my son. Your face grew distant but you, the essence of you, never left me. The mind can do amazing tricks to keep us sane. You were too precious to reveal to this miserly British family. Too painful to reveal to the man who stitched his life to mine. I kept you in the folds of my memory, tucked inside the shawl I wore over my past. Your father remained clear and recognizable, someone I wanted to curse each night, until I realized cursing the father would curse the son. I stopped immediately and began to pray each night, for the health and well-being of Abu, to ensure the health and well-being of you, my son.

No, I did not forget you. I forgot myself. Forgot my body once carried yours. I forgot my breasts once filled with milk, my elbow once cradled your head. I forgot I was a mother.

I change into dry clothes, then put the string around my neck and feel the pouch dangling between my legs, banging against my knees. I pull the string up and tie a loop so that the pouch settles against my hip. In the front closet I find a loose jacket and wrap myself in the folds, covering the pouch. Hunger seizes me, and I leave the house.

MAYFAIR

Martin waits in the doorway of Talcott's club until the rain ends. For the first time in his life he feels lost. He is only blocks from home, but he hesitates. Talcott will speculate about his interest in the tribe. He's not sure he can count on the discretion he takes for granted with Richard. Sun breaks through the clouds, hits the railing, and for a moment Martin is blinded. He shakes out his hand, steps onto the walkway, then turns towards Green Street.

The minute he opens the door he knows Alice has been there. Something in the air. He enters the kitchen and sees the brown packaging on the table. There is a dank smell to the paper. He lifts it and grimaces. He knows she's not there, but still he calls for her. No response. Martin sinks into the chair at the table and puts his head in his hands. Where is Alice? What is she doing? Martin reaches out and spreads the brown paper out on the table. A pair of gold earrings appears. They aren't familiar to him; Alice doesn't like to wear gold. He remembers the photo Richard showed him. This must be the packaging for the pouch. Alice must have the pouch now. What did Richard say? That the pouch is proof of Abu's death? What did the Reverend Mother say? That the pouch would be delivered. Then what? Martin sinks into the chair and feels his eyes burn suddenly with tears. He is exhausted and fearful, two states he has successfully avoided most of his life since the trenches.

"Captain, Talcott has been hit!" Martin dashed down the trench just as a blast pushed the air out of his lungs and threw him on top of Talcott. Dirt blanketed them, turning the sky from noon to midnight. Then the screaming began.

Martin puts his hands over his ears. He is dirty, filthy. He gets up and heads to the bath, where he stands under the shower until the battlefield is washed off his body and he can think. Alice is in the city. She has been to the house and will no doubt return at some point. Why did she not contact him? He turns off the water. Of course. She thinks he's still in Paris.

Martin savors the feel of his freshly pressed shirt, pulls a tie around his neck and passes the ends into a perfect knot, then selects a lightweight herringbone jacket to coordinate. He walks to the phone and dials Edith.

"Alice was here," he says when she answers.

"Should we come up to town?"

"No, stay where you are for now."

"Are you sure—"

"Yes, I'm sure."

"Of course," Edith says. He is grateful she doesn't press for more, that she seems content to follow his directions.

SOHO

"*Inshallah*, Miss Aleece."I am at Tariq's restaurant, the place I used to turn to when my direction was unclear. Since we sold the studio around the corner, my visits have been few and far between. Tariq bows deeply and I know if I were a man he would hold my hand, then let it go and touch his heart.

"Please sit, so good to see you again. It has been a long time. I am making tea," he says. He always saves me a place in the back near the kitchen, where we can talk while he peels carrots and slices onions and folds bread.

I smell meat. I see something on a spit in the kitchen behind Tariq. Cooking in the desert was done over a campfire, by slaves. There have always been slaves in the desert, and I'm quite sure there still are. It's the natural order of things. Outrageous, we think, in our comfortable society. But a fact of life in a land where there are beasts of burden and selling your child to a caravan is a way to save the rest of the family, and if the child is clever enough, a way to start over once the caravan has transported him like a seed across the sands, to take root and flourish by the sea.

Tariq brings the tagine to my table, lifts the lid, and smiles when I swoon. He leaves me to dine alone, then returns with the tea. *Aleece* he says. I come for Tariq's voice as much as for his meals. *Aleece*. It wafts over my tired old bones; my shoulders relax, and I smile into the eyes of a man who knows peeling carrots and onions and tomatoes is as important as conducting Parliament.

"*Shukran*," I say as he stands above the table and lets the stream of tea gather air as it flows down to the glass.

"No 'thank you' for my duty," he says and we both smile.

Please and Thank You were ground into me at an early age, then chiseled out of me in the desert. Desert people do not say please and thank you. Why thank people for what is their duty? Imagine—it is a duty to be kind to one another.

Tariq sits down and bows his head to me. "Miss Aleece, you are on a journey?"

"Yes," I say, marveling once again at the man's ability to read people.

"Your feet are not solid on the earth," he says. "Your world is in change."

"Yes . . ."

"Where is your journey?"

"Home."

"Home?" He shakes his head. Home is blocks away. He nods toward Mayfair and shakes his head again.

"No, not that home," I say.

"What home?"

I nod towards my studio.

"Ah," he says and puts his hand on his heart.

"Yes," I say. "That home."

"Good," he says, and raises the glass of tea to his lips. "This Abu you would talk of, he brings us home."

I rise from the table, and this time Tariq stands.

"*Bismallah*, Miss Aleece," he says, and touches my hand, then his heart, then my hand again.

I lift my hand to my lips and we both close our eyes and bend in a slight bow.

"*Bismallah*," I whisper, and Tariq holds the door for me.

Martin pushes open the restaurant door, turns, shakes out his umbrella, and places it in the holder just inside the threshold. Tariq bows slightly as he calls out, "Good evening, Sir." The restaurant is empty of customers but filled with the aroma of onions, cumin and roasting meat, the aroma that drew Martin in from the street. He raises his index finger to signal he is alone, and Tariq leads him to a table by the window. The room is warm and the seat comfortable. On the white-washed wall a photo of camels trekking across a desert stares down. The window frames are painted a brilliant blue, and the tables are covered in bright cloths. Martin takes all this in as he pulls out the chair and seats himself. Before him is a hand-painted piece of pottery: three tiny *tagines* attached to a handle. He lifts one lid. Salt. The next. Pepper. The third. Cumin. Have I been here before? he thinks.

Tariq places a plate of olives on the table alongside a hand-written menu. "Would you like tea?" he asks.

Martin startles. Olives and tea. I have been here. With Alice? This would be her kind of place. This is Soho, is it not? Only a few blocks from Talcott's club. Was I here with Talcott? Slipping, he tells himself. You're slipping. Stay aware, stay focused. "Tea, yes, tea," he says and notes the accent, the Northern African face, and the warmth of the atmosphere. "And the special," he says, pointing to the line at the top of the menu.

Martin sits in silence, his hands smoothing the soft cushion of the cotton covering the table. Alice a murderer. A mother. Does one negate the other? He picks up the spoon and twirls the bowl in front of his face. All his years as "advisor to the government," working alongside intelligence—never within, always discreetly alongside—and he did not know a murderer slept in his bed?

Alice came to him full blown in beauty, intelligence, and appetite for life. After the war, his months in hospital, he questioned nothing, grabbed what she offered like the rope thrown to a drowning man. Then came the call from the Home Office and the chance to work with Richard again, and life with Alice became a fanciful background to the black-and-white craziness of the world.

The tea arrives, carried on a silver tray by a young woman in a *jellaba*. Martin smiles at her and nods his head, then realizes he is still twirling the spoon, which he jerks back, hitting the glass on the tray. The young woman deftly catches the glass with her other hand and places it in front of Martin, then steps back and turns in one fluid motion. Not a drop has spilled. Martin turns and sees Tariq watching him intently. Empty restaurant, solicitous Northern African, what should I deduce? Martin is tired. Tired of the constant vigilance, the belief that there is always a negative to the black-and-white picture in front of one. Maybe this is just a quiet little restaurant off the beaten track.

Tariq places a large *tagine* in front of him and lifts the funneled cover. Martin breathes in the fragrance and sighs. Alice, he smiles, essence of Alice. He picks up the bread and tears at it as if he has not had a meal in days.

Tariq stands back and smiles. "A good appetite," he says, and leaves Martin in peace.

People are afraid of the wrong things. Edith thinks Alice is nutty again. She wants to keep the family safe. Keeping people safe is a fiction. Alice knows that. I know that. Trying to remain safe has cost the lives of countless innocent bystanders. Accept people for who they are. That's the only safe thing. An odd thought for someone who makes his living in the intelligence community, but it's how I've always operated. Or so I always thought. Who did I think Alice was?

Martin taps his finger on the tablecloth and thinks of Reverend Mother. She knows more than she is saying. She's not what she appears. He turns to ask for the check and Tariq is already beside the table. A bow, a small plate with a discretely folded piece of paper. Martin lifts it from the plate and drops a generous tip with a clattering of coins. Tariq bows from the back of the restaurant as if he can calculate the amount from the sound.

DUCK LANE

B ECAUSE WE ARE SET ASIDE from the continent, we are able to maintain our aloofness. We can sit quietly on this island, to the left of a continent with a jumble of languages floating across it. We can drive on our own side of the road. We can speak our own King's English. We have fought off the invaders, twice in my own lifetime, and now we watch as the children prance and dance in our streets. And here it is. Duck Lane. My studio in Soho. Why did we sell it? I stand back from the doorway and try to read the graffiti on the wall. "US out of Nam." Who is Nam? I push open the door and step into the hallway. The smell of paint, the overcast aroma of sweat and toil. And now it hits me. Of course. My eyesight. The canvases are gone. Sold to the new tenant. The paintings are gone. Given away. Unsigned. Except the Amenokal. Is that still in the hallway?

"Hey Lady," a hairy young fellow grunts.

"Hey," a golden-haired girl at his side whispers.

I step out of their way and lean against the wall. My heart is racing again. It is hot. Hotter than Tamanrasset. Water. I need water.

The hairy boy and the golden-haired girl turn to me. "Are you all right?" she asks.

"I used to work here," I say, pointing out my painting in the hall, and they nod approvingly.

"We heard about you, about your work. You never sold anything—I mean you didn't put your work up for sale," the fellow says.

"It was not for the world," I say.

"Cool," the girl says. Her irises are so large her eyes look like black marbles. She stands one foot away from the canvas and sways her hips.

"Please," I say, "is there water?"

The fellow hustles about and finds a paper cup, then fills it at the water fountain and brings me a chair.

"Thank you," I say. "You are most kind."

"Will you be all right now?" he says.

"Yes, yes, I will be fine."

"There's our place." He is pointing up the stairs. "You can crash there if you need to rest. The door's never locked." He reaches out his arm to the swaying girl and sashays her out the door.

Yanks. They are always so open—stay here, use this, and these young ones today, so trusting. It's the desert hospitality that has arisen today—always care for the traveler among you.

I climb the stairs, then stand in the doorway and stare at the mattress in the corner.

THE OFFICE

MARTIN RETURNS TO HIS OFFICE. Miss Patchett has left all in order. He stands for a moment enjoying the quiet, then picks up the phone and dials. "Talcott," he says, "any news? The Sisters of Blessed Mercy? When was he there? Yesterday?"

Martin drums his four fingers on the side of his pocket listening to Talcott rant, then flattens his hand out on his stomach.

"Yes," he says. "You'd think a man in robes would be hard to lose. Those Tuareg, though, they're hard to track."

Talcott continues to rant. *Really*, Martin thinks, talking like this on an unsecured line? "Talcott, thank you." He tries to end the conversation but Talcott is still talking—Paris . . . the bloody French, can't be trusted . . . Then he hears the words "but we have him now."

"You have who?" Martin's voice rises despite himself.

"We have the son. We don't quite know what he's up to, he's travelling with someone, but he'll be headed back to the Sahara and we have him in the crosshairs. We can set a trap."

"Are you sure he's going back to Africa?"

"Can't give details, you know that, but we caught up with him, we'll have him soon. You can be sure of that."

Martin shakes his hand out in front of himself as if flicking away a dust mote. Talcott never did follow protocol, but that's what makes him useful at the moment.

"Talcott, a favor if you will." He hears a breath pulled on the other end of the line. He's never asked for anything like this before. He can imagine Talcott's tongue hanging out like a particularly eager dog.

"Track him, but don't pick him up. I don't think he's headed back to the desert. Let him take the lead. And keep this to yourself please."

"As always," Talcott says.

"Thank you," Martin says with real fervor. "I'll be in touch."

THE STUDIO

WHO WORKS HERE? That silly young man and his girl-friend? And why not? Who is to say who is an artist and who is not. The canvases are well put together, the brushes are clean, and the paint is here.

I pick up a brush and walk it along the white wall, holding it over my head, creating a line straight across the room. Circles appear above the line, then features: eyes, ears, nose, mouth, then hats, hair, wigs: a row of heads along the line.

I stand back and look at what I've painted.

Why did Edith never say anything before? How did she and Mother get themselves home from Marrakesh? And James? Is that what set him afire to join the army? Revenge?

I need a larger brush. There is one in the bucket on the right. Perfect. I swathe the wall in blue, covering over the line of heads. I shake my upper body. We're good at covering over the past, aren't we? I watched Mother diminish, watched Edith grab her man and vault into motherhood and family. Would things have been different if we had told each other the truth? Perhaps. Or perhaps I would have entered Vincent Grove much earlier. I needed space and light. There are no secrets in the desert. There is nowhere to hide from the light in the desert. Yellow, I need yellow.

And now I have a green wall. Of course, blue and yellow become green. The sky and sand have become the color of

Islam. Ha! I need a smaller brush. And yes, there it is, waiting for me in the bucket. These artists are so generous. Let the line flow. Music starts up next door. No doubt the lovely aroma of *kif* will follow. Just let the line flow, follow the line.

"You are woman," the boy said. "Your body is in tune with the world."

I thought he was silly. I was totally out of tune with the world, definitely out of tune with the world of the desert. The men knew how to read the changing sand, how to smell the wind.

"You know the animals," the boy said. "They trust you. They come to you."

"They spit at me," I said.

The boy laughed. "Of course they spit. They are camels. Camels spit. You know the world," the boy said again.

Funny how that comes back to me now. And I have to wonder who was leading whom out of the desert. I turned to the boy to help me escape. Was he turning to me? A slave, and a white woman. The lowest level of life on the Sahara. Or so I thought. Abu must have known every step I took, and he let me take them. Even when the boy betrayed me?

Whatever happens, you will always be safe. Abu's words. Of course, I didn't believe them. Or I didn't really hear them. Hard to believe one could be safe crossing the desert alone with a slave-boy. Safe in a harem. Safe after murdering a man. Abu was aware of my decision. He must have known I would leave. He did not try to stop me. Would he have stopped me if I took our son? *Whatever happens, you will always be safe.* And maybe on some level I knew that, as terrified as I was crawling across the desert. As horrified as I was at the boy's betrayal. Still, I took action. I moved forward. By all rights I should have been dead. A woman killing a man. No need to even call the authorities. Just get rid of her body.

The music grows louder next door and startles me out of a deep vision of color, of the lines that used to flow across my studio, from floor to wall, to window to canvas. I rouse myself from inside red, glorious red. I awake from silence to an unnatural beat that threatens to break through the wall. I put my hand on the wall and allow the vibration to travel down my arm to my armpit. Haddad. I put my hands over my eyes.

"It's a long and winding road." The words come up out of the music.

Life is a mirage. Abu said. *Illusion. Life is not solid. We are not solid on this land. We must be in motion. The tribe must move to survive.*

In the night, in my dreams, in my wild breathing at midnight, my body always told me Abu and my son walked the earth. When the telegram arrived, it was not news. My body had already told me Abu was gone. My dreams were dry, icy, my body needed more blankets, heavier layers. Two nights I lay awake as my body told me. When the telegram arrived, my body went cold before I opened it. My shoulder twitched, the spot where Abu first touched me. The mark later left by Haddad. A tremble that shivered into a shard. Abu was gone.

I shift the pouch to hang in front of me as I continue to paint. It swings back and forth as I move along the wall, setting up a rhythm. When I can't reach above the line I first drew across the wall, I look around for something to stand on. Finding nothing, I pick up a ball of twine and unravel it, tie a large knot on one end, and dip it into the red paint, then stare at the wall. Then it comes to me. I pull my arm back and whip the wall with the string, slashing the figures with tight, wiry lines of red.

I work on into the night, using every brush in the jars on the counter, carefully setting each back in the container from which it came. When my arm begins to throb I lower it beside my body and shake it out, then allow the shaking to take over my whole body. The pouch slaps against my midriff and I pat it with my hands, like a drum, like a *tende*.

I pull the pouch over my head and see the paint from my fingers has created a new pattern on it. I laugh and sit down on the floor, letting my skirts fold away from me. My fingers fumble as I open the pouch again and look at the marks on the inside flap of leather. Is that a blood stain? Or is that from my fingers? I lift the pouch to my nose and wait for the image of a body in the sand to recede, wait for the fear to subside. Is that how he died? A violent death? A desert death? I hold the pouch to my heart and rock back and forth, murmuring, keening quietly.

When the music on the other side of the wall stops, I stand and stretch. I pick up a tube of paint and walk to the window, then use my finger to cover the glass with wide strokes of cerulean. I bend down to Abu's pouch and pull off a leather strand, dip it in the pot of yellow standing on the sill, then carefully work yellow streaks through the blue.

THE OFFICE

June 12, 1970

THE LORRY OUTSIDE HIS OFFICE inserts itself into Martin's dream. He startles at the sound of the high gear and awakens from the battleground to find himself fallen across his desk. He rubs his eyes and stretches his arms, then rises from the desk and looks at the clock: 3 a.m. He fumbles in his pockets, pulling out the receipt from last night's dinner. He unfolds the paper and reads:

the Studio

Of course—that's where she would go—back to her art; but the studio, they had sold that a while ago. He must have made a note to himself last night. Martin folds the paper and places it on his desk, then walks across the room and locks the door. Five minutes later he emerges from the office in a pressed shirt and clean jacket.

Martin walks the streets of Soho, an oddity among the partiers and demi-monde staggering along. His nose twitches at the smell of vomit, urine, and strong liquor. He keeps his eyes straight ahead and crosses the street to avoid passing the most scandalous storefronts and seediest doorways. London needs its fog again, he thinks, to blur these vagaries of society. When he reaches Duck Lane he stands in the hall, taking in the smell of turpentine, paint, and the ubiquitous aroma of weed that seems to float through London these days. He stretches out his fingers and steps forward, as nervous as he was on his wedding day.

Why do they make the man wait at the altar? Martin's heart is pounding. He was the one who wanted the church wedding. Alice would have walked off with him, she said as much. But here he stands in front of friends and family, waiting for Alice to be presented to him. A barbaric tradition. She is not dinner on a platter, but she will be conveyed down the aisle trussed up in white. There is a hush throughout the congregation as the organist starts playing the processional. Martin turns and locks eyes with Alice. There you are, he says aloud and smiles. Here I am, she says. Life began then.

Martin walks quietly down the hall to the open door of the studio. Alice is painting. He stands still and watches. On the walls are vague figures. He squints and feels his logical mind push at the scene. Are those camels? A line of camels? Is that a man in robes? Or a sun above the horizon? He watches her body moving forward, back, side to side, bending, swaying as she works. It's not a dance exactly, but a communion with color. Martin watches the images mutate as Alice dips the brush here, there, and overlays color on color. He has always found her work mesmerizing. Martin is caught up in watching the kaleidoscope before him, waiting for the colors to coalesce, to settle, for the figure he first glimpsed to re-emerge, waiting for something, anything, to make sense.

He can't stop looking at the blot of blue in the center of the wall. Then he realizes it's not a wall, it's a window. As he watches,

Alice swings back with a large brush and washes over the blue with yellow, then picks up a smaller brush and dabs at the edges. The colors merge into green and she moves away, swinging the brush wildly along the wall. Water, he thinks. It's water, moving like a tide coming in, pressing against the edge of the wall. He can almost feel the surge. He startles when she returns to the center of the wall and stands silently. When she lifts the brush to the wall, he realizes he has been holding his breath.

I take the brush and continue the line along the wall, to the corner, and then along the railing to—MARTIN. I drop the brush and he steps into the room. He is smiling. A larger smile than I have ever seen on his face. My fingers reach out and touch his sleeve, pressing into the initials embroidered on the cuff.

"I found you," he says, pulling me into an embrace.

"I'm sorry," escapes from my lips. "I'm so sorry, please forgive me."

He shushes me and leads me to the ragged sofa.

"Shhhh." Martin places his hand gently on my cheek as he sits down beside me. I begin sobbing.

"There is no need to explain. I know. It is all right."

I lean into him and wipe my face with the perfectly pressed handkerchief he hands me. He is staring at the walls and window. Suddenly I realize I have defaced someone else's property. "Oh my God," I say. "What have I done?"

"You have done well," he says. "It's beautiful work."

Alice sits back and stares at Martin. He is looking carefully at the walls, at the colors she has used, the layers that reflect light, that meld into each other and suggest rather than delineate. Who is this man? What have I done, she thinks? All these years he has stood by me, has seen me, has accepted me.

"Forgive me," she says. He looks at her with puzzlement.

"There is no need to explain," Martin says. "We all have a time, a place that defines us, that haunts us. That comes back to claim us."

Alice shifts her body and the pouch falls to the floor beside the sofa. Martin looks down but does not touch it. Alice feels herself blush.

"When did that arrive?" Martin asks.

"Today. It was at the house. Do you know what it is?"

"I do," he says quietly.

This is a man who works in the intersection of clashing cultures. Why did she think he would not understand? He understands the shoe pounding on the table. The swords carried into the peace talks. The words spoken to cover thoughts.

"I know who Abu is. And what this pouch means," he says quietly. Martin looks at her as if there were a wall of glass between them that could shatter with the weight of sound. Alice reaches out her hand and laces her fingers through his. He closes his eyes and squeezes her fingers gently.

"Alice," he says, gazing down. "I did some research this week." His voice is kind, gentle. Not threatening, not commanding, not the voice that brings clients to their knees, or puts a member of Parliament back in his seat. His voice is calm. And quiet. And new.

"What do you know, Martin? Look at me."

His eyes flip open like the owl outside her window in Devon. Penetrating, direct, enlarged with the question.

"I know Abu rescued you twice."

"Twice? He took me from the driver. He rescued me from the driver—once."

Martin lowers his eyes and takes a breath.

"Haddad," he whispers.

Alice gasps and pulls her hand free.

"Haddad," Martin says aloud.

"Abu knew?"

"Yes," Martin says. "It was Abu who delivered you to the Sisters of Blessed Mercy."

Everything lets go. The invisible geography of their lives opens up, and Alice feels the space between Martin and her disappearing. All the moments of the past begin to line up behind that sentence. Abu knew? He knew about the murder? And Martin—Alice looks up at the man who has stood by her for the last fifty years.

"I'm sorry," she says. "I'm so sorry, I"—her throat closes, the tears stream. "You don't know—I'm so sorry—you don't deserve this—Martin—"

"It was not murder," Martin says firmly. Alice's shoulders begin to shake.

"It was clearly self-defense," he says.

She looks up, startled, then claps her hands together, startling the both of them. "Of course it was," she says loudly. "There is no other law in the desert. One defends oneself against all elements. There is no law, no recourse, no torts and decrees and magic Magna Carta. There is only survival in the desert—" She was standing now, ignoring the pain shooting up her leg. "It was not a defensible action," she says. "It was murder. I killed a man. With his own dagger. I took the life from him, wore his blood on my body." Alice lifts her head. "And I would do it again." She slashes her arm in front of Martin's face. "I'd do it again," she says loudly, reaching for the pouch.

"Yes," Martin says, "Yes, of course you would."

She stares at him. "I have done worse," she says, clasping the pouch to her bosom.

He waits, feeling the blood drain from his face.

"I have denied—"

"Denied what?"

Alice's lip is trembling but her eyes are locked directly on Martin's. "I have denied my child."

"Shhhhh, it is not so." Martin stands, wraps his arms around her and rests his chin on her head. They sink to the sofa in a tight embrace. In the middle of the stolen studio, in the middle of the night, in the middle of their splintering world, Alice presses against Martin, still holding Abu's pouch. It is grotesque to him but he does not react when she hands it to him. The smell is strange. Sweet and stale at the same time. A smell from the trenches. He shivers at the memory of lifting what he thought was a leather bag and seeing an arm pull away from a body. He swallows hard, then places the pouch down beside them.

Alice and Martin lie like spindrift, his long arms around her tender body, her five paint-stained fingers wrapped through his four manicured digits. In time they fall asleep, their bodies loosen, and the pouch slips to the floor, taking its feverish history with it.

THE STUDIO

MARTIN AWAKENS FIRST, startled by the light from the window—a strange yellow glow peering through the blue Alice folded onto the glass the night before. He takes in the smell of Alice, the feel of her hair against his neck. He hears a bell. So clear he looks about for its source at the same time that he knows only he can hear it. It is a call. He does not believe in such things, neither does he dare to ignore them. A bell at dawn.

Alice stirs beside him. He lifts himself gently away from her, keeping their fingers entwined. When she opens her eyes, he takes her fingers to his lips and keeps them there.

Alice sits up and looks to the window. "Progeny is coming," she says.

"That's not clear—" Martin begins.

"Progeny to arrive June 12, that is what the telegram said."

"Yes, I know, but I have been in touch with sources—"

Alice holds her breath. Martin has sources. Of course he has sources. "What have your sources told you?" she asks.

Martin looks at the face before him. Stripped of pretense. Open. Unafraid. He looks down at the pouch on the floor, its string flung away from it, a paint-spattered brown snake against the gray cement.

Alice grabs the pouch and a cry escapes her. "It should not

have come to me," she gasps. "Why was it sent to me? What does this mean?"

Martin reaches out to hold her but she pulls away. "He is coming. I know he is coming. The telegram said so. We must be there." She turns abruptly and begins gathering herself together.

Martin looks about the room calculating how and when to return to make amends for the damage. It's not really damage, he thinks, it's art. But there's every likelihood whoever owns the studio now will not see it that way. Especially when they realize the wife of an OBE recipient was the perpetrator—the artist.

Alice picks up her coat and turns to looks at the walls. "Don't worry," she says. "I have met the new tenants. We will be able to work this out." She is standing tall, her voice is strong, and her eyes are clear. She looks decades younger. Martin takes her hand and closes the door quietly behind them.

GREEN STREET

M ARTIN STEPS ON AN ENVELOPE on the floor as he crosses the threshold. He slips it into his pocket and follows Alice to the bath, where she runs warm water and pours in her favorite bath salts. "I'll join you in a minute," he says, then steps to the garden window to read Talcott's note. *We lost him. Suspect is slippery. May be in disguise. Last seen at British Museum.* Martin stifles a laugh. A handwritten note. He imagines Talcott wandering the city like a latter-day Sherlock, magnifying glass in hand. Then he realizes Talcott is working this himself, as he asked, keeping this to himself, and he is grateful.

Martin turns to the window and sees the early morning light illuminate the chimney pots across the lane. He squints and sees the light the way Alice put it on the walls. He didn't think the son would be able to enter the country, particularly with Talcott's people on the case. Talcott must have taken them off it—another slice of gratitude. And the son, making his way here, he just might make his way here.

Good Lord, will you look at that! Martin raised the periscope and saw a figure in the midst of the smoke and flashes of fire. It's a Kraut! Talcott yelled. Walking across the battlefield. Martin could see the helmet, the tall gait of the man outlined by the flares. He was walking straight across no-man's-land, straight through bullets and smoke and bodies dropping beside him. Martin put down the periscope and raised himself gingerly up the ladder to peer over the rampart. The soldier was still there, still walking calmly forward. The firing died down as they watched the tall figure cross the muddy field without a stumble. It was the best sight of the war. One man walking fearlessly forward.

Martin hears Alice humming in the bath. He puts Talcott's note in his pocket and begins undressing, letting go of the memory, forgetting whether the soldier made it through to the other side or not.

Alice and Martin sit at the breakfast room table listening to Brahms's *Requiem*. Alice is calm. Martin is agitated. When the post clatters through the mail slot he jumps, then tries to walk down the hall slowly. Alice looks up as he places a blue envelope on the table in front of her. There is no return address. Martin hands her his letter opener and she slices through the lip of the envelope, then hands the paper to Martin. "My eyes are too tired to read," she says. She seems preternaturally calm, detached, but she looks brighter than he remembers ever having seen her.

It is typewritten on plain foolscap. He begins to read:

My Beloved Son,

I have spoken the language of your mother. I have told you the stories of your mother. I have recited the songs of your mother—the rhymes of nursery, the Dickens man, and the poems of her friend Shakespeer. All this I have given you, a man of the desert. You were born to the Sahara but the Sahara is no longer your destiny. Amaya is the spirit of your mother. She smiles with the eyes of your mother, dances on the legs of your mother, speaks in the voice of your mother. The world is pressing in on our people, on our tribe, on our life. I give you these words:

Alice George Hightower
Green Street
Mayfair
London

These words are for you my beloved son, son of my beloved Alice. You must do what you desire. *Inshallah*

Martin looks across the table at Alice. Her eyes are closed. The language would be laughable if he had not once sat in a café in North Africa watching people line up to recite their missives to the professional letter-writer. He marvels at the thought of the power in the fingers of the man who sat cross-legged on the street, typing on an ancient machine set upon an upturned crate.

"There is more, is there not?" Alice asks.

Martin turns the paper over and sees handwritten letters, perfectly printed:

My Beloved Mother,

These were the last words from my father the Amenokal of Ahaggar. My beloved mother my desire is to meet you. *Inshallah*

Alice smiles. "He is announcing his arrival. He is explaining his purpose. He is sending me his entreaty."

"Entreaty?"

The Tuareg do not barge into a person's life. You prepare yourself for meeting. You prepare people to be met. In the desert, after days of the men straddling the camels with their *tagelmusts* falling low or even off their faces, with their robes pulled up above their knees, at some unfathomable hour they stopped the caravan, rested, washed, and dressed in their finest robes. Within the hour another caravan arrived and was greeted as honored guests. I never could figure out how they knew a party of strangers was arriving. The only people ever surprised in the desert were the French Legionnaires. The only people unprepared for the arrival of the caravan were the people they raided.

"He will be here soon," Alice says.

Martin stares at her. She is a different woman.

Alice and Martin sit on the bench in the garden. "Should we be inside?" Martin asks. "To hear the doorbell?"

"No," Alice says, and takes Martin's hand. "He will come to the oasis."

Martin doesn't remonstrate. This is Alice's story now. He sits beside her looking across the garden, feeling as if they are on a ship at sea waiting for the sight of land.

Alice grips his hand and draws in her breath. Someone is coming up the lane. The top of a head is moving along the wall, a splash of blue against the brick wall. Alice shuts her eyes. *Heads along the wall. Black V's in the sky Van Gogh painted. Black in the harem. White in the Sisters of Blessed Mercy. Black in the tent. White in the palanquin.* She opens her eyes and all is blue again.

Martin rises and walks quickly to the garden gate. He opens it and moves aside as a man in a dark robe bows before him. Martin turns to Alice, who is standing now, clasping her hand over her mouth. A sound begins to escape her lips, a tiny wail, almost a whistle. She drops her hand from her mouth and opens her arms. Rashid walks forward, and Martin watches mother and son embrace.

Martin turns back to the gate and stumbles at the sight of

Alice, in a long blue dress. He turns back to see Alice and her son embracing, then turns again to the gate. What is he seeing? His eyes are wet, he blinks hard. It looks like the window Alice painted last night.

Alice and Rashid turn and Alice falls forward, but Rashid catches her. *It's a mirror. It is me the day I went into the desert. LA, it is a mirage. But there is no horizon, no shimmering sun, there is only blue and yellow.* Martin comes towards her. He steps up beside her and puts his hand softly into the dip of her back, and she is at the tea dance. She turns her body towards him but he is not bending to take her hand, he is holding her upright and extending his arm to the yellow and blue that is moving towards her. Her son is calling to her from far away. Martin takes her hand, and with his touch everything comes into focus.

"My beloved Mother," Rashid says. "This is your granddaughter, Amaya."

DEVON

1973

Edith, Jane, and Benjamin joined us the day after Rashid arrived. I was relieved to let Edith take charge of the house. She and Jane set to work making a grand meal, Benjamin and Rashid delighted in each other, Martin played the piano, and Amaya and I sat together in the garden. I knew Rashid the minute I saw him, but Amaya was a revelation.

Edith embraced me in the kitchen. "I never thought I'd see you again," she said.

"What—"

"Amaya is you. She is the person I was looking for when you returned from the desert."

My arms were suddenly weak. I lowered the flowers I had brought in from the garden onto the table. Why do people do this? "She looks like you." "She reminds me of you." At some point each member of my family had whispered that to me.

"Do you think so?" What else could I say? I saw the resemblance, the hair, the eyes, the face. But what did they see? Amaya was vibrant. She laughed with Benjamin, she slipped easily into the kitchen preparations, she sat at the piano and delighted at the sounds that came forth when she struck a key. And she gathered herself into an imposing force the one time Rashid disagreed with her. They saw me. I saw Abu.

Of course the first place I took them was Tariq's restaurant. The four of us, Rashid, Amaya, Martin and me. I should have told Tariq we were coming, but I knew he would have closed the business and set up a feast just for us. As it was he did just that. I could see that Martin was relieved when Tariq turned the sign on his door to "closed." The walls echoed with our different languages. Tariq brought his wife and son out, their robes sweeping by the windows, and Rashid insisted they join us. Amaya was on her feet back and forth to the kitchen helping them; then Rashid and Tariq cleared the tables away, tossed pillows on the floor, and as the lowering sun painted the walls gold, I took Martin's hand and sat him down in my former world.

Rashid stayed for a week. Martin was on the phone at odd hours and advised Rashid to stay within our walls, but I knew he could not be confined. On the third day he dressed in one of Martin's suits and removed his blue *tagelmust*. When he appeared at my side, I tried not to cry out at the sight of a Tuareg without his *cheche*.

Rashid took my hand and led me into the garden. We sat side by side on the bench facing the back wall.

"Tell me," I said, "how did he die?"

Rashid turned to look straight at me. "He died a good death," he said, and I knew there was no more to be said.

"And Amaya?" I asked. "Who is her mother?"

"Her mother died in childbirth."

I gasped. He shook his head slowly, still looking straight at me. "Amina raised her," he said. "As she raised me."

"Layla?"

"She was not worthy." And for the first time he looked away.

"Amina," I said. "Is she still—"

"She is aged. She is tired. My father always wanted Amaya to come to you. We talked of it many times, but Amaya was not ready."

"And she is now?"

"She is no longer a child of the desert. The desert world is changing, we do not see what is ahead."

"What is happening?"

"It is better that you ask that question of Martin," he said.

In the ensuing days we walked through the park, we stood in front of the palace, we had tea at the Savoy. Even with his blueish skin, Rashid did not draw attention. Amaya always did. I presume she always will. I understood immediately why Rashid had brought her here. She is a rare species and needed a bit of the greenhouse life to blossom fully. I promised him I would find the right education for her and I would never prevent her from returning to the desert.

I drank in the sight of them striding through the park and kept my gasp to myself the few times my sight flashed out. We stopped in the Serpentine Gallery and Martin said we should make a studio in the house, which we did. In the months that followed, Amaya joined me in playing with paint and if she noticed my failing eyes, she did not say so, just carefully managed the pots and brushes herself.

Amaya was stunned by our fruit. She knew dates and pomegranates and lemons, of course, but apples and bananas and pears and gooseberries—those were a revelation. We went off to the farmer's market one week and when we came home, after lunch at Tariq's, she arranged her treasures on the table and sat down with her paints. On a leaden London day, she brought the light of the desert to the canvas and illuminated the fruits in a way I had never seen before.

When my son and I parted for the second time, my heart remained still. Martin was more upset than I. He knew there was great reason to fear, but I had the desert inside me again, and there is no place for fear in the desert. There is only sky and sand and sun and moon. There is only mother and son and grand-daughter. There is only love and death.

Inshallah

ACKNOWLEDGMENTS

This book would not have materialized without the support and love of a generous community of writers. A particular thank you to those who were there in the beginning and believed in it long before I did: Dorothy Allen Brown, Karen Findlay, Caryn Markson, and Christine Menard. I am blessed to be part of the Great Darkness, a group that has been writing together weekly for longer than most of us can remember: Marianne Banks, Joan Barberich, Jennifer Jacobson, Lisa Drnec Kerr, Patricia Lee Lewis, Edie and Alan Lipp, Pat Riggs, Morgan Bubbla-Sheehan, Jacqueline Sheehan, and Marion Van Arsdell. I am also grateful to the members of my monthly manuscript group who read this story in many different iterations: Marianne Banks, Kris Holloway-Bidwell, Lydia Kann, Ellen Meeropol, Dori Ostermiller, Pat Riggs, and Jacqueline Sheehan. Other generous readers/supporters along the way include Jean Brandt, Seth Fischer, Plynn Gutman, Leslea Newman, Mollie Traver, Anne Dubuisson, Susan Markman, Loraine Millman, and Susan O'Neill.

Time and space for writing were graciously provided by Dorothy Allen Brown, The Turkey Land Cove Foundation, and La Muse Retreat. Thanks are due to Sherrill Layton for her expertise in reviewing the Arabic phraseology. A huge thank-you to Mary Bisbee-Beek who has been a steady guide through thick and thin.

Blue Desert was incredibly lucky to have landed in the hands of the talented and passionate team at Rootstock Publishing: Stephen McArthur, Courtney Boynton Jenkins, Samantha Kolber and Nancy Disenhaus, for whose editorial guidance I shall be forever indebted.

It was a true pleasure to work with the creative designer Lisa Carta, who brought this book to life visually.

BIBLIOGRAPHY

The following books were invaluable during the writing of *Blue Desert*

Bensusan, S.L., *Morocco*, London: Adam and Charles Black, 1904.

Bodley, R.V.C., *Wind in the Sahara*, New York: Creative Age Press, Inc., 1944.

Bowles, Paul, *A Hundred Camels in the Courtyard*, San Francisco: City Lights Books, 1986.

_____ *The Sheltering Sky*, New Jersey: The Ecco Press, 1977.

Briggs, Lloyd Cabot, *Tribes of the Sahara*, Cambridge: Harvard University Press, 1960.

Butler, Henrietta, ed., *The Tuareg or Kel Tamasheq: the People Who Speak Tamasheq and a History of the Sahara*, Unicorn Publishing Group, 2016.

Cecil, Robert, *Life in Edwardian England*, New York: G.P. Putnam's Sons, 1969.

Davis, Robert, *Pepperfoot of Thursday Market*, New York: Holiday House, 1941.

De Villiers, Marq and Sheila Hirtle, *Sahara: a Natural History*, New York: Walker & Company, 2002.

Eberhardt, Isabelle, *In the Shadow of Islam*, London: Peter Owen Publishers, 1993.

_____ *Prisoner of Dunes*, London: Peter Owen Publishers, 1995.

_____ *The Oblivion Seekers*, San Franciso: City Lights Books, 1975.

Emily, Shareefa of Wazan, *My Life Story*, London: Edward Arnold, 1912.

Fisher, Angela, *Africa Adorned*, New York: Harry N. Abrams, Inc., 1984.

Gautier, E.F., *Sahara the Great Desert*, New York: Columbia University Press, 1935.

Gerster, Georg, *Sahara Desert of Destiny*, New York: Coward-McCann, Inc., 1960.

Lady Grove, *Seventy-one Days' Camping in Morocco*, London: Longmans, Green, and Co., 1902.

Mrs. Humphry, *Manners for Women*, London: Ward, Lock & Co, Reprint by Pryor Publications, 1997.

Keenan, Jeremy, *The Tuareg: People of the Ahaggar*, London: Sickle Moon Books, 2002.

Langewiesche, William, *Sahara Unveiled: A Journey Across the Desert*, New York: Vintage, 1997.

LeClezio, J.M.G (C. Dickson translator), *Desert*, Boston: David R. Godine: 2012.

Lindquist, Sven, *Desert Divers*, London: Granta Books, 2000.

Maxwell, Gavin, *Lords of the Atlas: Adventure, Mystery, and Intrigue in Morocco, 1893-1956*, New York: Lyons Press, 2000.

Motley, Mary, *Morning Glory*, New York: St. Martin's Press, 1961.

Nicolson, Juliet, *The Perfect Summer: England 1911, Just Before the Storm*, New York: Grove Press, 2006.

Novaresio, Paolo & Guadalupi, Gianni, *Sahara*, San Diego: Thunder Bay Press, 2003.

Porch, Douglas, *The Conquest of the Sahara*, New York: Knopf, 1984.

_____ *The Conquest of Morocco*, New York: Farrar, Strauss, Giroux, 1982.

Rodd, Francis Rennell, *People of the Veil*, London: Macmillan and Col, Ltd, 1926.

Seligman, Thomas K. and Loughran, Kristyne, eds. *Art of Being Tuareg: Sahara Nomads in a Modern World*, Los Angeles: Cantor Arts Center for Visual Arts at Stanford University, 2006.

Tuchman, Barbara, *The Guns of August*, Random House, Reprint, 2009.

Ward, Edward, *Sahara Story*, New York: W.W. Norton & Co., 1962.

Wharton, Edith, *In Morocco*, New York: Charles Scribner's Sons, 1920.

BLUE DESERT

Book Group Discussion Questions

※ Did you find Alice's motivations and decisions at various points in her life believable in light of her experiences? Surprising?

※ What qualities did you see in Alice as a teenager that contribute to the decisions she makes, and to her survival, in the desert? Where do you see the seeds, in Alice's earlier life, of the courage and independence she shows during her desert experience?

※ What elements of Alice's relationship with Edith seem universal to relationships between sisters, and what elements seem to arise from their particular life experiences?

※ How did you react to the figures who are neither in the aristocratic world of Alice's English family (e.g., Kate the cook) nor in the tribal group (e.g., those who work in the compound and interact with Alice and her family in various ways)? Do they help to reveal aspects of their cultures through their words and behavior?

※ Where do you see Alice's growing understanding and admiration of Abu and awareness of his personal qualities?

❋ What seems to be Edith's way of coping with her own Moroccan experience and its aftermath? Does it seem to have served her well?

❋ How do Martin's WWI experiences and Alice's desert experiences make them well suited for each other, despite Alice's feeling that she has never given him her full self?

❋ Amaya and Rashid appear very late in the book, after the telegram initiates a long period of suspense concerning Alice's "progeny." Were you surprised by any aspects of Rashid's behavior or attitudes? Speculate about all that's unsaid about Rashid's life and the ways his life experiences would have shaped Amaya. What aspects of Abu's and Alice's character seem evident in Amaya?

❋ Abu is a central figure but remains to some extent mysterious and unknowable. What scenes and behaviors helped you understand Alice's attraction to and eventual love for him? What scenes surprised you or revealed unexpected aspects of Abu's character?

❋ Abu's pouch contains the gold earrings of his wife Layla. How did you feel about this, and in what way is the character of Layla further developed at the end of the book? What untold story does Rashid's cryptic comment about Layla seem to suggest?

❋ How does Alice evolve spiritually or in her outlook on life during her time in the desert and thereafter?

❋ How does Alice's relationship with Edith evolve, from their girlhood to the book's close? What decisions or actions contribute to this evolution?

※ How does Alice's art help us understand her recovery and her ways of adapting to her life in England? What seems to be the role of painting and color in Alice's healing?

※ How are the characters of Rashid and Amaya meaningful in our understanding of the changes the Tuareg society underwent as a result of the two world wars? Do their characters offer an emotional resolution to the story that seemed fitting to you as a reader?